Water on a Sea Star

Annie M. Cole

To Rebecca,
May the Author of Life
guide you always
Annie Cole

∞INFINITY
PUBLISHING

Copyright © 2011 by Annie M. Cole

ISBN 0-7414-6537-X
Library of Congress Control Number: 2011924510

Printed in the United States of America

Published August 2011

INFINITY PUBLISHING
1094 New DeHaven Street, Suite 100
West Conshohocken, PA 19428-2713
Toll-free (877) BUY BOOK
Local Phone (610) 941-9999
Fax (610) 941-9959
Info@buybooksontheweb.com
www.buybooksontheweb.com

It is with deep love that I dedicate this book to my mother, Leigh, who taught me the joy of paying attention to life.

Chapter 1

Bell Bennier plantation

A forceful wind pushed across the shoreline, stealing its way up the embankment as it hurried toward the stately brick mansion known as Bell Bennier.

The house seemed strong, impenetrable with a defiant grace that stood and faced that which was sent her way as if divinely held there throughout the generations. Within the boundaries of this land called Bell Forest, the inhabitants have remained strong and resilient just as the brick and mortar of her structures and the long avenue of weathered oaks that usher you to her door.

A squeak of hinges intruded into the kitchen as six-year-old Sassy rushed past her mother, reaching the freezer as the screen door slapped against the doorframe. Pushing open the lid, she scrambled around in the bottom until she located the half-eaten Push-Up Popsicle she'd deposited there earlier.

"Maddie wants to be my sister!" she proclaimed, hurriedly and out of breath.

"That so?" Lou questioned, not paying the girl any mind. Busy with both hands in the biscuit dough, she folded it over and over methodically, stopping occasionally to push a loose strand of hair away from her face with the back of her arm.

"Ah huh, told me so this mornin…says 'cause that'd make *you* her momma." The spring on the screen door stretched out taunt before slamming shut as Sassy ventured back outside.

Lou stilled. For a long moment she stood staring down at the soft dough that formed around her fingers. Snatching her hands out of the wooden bowl, she moved to the sink, placing them under a cool stream of water as a hot path of tears ran down her cheeks. Grabbing the corner of a dishtowel from the oven handle, she dried her hands, blotting her face with the sleeve of her shirt as she choked back tears. "Mercy, mercy me," she whispered. Pulling a chair away from the kitchen table, she eased her weight into it with an exaggerated breath, pondering the revelation of her daughter's words. *Forgive me Lord for being so blind. I'm whatcha call blind in one eye and can't see outa the other.*

Heaving a weary sigh Lou got up and headed out the door, passing her boss, Jim Warren on the back steps. Shielding her eyes in the late afternoon sun, she asked, "Where's that boy?" Turning her "good" eye toward Jim, she waited for his response.

Lou's bright blue glass eye gleamed in the sun. It didn't seem to matter to Lou that her other eye was brown, matching her skin. She prized that blue eye. And, after the initial shock, most people just seemed to accept the oddity without question.

Jim turned to appraise her. "Jude? He's at the barn. Why, you need him?" He slapped his dusty hat against his leg as he studied his cook's expression. Few things pulled Lou away from the kitchen, and that fact alone was cause for concern.

"Yeah, I need him right this minute. I ain't fixing to have this." Her jaw was set. With both hands placed firmly on her hips, she scanned the area, looking for a glimpse of Jim's son, Jude.

"Whatever he did, when you get finished with him, send what's left over to me."

"Oh, that boy ain't done nothin wrong; I just need him to get that Kabobble thing out and take me over to Madeline's."

Jim contemplated her words, tugged at his earlobe and grinned. "I'll get the Kubota for you. Hold on, let me get Jude so he can drive you over." Jim reached around and unclipped the walkie-talkie from his belt. "Madeline all right?" he asked, before calling for Jude.

"From now on she gonna be! Yeah, she sure gonna be if I have anything to do with it." Lou's voice trailed off as her eyes scanned the field for Jude.

Jim heaved a sigh of relieve. *Thank you, Lord!* He'd hinted around for months hoping Lou would read between the lines and step in to help with Madeline. At the age of twelve, Madeline needed a woman's hand and there was no hand better that Lou's.

Jude eyed Lou cautiously as they approached the cottage. *What has Madeline done to light a fire under Lou? She never leaves the house with chicken left to fry.*

Lou's lips were pulled in tight forming a straight line. It was frightening to see the determined look on her face.

Jude rolled up near the back steps of Bay Cottage and killed the motor. Taking a deep breath, he held it in, pushing air from cheek to cheek as he nervously waited for the showdown.

Wasting no time, Lou slid out of the seat and headed toward the door. From the worn-out look of the steps, she decided to test them before putting her whole weight down on the shaky boards.

The door suddenly flew open and out stepped Madeline. Her face registered surprise as she looked into the bronzed and glistening face of Lou.

"Go tell ya momma you comin with me for awhile," Lou spoke directly. "Go on now," she said, making a shooing motion with her hands.

"Uh...Momma won't care." The word, *Momma* was unfamiliar to Madeline's lips and she stumbled over it.

"Well, come on then. We ain't got all day."

"I...I can't. I have to fix supper...for Aunt Della." Madeline shifted her eyes to hide her disappointment.

"Who?" Lou scrunched up her face and turned to Jude for clarification.

"Madeline's mother," Jude whispered, hoping Madeline wouldn't be embarrassed by the disclosure.

Lou studied Jude's face, as if to see if he was serious, then reached out and grabbed Madeline's hand and pulled her toward the Kubota. "Don't you worry none about that Miss Priss, I got plenty of supper. We'll fix that Aunt Della a plate and with some blackberry pie, too. Y'all can run it back down here before we eat supper."

The sweet scent of White Shoulders perfume permeated Lou's entire being. Madeline inhaled deeply of the familiar and comforting scent as she slid past her, taking a seat next to Jude.

Lou climbed in beside her, noticing Madeline with a fresh eye. Her hair was all stringy and matted with no particular style. Her fingernails were embedded with dirt and a grainy string of "Granny Beads" encircled her neck. Giving her the once over, she noticed a patch of red bumps clustered around her knee. "Do they itch?" Lou asked, indicating the angry red blisters.

"Yes ma'am," she nodded.

"Looks like you got yourself a good case of chiggers. You got them anywhere else?"

Madeline looked down at her hands. "Yes ma'am."

"Well...I'll fix you right up after supper. Now get me home, Jude. I got chicken to fry." Bracing herself, she held on tightly to the seat as Jude cranked the Kubota.

Embarrassed, Madeline cut her eyes to Jude who reassuringly patted her on the leg before turning his attention to the rutted dirt road.

Shortly after the dinner dishes had all been cleared away, Lou set about tending to Madeline. She instructed the young girl on how to properly care for her personal needs, telling her everything a young girl of twelve needed to hear from her momma. But, since Madeline's momma was crazy, Lou surmised, it fell to her to prepare the girl for the changes that would soon take place. After a good scrubbing, Lou sat the girl down and began her lecture.

"*Never* and I mean *never* go out of the house without takin a bath, washing your hair and brushing your teeth," she admonished. "And another thing...your fingernails look like you been diggin for grub worms. Take this soft brush and scrub them clean, every night." Lou held out a small fingernail brush before picking up the hairbrush. Holding the brush in mid-air, she asked, "What size you wear, Missy?'

Madeline shrugged, "I'm not sure." She smoothed the front of the faded out Old Navy T-shirt with her hand, remembering it had once belonged to Jude.

Pursing her lips, Lou appraised her frame. "You look about the size of my niece, Precious. Her momma buys her these prissy clothes and that girl wouldn't be caught dead in 'em. They just hang in her closet with the tags still on 'em…that Precious." She pulled her head back giving Madeline a concerned look. "Keeps her head under a car hood most of the time. Her daddy done ruined that girl with all that boy stuff." She shook her head in disgust. "Even took to calling her Pete, can you believe that?"

Lou hummed as she worked the hairbrush through Madeline's freshly washed hair. "*Mm mm*, you sure do have a head full of pretty hair. Just look at it, all glossy and smooth." She pulled the brush back and let the hair fall into the sunlight. "It's the same color as a jar of clover honey sittin up on the windowsill, just catchin the mornin sun." She picked up the scissors and made a clean cut across the bottom of Madeline's hair, removing the dead jagged edges. "I'm calling my sister tomorrow to see about them dresses. I'm thinkin I got myself a diamond in the rough!"

A light knock sounded on the door as Jude peered inside.

"Look here, Jude. Let me show you what a girl is supposed to look like!" Lou gripped Madeline's shoulders and slowly turned her around.

Madeline's long shiny hair fell in smooth waves across her shoulders, framing her softly tanned face. *Has she always had green eyes?* Full lips that turned up slightly at the corners gave the impression she was up to something. Jude swallowed hard, finding it hard to turn his eyes away. He'd lost the ability to speak.

A loud peel of laughter rang out as Lou threw her head back with joy from the look on Jude's face. "Best be gettin' use to it, boy. From now on, Miss Madeline here is gonna be a little lady. She gonna look like one anyway," she said, with a wink. "Next...I'm gonna get my hands on that mangy cockle burred nappy headed poodle of hers! You just hide and see if I don't!"

Chapter 2

Eight years later

*A*s on a day when the east wind blows, change came suddenly to Bell Bennier. Samuel Warren closed the thick folder in his hand and tossed it onto the mahogany desk. *The responsibility of it all falls to me; Jude, the plantation, all of it falls to me.* He leaned back and drew on his cigar thoughtfully, staring out the study window. Clusters of white snowy hydrangea blossoms bobbed their drowsy heads in the breeze as if agreeing with his assessment.

Samuel and his father, Jim Warren, had not always seen eye to eye. But, their love of family and love of the land could never be questioned. Jim Warren knew that about his son. He also knew that Samuel loved Bell Bennier plantation and the surrounding land better than anyone; it ran deep in his blood. His last wishes were for Jude to finish school and for Samuel to return home, where he belonged, according to his father.

Everyone around those parts knew the plantation as Bell Bennier and the surrounding lands as Bell Forest. Bayou Bell, a meandering marsh creek, ran along the northern half of the property separating lands to the north, which were once part of the original Bell Bennier plantation and now belonged to Michael Christenberry and St. Thomas Monastery. Bayou Bell held its own secrets.

Leaning forward on the desk, Samuel tapped out his cigar. *Jude will fight me on this.* He thought back to earlier remarks made by the ranch hand, Greenberry White. He'd told Samuel that Jude would never leave home, because he'd never leave Madeline Linville. *Could little Maddie really have such a powerful draw? Could any woman?*

A knock at the door interrupted Samuel's thoughts. "Come in." His deep voice reverberated across the room now filled with late afternoon soft and smoky light.

As the study door opened, Jude stuck his head inside. "Am I intruding?"

"No, no come in. I was just thinking about you."

Jude's gaze narrowed. "This can't be good."

Samuel pushed out a chair next to the desk with his foot. "Sit down...let's talk."

Jude walked out of the study a short time later as Samuel ran his hand down his face and let out a weary breath. *Issue resolved. Jude will attend college in the fall and begin pursuing his dream of becoming a marine biologist. The only concession, I have to stay here for the next four years. Well...you got what you wanted, Father...for now, anyway.*

Jude surprised Samuel by holding firm to his terms. He would not even consider leaving home without the assurance that Madeline would be taken care of. But, not just looked after, looked after by Samuel.

Later that afternoon, while walking the grounds, any second thoughts Samuel might've had about his agreement with Jude began to fade. Inhaling the scent of the place, the timeless and familiar Bell Bennier scent of sea mingled with the pungent smell of old boxwoods and cut hay began to revive his senses. Ancient moss draped oaks, bent with time stood watch, caressing him with their shawl of gray as he passed beneath the low-lying branches.

Samuel's heart picked up a beat as he neared the stables. Of all of the places on the plantation, this was by far his favorite. This was the place of his boyhood memories, the place where he seemed to possess complete peace of mind and physical contentment. Horses, tractors, farming implements stirred his blood. Nothing pleased Samuel more than working with his hands on the land, and not just any land, but his land. The utter naturalness of the barn brought ease to his mind. Almost instantly, the heavy obligation of his new set of responsibilities lightened as he stepped into the darkened barn. Looking around, he smiled, inhaling deeply of the musty familiar scent. Hay, oiled leather and whiffs of manure hung on the air. *Ah...I'd almost forgotten.*

A movement from the corner of the barn caught Samuel's attention. "That you, Greenberry?" he asked, squinting in the dim light as his eyes adjusted.

Greenberry never looked up; just kept right on working with the saddle he was cleaning. "Who's that woman you've got up there?" Greenberry made a motion with his head in the direction of the house. "That your wife?"

Greenberry White was a man of few words. In all of the years he'd worked on the plantation, Samuel could count on both hands the number of times the man had ever said anything. He gestured mostly or mumbled incoherent words under his breath.

Understanding registered with Samuel. "Oh, you mean Willa. She's my cook. I brought her down to see if she'll like it here. She lost her husband a few years back and I thought a change might do her good. Her daughters are grown and married, scattered all over." Slightly amused, Samuel leaned up against a stall, waiting for a reaction from the old farm hand.

"Mmm." Greenberry nodded once, then resumed his work.

A somewhat complicated man, Greenberry stood around six foot with a solid sturdy frame. His light brown hair was beginning to gray at the temples calling attention to his ice blue eyes. His weathered look reminded you of an old Marlboro cigarette man. Not once had the man ever mentioned a woman. Greenberry seemed to prefer solitude, living peacefully on the property in a small house tucked back into the woods. The highlight of his day was to turn in around sundown with a good paperback western. Still, Samuel wondered if Willa had caught the eye of the old cowpoke. *She's an attractive woman by anyone's standard,* he thought.

As if on cue, Willa stepped into the barn. Her ash-blonde hair swept up loosely on her head, landing softly around her shoulders. Wearing a pair of faded jeans and an oversized white collared shirt with the sleeves rolled past her elbows, she looked much younger than her forty-eight years.

"There you are," Willa said, slightly out of breath. "I've been looking everywhere for you. I need to know how many people to expect for supper." She glanced around Samuel's shoulder, noticing Greenberry for the first time.

Greenberry tipped his hat and then quietly made an exaggerated circle around her and left the barn.

"Cook enough for twelve. I'd rather have too much than not enough. Out here, you never know who might drop by around suppertime. Once word gets out about the way you cook, I'll expect even more." Samuel smiled, then winked. "I saw a few men out in the field earlier. I'll go find out if they're staying for supper and let you know." He turned and headed in the direction of the horses.

Willa gave a quick nod and smiled. "That'll be just fine." As she neared the barn door, she let out a cry. Lying across the ground, blocking her path, stretched the longest black snake she'd ever seen. Frozen in fear, she could only stammer, "Sssnake!"

Before Samuel could cross the barn to reach her, Greenberry came out of nowhere, picked up the snake and tossed it out of harms way. "That's Charlie ma'am. He looks meaner than he really is. He's just showing off in front of a pretty lady," he drawled.

Greenberry's face lit up with a look Samuel wouldn't have believed possible for the old codger. He acted almost smitten and actually spoke in complete sentences!

"Thank you for that, I'm terrified of snakes! I'm Willa, Samuel's cook," she said, cautiously looking around on the ground before extended her small hand to Greenberry.

Greenberry quickly took it in his hard calloused one. "I'm Greenberry, the stable hand around here, mighty pleased to meet you, Ms. Willa."

"Will you be joining us for supper, Mr. Greenberry?" Willa smoothed away the loose hair from around her face glancing every so often around her feet just to make sure Charlie hadn't come back.

"Looking forward to it, and its just Greenberry, Greenberry White."

"Well, Greenberry, I guess I'll see you at suppertime then." With that, Willa stepped past him and headed toward the house, her eyes searching the ground before her.

Samuel twisted his lips to hide his ever-growing smile as he noticed Greenberry's attention on Willa's retreating form. He cleared his throat. "I guess pretty women are a rare sight way out here in God's country, huh, Greenberry."

"You're right about that," Greenberry responded, never taking his eyes off of Willa.

The late summer wind rustled the trees as they stood outside the barn. Samuel eyed the sky, noticing the ominous approach of ever changing dark gray clouds. "Looks like rain. I'll head out and check on the men, see you at supper." He tossed a grin Greenberry's way before turning to face the sky once more.

That evening after supper, as the last guest walked off the porch, Willa began untying her apron. "If you're sure," she questioned again. Samuel's repeated insistence that she turn in for the evening had finally won out over Willa reluctance.

"I'm sure, now you go on upstairs. I'm just gonna put on some coffee and relax awhile. It's been a long day."

Just as Samuel was pouring a steamy cup of coffee, he heard a light tapping on the front door. Putting down the coffee pot, he made his way to the door.

Chapter 3

Samuel yanked open the front door, then looked down into the most beautiful face he'd ever seen. There, in front of him, was a shivering and rain drenched girl, peering up at him with golden-green eyes. Cold air blasted from inside the house, causing her teeth to chatter. Holding tightly to the foil wrapped plate in her hands, she smiled, seemingly amused by the startled look on Samuel's face.

"Madeline!" Jude's excited voice called from the staircase.

Jude's words caused Samuel's eyes to widen. With sudden recognition, Samuel tilted his head. "Maddie?" he asked in disbelief.

"In all my glory." Madeline tugged self-consciously on her thin wet shirt before offering the plate. "Jude told me you were coming home. Hope you like chocolate chip?" She glanced toward Jude with a hint of a wink in her eyes.

Transfixed, Samuel could hardly believe his eyes. Where had the gangly, stringy-haired, scabby-kneed, chigger infested girl gone? And more importantly, who was this breathtaking creature shivering before him?

Madeline had grown into a beauty. Her long rich honey-amber hair fell in damp waves around a light olive complexion. Golden green eyes emitted glowing warmth as her soft full lips turned up slightly at the corners, drawing the eye to their mischief.

Taking a deep breath, Samuel took the plate and smiled, "My all-time favorite."

A smile of satisfaction crossed Madeline's face as she made her way over to Jude. He descended the steps quickly reaching her as she lifted up on her toes to plant a kiss on his forehead.

Samuel raised an eyebrow in surprised amusement at the exchange. "How about some hot coffee, Madeline, we keep this house freezing in the throes of August heat."

"Coffee sounds wonderful."

"Coffee it is then." Samuel shook his head as he stepped into the kitchen, finding it difficult to believe his little brother's playmate had developed into such a stunning beauty in only eight short years!" Returning, he extended a cup to her. Feather soft fingers brushed his calloused hand as she took the cup from his grasp, cradling it within her fingers.

Taking a seat on the couch, Madeline smiled as Jude plopped down next to her. "This should take the chill off." She shivered slightly, sipping the coffee.

"Oh...here." Jude lifted a quilt from the corner of the couch and draped it around her. "Pull your feet up and I'll cover them." Rubbing her feet through he blanket he asked, "Better?"

"Much." Madeline smiled, taking in Jude's face with tenderness.

Samuel dropped into his chair, watching the exchange through puzzled eyes. Seeing Jude so attentive to a woman caught him off-guard, especially this woman. He had never witness that side of his brother. *Can't blame him*, he thought, laughing under his breath as he reached for his coffee.

Noticing the smirk on Samuel's face, Jude questioned, "What?"

"I was just trying to remember the last time I saw Madeline." Samuel stroked his chin thoughtfully. "Must've been about...eight years ago. How old were you then, twelve...thirteen?"

Jude's lips spread into a slow wicked smile. "Yeah, and *you* were twenty." He cut his eyes to Madeline, then back to Samuel. "Remember when we stowed away in the back seat of your old Mustang? You had that big date with Jennifer Crosswhite."

Samuel nodded, rubbing the stubble on his chin, "The drive-in."

Madeline grinned mischievously, punching Jude lightly on the shoulder before looking back at Samuel. "You never would have known we were there if Jude hadn't complained about the car windows fogging up." She laughed, blushing slightly at the memory. "You were furious, too! I remember being so afraid of you. You told us that you'd deal with Jude when we got home and that 'Madeline needed a paddlin!'"

Samuel tossed his head back and laughed. "Yeah...I seem to remember something like that," he confessed. Sighing deeply, he feigned regret. "And that was the last time I ever saw Jennifer Crosswhite."

"She was all wrong for you, Samuel," Madeline teased. "We probably saved you from a lifetime of grief."

"Well, thanks to the two of you, I guess I'll never know." Lifting his eyebrows, Samuel met the challenge in her playful eyes, holding it there for a moment.

Madeline's heart seemed to skip a beat, uncomfortable with the scrutiny of his gaze. "Well, I better get going. I just wanted to welcome you home, Samuel. It's good to have you back."

Madeline's voice was distinct and Samuel remembered it like you'd remember an old song or a favorite childhood story. It was silky smooth and low, barley over a whisper. She got up, folded the quilt and draped it over the arm of the couch in a single fluid motion.

Jude stood. "Come on. I'll take you home." He yanked on his tennis shoes, grabbed his rain jacket from the back of a chair and walked behind Madeline to the door.

At the door Madeline stopped, turned toward Samuel and smiled. He caught his breath as she disappeared behind the out-stretched rain jacket. *My goodness...what has been happening out here since I've been gone?*

Madeline was a woman out of step with the rest of the world, but somehow managed to move forward nonetheless. She lived a sheltered life, very seldom ever leaving the confines of her home and the surrounding property known as Bell Forest. The tragic life of her mother clung to her like barnacles on an old sunken vessel, weighing her down with heaviness. If not for the providence of God and the Warren family, Madeline would have sunk to the bottom of grief and despair long ago.

Located just south of the small town of Moss Bay, Alabama, Bell Bennier plantation was home to the Warren family. Madeline Linville lived in a small cottage on the coast nearby. They'd been neighbors since Madeline's mother moved to the home, known as Bay Cottage, some twenty-one years earlier.

With the recent passing of her mother, Madeline now lived alone in the humble dwelling. It faced the western sky and witnessed the ocean's rush into the warm bay waters. Her home nestled against a maritime forest to the north and the Warren compound to the south and east. Twelve acres of remote coastal area belonged to Madeline with the surrounding three thousand acres belonging to the Warrens.

The plantation's name came from the French settler who built the majestic home and acquired the lands back in the early 1700's. As a result of financial hardship, the Bennier family sold off most of the land and the house to the Warren family decades earlier.

"It sure is good to have Samuel home isn't it Jude?" Madeline whispered as she turned the knob to the back door of her cottage.

"Yeah…but it feels strange having people in the house again. Samuel always travels with an entourage." Jude gave a half-smile, then plopped down on the porch swing. "Don't go in yet, come sit out here with me," he said, patting the seat next to him. "I have this feeling he's here to take charge. He still thinks of us as kids you know."

Madeline slid off her shoes and joined him on the swing, pulling her legs up beside her. The sky was inky black without a single light. But, after the cleansing rain, the air was fresh and easy to breath. "Samuel is a "take charge" kinda guy. But he loves you Jude, you know that."

"Yeah, I know. I will say this…that Ms. Willa of his sure knows how to cook; almost as good as you." Jude winked. "Almost."

Jude and Madeline had been inseparable since they were old enough to toddle out of the house. Growing up on the farm and virtually alone, they had bonded to each other like sugar on a gumdrop. With the vastness of the sea in front of them and fields and wilderness behind them, they'd had lots of territory to explore and countless hours to fill. Not many people understood their relationship, lest of all Samuel. It had often been the subject of controversy, but it didn't matter to either of them. They were best friends and it didn't matter what the rest of the world thought about it.

Around midnight, Jude cranked his Kubota and headed for home. Dodging mud holes in the well-worn dirt road that trailed from Madeline's home to his, a sinking feeling came over him as he looked down and saw the wooden planks that bridged the gnarled roots of a giant oak. Those roots had been a constant source of injury for Madeline. He thought back to the many times she'd stumbled on them, skinning her knees over and over until one day he'd decided to build a bridge. He'd set to work, spending the whole day dragging up leftover wood from all around the property. With sweat stinging his eyes, he'd worked until sundown on the makeshift bridge. With the construction complete, he ran up the steps of Madeline's back porch, yelling for her to come out. Grabbing her hand as she stepped through the door, he pulled her down the path, stopping as they stood in front of the bridge.

Madeline gasped. "Oh Jude…you did this for me?"

Jude beamed proudly.

"It's the best bridge I've ever seen in the whole wide world!" Madeline proclaimed, running across it, back and forth, back and forth until out of breath. She smiled up at Jude, her face nearly splitting with excitement and gratitude.

Jude's throat tightened at the memory and the thought of leaving her behind. Samuel was here though, and that gave him comfort. With a heavy heart, he drove across the wooden planks of the bridge and headed toward home.

Walking through the kitchen door, Jude pulled off his muddy tennis shoes, tossed his rain jacket on the back of the chair and made his way to the oven. "I thought I smelled cobbler. You have any trouble warming that up?" He pulled out a barstool and took a seat.

"Nah, I can work magic in a kitchen." Samuel tossed a carton of vanilla ice cream on the counter. "For your cobbler."

"Ah, you remembered," Jude teased. "I guess that's why you travel with your own personal cook, 'cause you're so magical in the kitchen."

Samuel playfully hit the back of Jude's head. "I called you to ask if Madeline wanted dessert, then I heard your phone vibrating on the bar." Samuel straddled his seat, scooped up a spoonful of blackberry cobbler and casually appraised Jude as he chewed. "So...tell me," he asked, swallowing down the first big bite, "what's been goin on out here since Dad died?"

Jude shrugged. "Same as usual, I guess. Why?"

"What about Madeline?"

"What *about* Madeline?" Jude eyed his brother suspiciously.

"What happened to her mother, aunt, whatever you want to call her?"

Few things irritated Jude more than people asking questions about Madeline. "She died a couple of weeks before Dad. That's why she wasn't here for his funeral. She had to travel down to Tarpon Springs, Florida for the burial and wait for all of the papers to get sorted out. She just got back. And, just so you'll know," he stopped chewing and looked pointedly at his brother, "Della was her *mother*."

With his spoon hovering over his bowl, Samuel studied his brother. Not much had changed. Jude was still as defensive of the girl as he'd always been. It was going to be a real challenge to tear him away from her and send him off to college, agreement or no agreement. *I guess that's understandable*, he thought. Their strange relationship had always nagged him, even as a boy. He should have known that the only way he could've persuaded Jude to leave for college was to promise to move down and commit to live there for the next four years.

Leaving his home in Charleston, South Carolina would be difficult for Samuel. But as divine intervention would have it, Samuel's business, Warren and Beckett Developers, had secured a rather large project some fourteen miles away from Bell Bennier. He was now in the process of setting up a small office in town to help organize the development.

"Hmm," Samuel mused, as he thought about the coincidence.

"Did you say something?" Jude asked, still a little annoyed at his brother for bringing up Madeline.

"Just thinking."

"About?"

"Aunt Della.

Everyone knew that Aunt Della was in fact Madeline's mother…everyone, that is, except Della. Whatever turn of events marred the life of Della Linville apparently happened

21

shortly after finding out she was expecting Madeline. The "break-down" as the locals called it, came after Della's mother moved her to her husband's old family home, Bay Cottage and left her to handle the care of her newborn baby alone in a sort of "exile" far away from her home in Tarpon Springs, Florida.

The existence of Madeline had been an embarrassment to Grandmother Linville, so she isolated them far away where it wasn't possible for those who mattered to ever come across them in public. She'd provided the essentials of life for her daughter: food, shelter and clothing. But not so much as a visit could be expected from the proud and self- righteous widow Linville. As the years went by, Della withdrew further and further from reality, often staring out at the ocean as if looking through a fog, trying to identify something familiar. She was present physically, but emotionally she'd checked out long ago.

Jude let out an exaggerated breath. "I'm freaking out, man. I can't believe I'm seriously considering leaving her. What's she gonna do without me?" Jude ran his hand nervously through his wavy brown hair.

Samuel listened, lifting an eyebrow. "Isn't that what I'm here for, brother? I think you know me well enough to know that I'll never let anything happen to her. You do know that don't you?"

"I know, Samuel. That's the only reason I decided to go in the first place. Besides, she really wants me to go, or says she does anyway. She wanted to stay up all night and talk about it."

Samuel narrowed his gaze. "Just what have you two had going on out here all by yourselves? Call me old fashioned, but do you really think it's appropriate for y'all to still have sleep-overs?"

"What do you know about it? We've always spent the night with each other."

"Maybe...when you were *ten,* Jude!" Samuel shook his head, exasperated.

"You don't know what it's been like Samuel. *You* haven't been here! You ran out on us, remember. While you were out making a name for yourself we've been stuck out here trying our best to cope with everything. So what if we stay with each other, what does it matter, who will know?"

"I know! God knows!" Samuel clenched his jaw, frustrated with Jude's attempt to justify his actions and angry with himself for leaving them all those years ago.

"You don't know how it is and you can't keep us apart, Samuel. Nothing will ever come between us!"

Chapter 4

*C*aressed by a cooling breeze, Madeline slowly made her way along the edge of the water, stepping just out of reach of the tumbling surf. Despite the risk of sand and saltwater coating her bare legs, she continued, bending down occasionally to pick-up a tiny shell, depositing it in the pocket of her fluttering white skirt. Her hair was gathered and tied loosely with a ribbon at the base of her neck.

Samuel watched from his chair on the wide veranda that ran across the back of the house. He sipped his drink, squinting as he observed her. *She's not a goddess... she's a sea nymph siren,* he thought. *The kind that lay on rocks luring a man off course!* Not able to pull his attention away from Madeline, Samuel was relieved to be distracted by the ringing of his phone. "Samuel Warren," he said, pressing the phone close to his ear so he could hear over the clamoring sea birds overhead.

"I'm on my way out. Do you need anything?" the no-nonsense voice of Breanna Behrens questioned.

"Nothing Bree, I've got it covered. Don't forget to invite the office help; I don't want to leave anyone out. We'll eat around 7:00."

"Okay, I'll see you soon."

Snapping the phone shut, Samuel mentally pictured Bree. Well polished and refined. He wondered how she would react to this place he loved so well; would she think it to remote, to off the beaten path and quiet for her fast paced life style.

Breanna Behrens was a newcomer to Warren and Beckett Developers. Tall and slender with shiny straight-cut blonde hair, she personified the polished professional business-woman. She excelled at her job. Known for her cunning business savvy and aggressive nature, Bree easily moved into the role of sales. Using her charm, persuasion and beauty, she quickly climbed the ladder and in the process, also managed to gain the attention of one Samuel Warren.

"Jude, hold up," Samuel called over his shoulder, catching sight of his brother bounding down the stairs toward the shore.

Jude stopped and glanced back. "Yeah, what's up?"

"Ask Madeline if she wants to have dinner with us tonight around 7:00. Some of our employees are coming out."

"Okay." With a wave of his hand, Jude continued on his way toward the shoreline.

Samuel watched in fascination as Jude reached Madeline. He saw him lift his hand to brush back a wispy piece of her wind-tangled hair. She smiled up at him warmly, lips moving. Jude lowered his ear to Madeline's lips, intent on catching the words before the wind blew them away. He pulled back and laughed, mussing her hair. Reaching around her slender legs, he lifted her onto his back in piggyback fashion. Madeline's arms encircled his neck as they made their way down the beach, slowly fading from view. *Doesn't that girl own a pair of shorts?* Samuel thought, irritated that his attention was drawn to the movement of her skirt caught by the wind.

The Warren home shared all that is sacred in the coastal South: family, friends, good food, and "easy to relax around you" hospitality. Nearly every event marked by the calendar was celebrated in comfortable style at the Warren home. Passed down from generation to generation, the timeless plantation was full of love and laughter. It had seen its share of grief over the years, but the strong ties of family kept its children returning to her secure shelter decade after decade.

Preferring to dine outside, Samuel adjusted the seating where the sea breezes would blow in from the bay for comfortable dining and catching a beautiful sunset. As he lit a Citronella candle inside a green glass table lantern, he looked up to see Madeline coming across the lawn from the direction of her home. She wore a sleeveless beige collared shirt with a matching skirt overlaid with lace. It drifted, bell-like to swirl delicately just above her knees. Her clover-honey hair spilled over one lightly bronzed shoulder. Madeline was stunning in her simplicity. No jewelry, no particular hairstyle, still…she was breathtaking. His beating heart seemed to pick up speed at each sighting of her; and the behavior disturbed him.

"There you are," Bree announced, as she swung the screen door wide.

Startled from his thoughts, he quickly turned toward Bree.

"Bart just drove up," Bree informed him, casually eyeing Madeline as she watched her ascend the steps. She turned away dismissively, moving back into the house without a word.

Embarrassed by Bree's rudeness, Samuel reached for Madeline's hand, welcoming her. "Madeline, you're a vision. He lifted her hand to his lips pressing a firm kiss."

Madeline smiled, remembering Samuel's reputation as a lady's man. "Is there anything I can help with?"

The warmth of Madeline's voice and her calming spirit filled Samuel with ease. "Oh no, no, you just relax. Please," he indicated a chair near the outdoor grilling bar. "Have a seat and keep me company. I've sent Jude to town to pick up a few more steaks. He'll be back shortly."

Samuel lifted the lid on the grill as gray smoke billowed out, curling near the high ceiling of the porch. "So," he cleared his throat. "Jude tells me you're designing a special soap just for him." Samuel speared the steaks, turning them over with a sizzle as a puff of smoke dissipated into the air. Waiting for Madeline's response, he glanced over his shoulder, noticing how she sat perched on the end of the Adirondack chair with her hands folded tightly in her lap with her feet pressed together.

"Yeah, I want to have them finished before he leaves for college. It took me awhile to find the right blend of fragrance to capture his essence. I think I've got it now." Madeline looked down; sadness crossed her face briefly as she thought of Jude.

Seeing the change in her countenance, Samuel quickly tried to lighten the mood. "I'd imagine some smells coming from Jude are hard to duplicate."

Madeline laughed at his comment, gracing him with a smile. "I try to express what the person or place means to me through fragrance. But, Jude means so much to me it's been hard to define him in terms of soap. I settled on an ocean blend, it's kind of fresh and crisp. I hope he likes it."

"I'm sure he will." Taking a deep breath, Samuel released it slowly, saying, "So…how do you go about getting selected to have a soap made for you? I'd really like to be up for consideration." He flashed a dazzling smile in her direction.

Madeline marveled at the differences between Jude and Samuel. Samuel was muscular and well defined with broad shoulders and a strong masculine face that seemed to boast a five o'clock shadow no matter the time of the day. Charm oozed out of him. His smile could melt you on the spot. The only similarities between the two brothers were their smoky blue-gray eyes and dark brown wavy hair. Jude's strong and lean body gave him the appearance of being much younger than his twenty years, while Samuel's hard good looks made him look older with an air of confidence about him.

Madeline eased back into the chair, gently tucking her skirt around the sides of her legs. "I'll give that some thought and get back to you," she said, with an impish grin. She relaxed, noticeably.

"Oh no, here it comes…your people will call my people kinda thing…right?" Samuel teased, flashing a bright white grin.

The screen door opened suddenly and Jude stepped out, spying Madeline. "Sorry I'm so late and you've had to endure Samuel's company so long." He shot his brother a grin. "I hope you still have an appetite."

Madeline pinched his arm as he plopped down on the armrest of her chair. "We've had a nice conversation. I was just beginning to enjoy myself."

"Until I showed up?" Jude questioned, glaring at Samuel suspiciously.

"You heard the lady." Samuel smiled, feeling suddenly lighter as he replayed her words over in his head.

Bree appeared from around the corner, sashaying up to Samuel as she handed him a drink. "I thought you might need this." She leaned into him, kissing his cheek.

Taking the drink from her hand Samuel sniffed it. "No thanks. I don't remember inviting "Captain Morgan" to the party. You know how I feel about alcohol. Where did you get this anyway...not from my house?" The scowl on his face spoke volumes.

"Don't be such a bore. Bart brought it, but don't worry, he left the rum in his car." Sliding into a nearby seat, Bree stared at Jude and Madeline. Taking a sip of the napkin wrapped cocktail intended for Samuel, she announced, "I'm Bree, Samuel's girlfriend." Tightening her lips into a thin smile that never reached her eyes, she extended her hand to Jude, stern and business like. "You must be Jude. Samuel's told me so much about you."

Taking her hand, Jude replied, "Nice to meet you, Bree...Samuel is certainly full of surprises. Oh, this is Madeline." Jude put his arm possessively around Madeline's shoulder and squeezed.

Bree's fleeting smile flashed and was over before they could blink.

"Well," Jude said to Madeline, as he stood up. "Let's go get your bathing suit so we can go for a swim later." Grabbing her hand he pulled her to her feet. "We'll be back for dinner," he called over his shoulder.

Samuel gestured with his fork, acknowledging the words, but never looking up. He was clearly annoyed. He sensed the storm clouds gathering and prayed things would not turn out the way they seemed to be heading. *Maybe this wasn't such a good idea after all.*

Pale light spilled from the porch windows and out onto the lawn; twilight was dissolving into night. The music and laughter from the house mingled with the night sounds of crickets and distant frogs as Madeline and Jude walked to the sea.

From the corner of the veranda, Samuel sat in the shadows, grateful no one had witnessed his escape from the crowd inside. His partner, Bart Beckett, who'd recently separated from his wife of ten years, was having a hard time coping with the loss. Drowning his troubles was not the answer. Samuel understood his friend's misery but refused to allow his poor judgment to affect anyone else. He took his car keys and collected the keys of everyone who'd wandered out to "Bart's Backseat Bar" that night. No one there was stupid enough or drunk enough to argue with him. So, with a house full of jovial partygoers, he sought peace and solitude in the shadows of his porch, cradling a steaming cup of coffee in his hands.

Catching a glimpse of his brother and Madeline, Samuel watched as they stood together in the ocean, lifting as each wave rolled through them. Madeline was draped in a gauzy cover-up that clung to her as Jude held tightly to her arms, pushing her upward with each swell. The moonlight reflected softly on their silhouettes, shimmering against their wet skin. *Why am I always spying on those two,* he thought, taking a slow sip of his coffee. *Has it really come to this?*

Resting his head on the back of the weathered Adirondack chair, Samuel pondered briefly what it must be like to be Jude.

"Poor Samuel," Madeline said, as she and Jude floated together in the ocean, "looks like he's going to have a house full of rowdy house guests tonight."

"Don't feel *too* sorry for him,' Jude said, wiping his hand down his face to clear away the salt water. "He asks for it. My brother is the patron saint of the barfly. He's always trying to help somebody, especially the down and outers...been like that all his life."

"Jesus was like that," Madeline said softly, lifting with the swell of the wave. "He never shied away from sinners or outcasts, seemed to prefer them actually."

"Yeah well, I wouldn't compare Samuel to Jesus," Jude said, laughingly. "But, somebody told him a story once that made a difference in his life. It was a story about a man walking along the beach where hundreds of sea stars washed ashore."

"You mean starfish," Madeline corrected.

"No, sea stars. Starfish are not fish; they're echinoderms, like sea urchins. The proper name for a starfish is sea star."

A glint of mischief shone from her eyes. "I'm just teasing. You've told me that a hundred times. I just like to see the marine biologist come out in you." Madeline ruffled his damp hair with her fingers.

Jude rolled his eyes. "Anyway, as the man walked along, he would reach down and pick-up a *sea star* and toss it back into the ocean. Another man walking up behind him laughed, saying 'you must be crazy...there are hundreds of sea stars out here, it can't possibly make a difference.' The man reached down and took hold of another one, tossing it into the sea saying, 'It made a difference to that one.'"

After a long moment, Madeline looked back over her shoulder toward the house. She knew from that moment on that she would never view Samuel Warren exactly the same way ever again.

Chapter 5

*T*he days rolled by with ease as Madeline busily worked with her soaps. With encouragement from Greenberry, she'd started the cottage industry of soap making three years earlier. He'd complained about his rough and dry hands being sore and chapped from the elements and hard stable work. So, Madeline set to work trying to find the right combination of emollients to help relieve his swollen and chapped hands. Finding the right mixture of cleanser and moisturizer, Madeline had presented it to Greenberry along with a special salve he could rub into his hands each night.

Pretty soon, nearly every fisherman and farmer along the coast sought Madeline out for more of the concoction. Madeline's liniments and salves spread by word-of-mouth. She began making salves for all kinds of ailments, everything from diaper rash to dishpan hands. But, only in the last year had she branched out to include scented soaps, hand creams and bath gels. Several new orders had trickled in, igniting a new sense of purpose within her. Driven by the demand, she'd set to work.

Night fell and the wind picked up, howling and whistling through the cracks in the door as heavy rain pelted against the windows. Madeline finished packaging the freshly cut bars and donned her pajamas. Padding through the house, she turned off lights as she made her way to bed.

Startled by a loud tapping on the door, she jumped. Looking through the glass panes she could vaguely make out the image of a man. "Who is it?"

"Samuel. I've been given orders to retrieve you," he called out, flashing an arresting smile that was recognizable, even in the dark.

Opening the door, she could smell the rain on his skin all mixed up with some faint scent of spice and tobacco. Having a nose for scents, Madeline decided that that particular fragrance was...well, extremely nice. "Oh?" she responded, keenly aware of him and the way his masculine presence filled the doorway.

"Jude asked me to get you...wants you to spend the night."

"Is he all right?" Madeline knew how Samuel felt about their spending the night with one another, Jude had informed her. She couldn't imagine what had caused his sudden change of mind. *Jude must be sick for Samuel to come and get me like this.*

"He has a slight fever, but otherwise he's fine. He says he feels better with you in the house. You know Jude, when he's sick; he's such a baby. I don't think I can listen to his whining another minute!"

Madeline twisted her lips to hide a smile. "Okay, I'll go change."

"No need for that, you'll just have to change again anyway. Come on, I've got you."

Before she could protest, Samuel picked her up effortlessly, cradling her close against his chest. All protests along with all reasoning ability came to a sudden halt.

"I used to carry you around like this when you were little, remember that?"

Madeline nodded. She was barely able to breathe much less talk.

"Guess we better blow out these candles first." Samuel leaned over the kitchen table, snuffing them out with a quick breath. "A clam basket chandelier...would you look at that. There's a shop in Charleston that would pay good money for that creation."

Finding her voice again, she said, "Yeah, I like the way the light shines through it leaving a pattern on the wall."

Nodding, Samuel remarked, "Canning jars with candles for porch lights, clam baskets for chandeliers...very creative of you Miss Maddie. Any more fire around that I should know about?"

She thought she was going to faint from his closeness and the heady scent of him. Catching her breath, she said, "That's it. Oh, wait...there is one next to my bed."

Samuel surveyed the room; he noticed a plush comforter and pillows tossed on a window seat. The glow from a votive candle illuminated the darkened corner as it flickered on the nightstand, casting shadows on the ceiling. "Your bed, I presume?"

"Yes."

As he neared the window seat he looked out into the darkened night, noticing the choppy sea and wide expanse of sky. "Nice view." He bent to blow out the last of the candles.

"I think so," Madeline replied, almost in a whisper.

Something stirred in Samuel at the sound of her words, making him question his tactics. It was surprising to him how the world seemed to tilt ever so slightly whenever Madeline was near. He'd learned lately to brace himself for support whenever she was around. *This may not be the wisest thing I've ever done.* Pushing her up close to his chest, he noticed her soft fragrance, all powdery and fresh. Deciding it might be best to leave before he noticed anything else about her, he made his way to the door.

Closing the cottage door behind him, Samuel couldn't resist pressing her close just once more as he made a run for the truck. After placing her gently in the passenger seat, he ran around to the driver's side and hopped in. The truck rocked with the weight of his body as he cranked the engine and headed toward home.

They splashed through mud holes and ran across ruts, the very same ruts Jude had always been so careful to avoid, Samuel seemed to purposefully hit. Madeline held on tightly to the seat, gripping the leather until her knuckles turned white. Her small frame bounced around on the truck seat, being nearly thrown to the floor.

"Whoa there, Maddie girl." Samuel laid his hand across her knee to steady her. "I'd better slow this thing down or I'm gonna lose you." He lifted his hand and backed off the accelerator at the same time. "I should've put rocks in your pockets to weigh you down a little more," he teased, trying to coax a response and was rewarded with a somewhat shaky smile.

Pulling up to the house, Samuel stepped out saying, "Hold it right there. I'll do the honors." He stepped around the truck and opened her door. Reaching in, he lifted her effortlessly from the seat and climbed the stairs to the front door. Looking down at her rain-splattered face with her cheek pressed into his chest and her eyes fixed on him, he held his breath. In slow motion he reached down and opened the door, prolonging the time he held her in his arms.

"Your precious package has been delivered," Samuel said, reluctantly releasing Madeline onto the couch beside Jude.

"Thanks, Samuel." Jude let out a sigh of relief as he smiled weakly at Madeline.

With an amused grin, Samuel plopped down into a chair and leaned back against it. He raised his feet to the ottoman. "Your wish is my very great pleasure."

Jude shot him a look. "Why don't you go get me an Advil."

"Let me," Madeline offered. She got up and walked bare foot into the kitchen, her pink nightgown swinging slightly around her knees.

"Something on your mind, Samuel?" Jude inquired, giving him a suspicious glare as he watched him watch Madeline leave the room.

"Yeah, I'm still confused about all of this. I mean, what's really going on here. Are you two...?" He let the question hang in the air.

"No!" he interrupted. "We're not. I don't understand what's so hard for you to understand. It's not like we haven't been best friends since forever."

"Well, if you can't look at her and understand my concern, you're..."

Just then Madeline appeared in the doorway with her hand stretched out toward Jude. "Here ya go."

"Thanks." Jude took the medicine and swallowed it down. Giving Madeline a sympathetic look, he said, "I know you're tired, why don't you go on up to bed." He was anxious for her to leave the appraising eye of his brother.

"All right, but you come and get me if you start to feel worse." Leaning forward, she placed a light kiss on his forehead, lingering there a moment. "You're right Samuel; he still has a slight fever. That medicine should help pretty soon," she said, patting the quilt covering his legs. "Well, good night guys. I'll see you in the morning."

They watched her climb the stairs until she disappeared down the hall. Hearing the door close, a moment later they heard the shower come on.

"Did she have on Tinker Bell pajamas?" Samuel asked curiously, turning his attention back to Jude.

"What?" Jude raised his head off of his pillow and gave his brother an incredulous look.

"Tinker Bell, is she wearing Tinker Bell pajamas?"

Shaking his head, he replied, "I don't know man, why on earth does it matter?" He dropped his head back down on the pillow, staring at the ceiling.

"Just an observation," Samuel shrugged. "I think it's kinda cute."

Jude rolled his eyes. After a long moment of just staring at the ceiling, he whispered, "I hope I'm not gonna have to worry about you, Samuel. It's bad enough the poor girl can't even go into town without that pack of dogs from high school nipping at her heels. Please tell me I don't have to worry about you, too."

"Don't go getting yourself all riled up, you know me better than that."

In one swift movement, Madeline turned down the bedcovers, hopped up on the bed and slipped her feet under the silky sheets. She loved sleeping at Bell Bennier and had come to think of the guest room as her very own. Turning off the bedside lamp, she sank down into the folds of the lightly scented sheets. *Willa, no doubt,* Madeline thought, as she inhaled deeply of the fragrant sheets. But, the comfort she felt made her think of Lou.

Until recently, Lou had been the Warren's cook and housekeeper. She had taken care of both Warren boys most of their lives. Jim Warren had hired her shortly after his wife, Josslyn Camellia, passed away.

Madeline loved the old housekeeper and knew without a doubt that Lou had been responsible for all of the little packages she'd found on her doorstep during her teenage years. Each package was a complete surprise. Sometimes there would be personal items; frivolous things like hair clasps or chocolate, magazines or fingernail polish. But, whatever the gift, the feeling of being cared for and loved left her feeling warm inside.

As a young girl, Madeline had wished a thousand times that Lou would adopt her. Although the woman was not much on open displays of affection, she knew Lou loved her by her actions and the interest she'd always shown in her life. She was happy for Lou and proud that she'd gone back to school to finish her nursing degree. Still, on nights like these, she missed her terribly.

Stirred by a balmy breeze, Madeline watched the floor length drapes move in slow random patterns across the polished wood floor as crickets sang their lullaby from the hedges below. The scent of wood polish and wild roses filled the air as she scanned the room for the source. Finding a crystal vase spilling over with the fragrant pink blooms, she smiled; pink roses and hydrangeas were her favorite flowers. Settling back against the pillow she listened to the sounds of the endless sea. The ocean is never silent. You can always hear its rhythmic sound on Bell Bennier, especially at night when the house is quiet and still.

All of the bedrooms at Bell Bennier face the sea and open out onto a veranda that stretches across the house. The constant crash of waves invokes a sacred rhythm much like a heartbeat…soon you succumb to it, as if under a spell. Your breathing slows and your eyes grow heavy until you drift pleasantly off to sleep with gentle breezes from the open door stirring your hair.

Madeline awoke to the sounds of morning echoing through the house. The smell of coffee wafted up the stairs and into her room, reviving her senses. Slipping out of bed, she opened the closet door and took out a bathrobe she'd noticed hanging there last night in her search for a towel. Wrapping the huge blue robe around her, she turned up the sleeves and tiptoed down the hall toward the kitchen, expecting to find Willa at the stove stirring her pots.

"Good morning. Did you rest well?" Samuel asked, cheerfully. He folded his newspaper, laying it aside. Getting up, he poured her a cup of coffee. "Cream and sugar?"

Madeline nodded as she slipped into a chair. "I slept so soundly, I don't think I even moved. I sleep so much better…"she caught her words, letting them trail off. The last thing she wanted to do was upset Samuel, knowing how he felt about her staying over. "Where's Willa this morning?"

"I gave her the day off. She needed a few things from town. Greenberry offered to drive her in and show her the lay of the land. Nice of him, don't you think?" He grinned.

The deep lines around Samuel's eyes told of an uneasy night. Jude mentioned that Samuel suffered from insomnia and that he seldom if ever had a complete nights sleep.

Roaming over the house and property at night, Samuel had alarmed Jude on more than one occasion. Once he'd caught a glimpse of a shadowy figure passing in front of his door. As he grabbed his baseball bat from the closet, he followed behind the darkened figure until he was aware it was Samuel.

"That robe looks better on you than it ever did on me," Samuel said, slowly sipping his coffee as he studied her in the pale morning light.

Self-consciously, she twisted the fabric closed around her throat, noticing for the first time the stitched initials, "SJW" for Samuel James Warren. "I found it in the closet. I hope you don't mind. I was ambushed last night and left the house without being decent." Embarrassment flushed her face.

"Please. I'm glad something of mine is useful to you. I only wish I could offer you more." *Did I just say that out loud?* He thought. *I hope she thinks I'm kidding.* Relief washed over him as he saw her smile.

Madeline stood up. "How about breakfast…Jude will probably sleep a while longer, but you'll need to eat before you head to work."

Samuel raised his eyes in surprise. "You'll cook for me?"

"I'd love to. Tell me; are you a big breakfast kinda guy? You want the works?"

"If you're offering, I'm accepting!" He placed his coffee cup on the table, rubbing his hands together excitedly. Standing, he moved to the cabinets and began opening doors, pulling out all sorts of things like molasses and salt and pepper. "How can I help?"

"You can help by staying out of my way. I know my way around a kitchen. You just sit down and finish reading your paper." She grinned and reached for the apron on the hook inside the pantry door. Tying the straps around her, she set out to gather all she needed from the large walk-in pantry. She loved the open styled kitchen. It was designed for easy flow and accessibility, yet still maintained a farmhouse feel. The dark wooden floors were polished to a glossy sheen, accentuating the shiny stainless steel appliances. Smooth granite counter tops curved around the room pulling everything together. Open French doors led out to the ground floor veranda allowing the fresh ocean breeze to filter inside.

The clanging of pots and pans was music to Samuel's ears. He perked up at the first whiff of bacon and couldn't wipe the smile from his face. "It's been a long time since anyone's cooked for only me," he noted. "Willa cooks for an army."

Madeline looked back over her shoulder. "What about Bree? Doesn't she cook for you?"

A laugh escaped his lips. "Oh no, not Bree...her talents lay elsewhere." Seeing what looked like embarrassment cross Madeline's features, he quickly tried to recover his meaning. "She's an excellent sales person. I don't think our company would be as successful without her. She's really an asset, but there's not one domestic bone in her body."

"Oh, I see. Tell me about your business, what do you do exactly?" Turning her attention back to the skillet, she continued moving the bacon around in the pan.

"We do real estate development. We bridge the gap between builders and users...buy land, develop it, finance real estate deals and then line up builders to build."

"You mentioned that Bree is in sales, what's your job?"

"I handle the initial phase of development...oversee the building of roads and installation of utilities, spec houses, things like that."

"Sounds risky, what are some of the risks?"

"Cost overruns, bad weather, too few sales per month, higher cost…"

Madeline turned to him and grimaced.

"Everything worth doing has risks, Madeline, no exceptions. Even Columbus took a chance." Smiling, Samuel sipped his coffee. He'd gathered from Jude that Madeline liked to play it safe, seldom even venturing into town.

Trying to show vague interest, Madeline asked, "So…tell me about Bree. Besides being really beautiful and obviously smart, what attracted you to her?" Madeline was curious about the seemingly mismatched couple. Normally she would not have been so bold, but his good mood and the easy flow of conversation gave her courage to ask what she'd been wondering.

"Truthfully?" he smirked. "It's hard to resist a leggy blonde, especially one with business savvy. She's also a pretty good kisser." Even as the words left his mouth he regretted them. Changing the subject, he asked, "So, what about you and Jude? Please," he held up a hand, "I don't think I can stand to hear about what kind of a kisser he is…I'd lose my appetite."

"Well you don't have to worry about that," Madeline smirked. "The first and the last time we ever kissed on the lips was about ten years ago. I was curious enough to ask him to kiss me to see what it felt like. He told me he'd have to think about it. So, after about a week and much deliberation I'm sure," she raised her eyebrows, smiling, "he told me he'd give it a try. He leaned toward me with his wet lips pressing into mine all slimy and reeking of spearmint. I pulled away gagging and spitting on the ground." Madeline giggled. "Poor Jude, I don't think he's ever gotten over that. And I can't *stand* spearmint to this day!"

Samuel was shocked, had he heard right? Did she just say that they never kissed? He had always been confused about their relationship, but now he was down right dumbfounded! Sure, he knew he had a shallow relationship with Bree, but a relationship without physical attraction was...well certainly a relationship that was way *too deep* to his way of thinking! He studied her, narrowing his eyes as they raked over her. *Jude must be an idiot*, he surmised, as his mind began to think of all kinds of explanations for the odd behavior.

"Well, eat up," she said, placing the breakfast dishes down before him. The look on Samuel's face was worth all of the effort it took to prepare the meal. His eyes danced with delight as he dug-in, smiling and rolling his eyes as he chewed.

"Aren't you going to eat?" he asked, watching as Madeline sat down across from him, cradling her coffee cup.

"Nah, I never eat breakfast. I usually eat lunch about mid-morning each day. Technically, I guess that would be called brunch wouldn't it?"

He swallowed down a big bite. "You mean you fixed all of this just for me?" he asked, beaming. "Tell me, how did you learn to cook like this?"

"*Lots* of practice...I took care of Aunt Della...I mean Mother," Madeline clarified. "So, I had to learn how to cook early. I bought an old "Cotton Country" cookbook at a yard sale for fifty cents and I studied that book like it was the Bible." She brushed back a wispy piece of hair from her brow. "Poor Mother, she had to endure a ten-year-olds feeble attempt at cooking...crunchy eggs and all."

Poor mother, Samuel thought! *Poor Madeline for having to play nursemaid to a mentally ill woman at the age of ten!* "Well, that explains it. All of your efforts have certainly paid off well for me."

Chapter 6

*W*hy is it that Madeline never goes to church with you?" Samuel asked Jude as he bent down to tie his tennis shoes.

"She goes to church."

"Oh…where?"

"Down the beach." Jude began walking off.

"Want to try again," Samuel shouted after him. "You know good and well that there is nothing *down the beach.*" Beginning to feel annoyed, he glared at his brother's retreating form.

Jude stopped and turned back to his brother. "She has her own beliefs, man. She's fine, leave her alone…just because someone worships in a different way doesn't make them wrong or bad or whatever…" With a wave of his hand, he dismissed his brother and walked off.

Mystified, Samuel was a little more than curious about Madeline's so called beliefs. He knew it was pointless to inquire further. He saw his brother's defenses shoot up at the first mention of Madeline.

Stepping out into the fresh morning air, Samuel stretched and flexed as he prepared for his morning run. Heading down the beach, his lungs drew in the salty air as his heartbeat accelerated bringing his whole body to pulsating life.

He caught a movement from the corner of his eye. From a patch of sea oats he recognized Madeline's hair as strands of it lifted in the gentle morning breeze. He couldn't see her face, but there was no mistaking who it was, *no* one had hair that particular color. He kept running, but glanced back over his shoulder every so often as he wondered what Madeline could possibly be doing behind the sand dune.

The place was well hidden behind brush and sea oats. A rounded sand dune obscured the area from view and you'd most likely pass right by without a second glance. Samuel made a mental note to check it out on his way back, only if she'd gone, that is.

A half-hour later as Samuel neared the place behind the dunes, he slowed his pace, placing his hands on his thighs as he steadied his breathing. He stepped cautiously near the hidden spot. Sand pipers scurried around him just out of reach, but no other presence was visible. A light breeze bent the sea oats, rustling them softly. Everything was peaceful; nothing disturbed the tranquility of the scene.

Samuel peered over the dune, then searched the area again for a sign of Madeline. When he was sure she was nowhere around, he stepped near. A crucifix caught his eye, sticking out of the sand as it leaned forward slightly from the weight of the impaled figure of Christ. Twine crisscrossed around the wood and seemed to be holding the whole of it together. Just beneath the cross, stuck down into the sand, stood a tall red glass cylinder with a candle deep inside. The smoke from the extinguished flame still hung on the air. His eyes roamed over the area; it was then that he noticed the dimpled impressions in the sand in front of the cross. His throat constricted. Suddenly, Samuel felt as if he were intruding into something very private, something sacred.

Easing away, he stepped back, making his way to the firmer, wet sand near the shore. Pausing briefly, he peered back over his shoulder to the little sanctuary in the sand, then slowly made his way back home.

Lost in thought, Samuel walked up the porch steps and into the house as Jude came down the stairs, clean and freshly shaven.

Adjusting his tie, Jude eyed his brother skeptically. "Seagulls dive bombing you again, Brother," he asked, glancing up at Samuel's wind tossed hair.

"Funny." Raking his hand through his hair, he tried to smooth down the tangled waves of hair.

"You comin to church?" Jude asked.

"Yeah, let me jump in the shower...I'll be ready in fifteen minutes."

After his shower Samuel began dressing, his thoughts circling around what he'd discovered on the beach. The little alter in the sand was a foreign concept to him. *What a strange way to worship. So,* he thought. *Just because something is different doesn't make it wrong. Her focus is clearly on Jesus.* Still, something troubled him.

Pulling into the recently paved church parking lot seemed odd to Samuel. His ears were prepared to hear the familiar crunch of gravel and shell beneath his tires; instead they found the noiseless and smooth feel of fresh asphalt. Samuel and Jude hopped out of the truck and rushed into the church. The smell of hot tar hung thickly on the air as it followed them into the foyer. They hurried down the aisle to the opening song, *'Come Thou Font of Every Blessing'*. Glances from smiling members, not surprised by the tardiness, nodded in recognition as the men passed.

The Warren men were always the last to arrive. It was a tradition, like potluck on Wednesday nights or little pillows on the seats of the most faithful matriarchs. "Southerners hold fast to their traditions," Pastor Nathan once remarked. "I purposely sing all three verses in the opening song in order to make adjustments for the Warren family's tradition of coming to church fashionably late."

Samuel was just getting to know Pastor Nathan, and what he knew of him, he liked. He'd first met Nathan during his father's funeral and knew immediately that he liked his brand of Christianity. Never leaving their side, Pastor Nathan encouraged the brothers in the faith, reaching out to them with love and support and a ready hand to assist them with all the matters of laying someone to rest.

Looking around the congregation, Samuel recognized most faces. He spied Michael Christenberry's muscular form a few rows in front of him. Michael was his closest friend and had been since they were boys. A small woman with hair the color of golden wheat was standing next to him. *Must be his new wife*, Samuel thought. They shared a hymnal and glanced at each other adoringly throughout the entire song. He watched as Michael reached around and pulled her smiling figure closer, pressing her into his side. It was good to see his friend look so happy. After the tragic loss of Michael's first wife in a terrible automobile accident only four years earlier, Samuel was beginning to doubt whether his friend would ever truly be happy again.

With the rustling of paper and the movement of pews, everyone sat down, waiting for Pastor Nathan to deliver his sermon.

"As many of you know, this is my last Sunday as your pastor," Brother Nathan calmly stated. A hush fell over the congregation. An occasional sniffle could be heard from the crowd. "I'm leaving the pulpit, but not the church. I plan to stay on and help out in any way that I can. Serving the Lord is a privilege each of us share and there are many ways to serve Him. Our new pastor, Brother Thad, as he prefers to be called, has graciously asked me to oversee the church grounds." A low rumble of laughter spread throughout the church. "Somehow he's under the impression that I like that sort of thing," he said sheepishly. "As a matter of fact, it's been reported that I actually prefer our annual workday to Easter!" Knowing nods could be seen everywhere. "Let me assure you...I don't. For without Easter, we would have no hope." Thus began the last sermon of Pastor Nathan.

After service, Jude leaned over to Samuel to explain why Pastor Nathan was stepping down as Pastor. "He's getting married next month."

With raised eyebrows, Samuel responded, "So I take it his fiancée doesn't like the idea of being a pastor's wife."

"No, nothing like that...she's a divorced Catholic," he whispered, in a hushed voice.

"She's Catholic?" Samuel questioned, turning to Jude for clarification; not at all sure he'd heard him correctly. "Well, what about that. How did that happen?"

Jude shrugged. "Who can figure love? That's her over there," he motioned with his head toward the back of the church.

Following Jude's gesture, Samuel noticed a pretty, slender woman with long light brown hair. Her back was to the wall and her arms closed tightly around her bible. At her side was a little girl, a miniature replica of her mother.

Distracted momentarily by his observation, he didn't hear as Michael approached from behind. Suddenly, two strong arms wrapped around Samuel's shoulders, squeezing.

"Michael? The Lord is watching you!" Samuel strained his voice and smiled as Michael released him.

Michael grabbed Samuel's hand in a firm grip. "Good to see you Samuel! I heard you were coming home." Michael motioned for his wife. As she stepped closer, he wrapped his arm around her possessively, beaming proudly. "Samuel, I'd like for you to meet my wife, Telie."

"You poor, poor woman," Samuel said, shaking his head in sympathy as he reached for her hand. "What did you do sweetheart, make a bargain with God?" He lifted up a hand halting her response. "I know, I know, you told Him that you'd do *anything* for Him...go to Africa...marry Michael...anything!"

Telie grinned widely, winking at her husband. "That's exactly what I did."

Michael held his wife closely. "Come by and see me, Samuel, we need to catch up on things."

"I was planning on it. Put the coffee on and I'll drop by in the morning. And oh, Telie, you will join us won't you? I'd much rather gaze at you first thing in the morning than Michael."

Shaking hands firmly, Michael replied, "I see you still have an eye for beauty my friend, but this one's mine and there's no way she's coming around you; morning, noon or night!" With that said, Michael ushered Telie toward the back of the church, smiling over his shoulder.

Caught up in the conversation with Michael, Samuel had forgotten his bible. He reached down to retrieve it from the pew and felt a tug on his sleeve. Glancing around, he saw Mrs. Feldman, with her signature sweet smile aimed in his direction. "Mrs. Feldman! It's so good to see you!" Giving her an easy hug, Samuel released her gently. He could feel her delicate bone structure through her clothing.

Her shinning blue eyes danced at the sight of him. "Samuel, you're a sight for sore eyes, my boy. You remind me so much of your father."

Samuel stiffened under the comment. He'd never liked being compared to his father. "How are you Mrs. Feldman? You're looking well." Her tiny frame looked surprisingly strong and erect. She had to be fast approaching seventy years old by now. He'd always liked Mrs. Feldman and often thought she must've had the patience of Job. She'd been his fourth grade teacher as well as his Sunday school teacher during his rambunctious boyhood days.

"I'm very well, Samuel. Tell me, how are you and how is our Madeline? I think of her so often."

Surprise registered on his face. "Oh…you know Madeline?"

"Why heavens yes. I was her fourth grade teacher, same as you." A sympathetic look crossed her face. "Madeline has always been special to me…*and* to your father."

Curiosity was getting the better of him, although he didn't care to hear about his father, he was more than a little interested to know more about Madeline. "Why is that Mrs. Feldman?"

"Oh…well I guess I've always had a soft spot when it comes to the girl. She endured a particularly rough class of snobs. For some reason, Madeline never measured up to their high standard." She looked toward the ceiling thoughtfully, with a crooked finger under her chin. "I remember one day, all the girls in my class were invited to Robin Chamber's spend the night party. They all had their sleeping bags and over night cases, all except for Madeline. She was never included." Mrs. Feldman shook her head. "In all my days of teaching, that was the hardest thing for me to endure. I kept a lump in my throat for that girl most of the year. If it hadn't been for your father..." her voice cracked, before trailing off.

"What about my father?" Samuel leaned on the end of the pew, casually crossing his leg as he listened intently to her story.

"Well, I told your father about what happened...the next Sunday after church. After that, things began to change. I remember seeing the set of his square jaw and the determination in his eyes as he walked out of the church that day. Jim was madder than a whole nest of hornets. Well, Madeline just bloomed after that. Over the next few years, I saw a remarkable change in the girl. I don't know what he did, but whatever it was, it worked!"

What about that, Samuel thought, finding it hard to believe his dad was ever sober enough to make a difference in someone's life.

Chapter 7

*T*he soft light suffusing through the room seemed to emanate from the Robin's egg blue walls rather than the large seaside windows. A worn and weathered antique table stood in the middle of the room atop an earthy sisal rug. Glass apothecary jars of colorful herbs, sweet almond and coconut oils in a myriad of brightly colored bottles filled the table haphazardly. Molds and scales cluttered one end of the huge table; only the sodium hydroxide was placed high on a shelf, out of the way and guarded. Everything Madeline needed to create her soaps and salves was within the summery room. She reached her slender hand into a jar half filled with tiny seashells. Drawing one out, she threaded the small, perfectly round nature-made hole with twine then tied it tightly around the wrapped soap bar.

"There, that should do it," she said out loud, placing the last bar of soap in the overflowing box. She'd stuffed everything she could think of inside the package; cookies, socks, pictures and of course, soap.

"Hello to the camp!" Jude said, mimicking his father's favorite greeting. He rushed inside, grabbing Madeline in a tight hug. "Come on...I'm about to leave."

"Here, take your package." She slid the large box off the table and into his hands.

"Good grief Madeline, what's in here, the kitchen sink?"

"Everything but."

Once outside, Madeline heard Jude's car idling steadily on the pebble drive. The door was open and the backseat was overflowing with an assortment of pillows, blankets and suitcases, and even the rusty old fan he'd had all his life. So much of him was leaving in that car. Jude leaned over the backseat and placed Madeline's package on top, mashing it down to secure it firmly. When he turned around, he saw tears in her eyes.

The sound of Samuel's truck door slamming pulled their attention away from each other, but only for a moment.

Samuel watched as Jude reached for Madeline's hand, smiling at her as if they shared a secret no one else knew. A thought danced around in his head. *They probably do have secrets no one else knows about.*

Jude wrapped his arms around Madeline, squeezing tightly. "I'll call everyday. Keep your cell phone within reach. Samuel is right here if you need anything. I've asked him to keep a check on you so behave and *don't* give him any trouble." He winked back at Samuel. "We've already talked about y'all coming up to see me in a few weeks." He kissed her forehead. "It won't be long, you'll see." With that, he slammed the rear door shut and reached out and clasped Samuel's hand, giving it a firm squeeze. "Take care of her, man." With that said, he climbed into the car, shut the door and drove slowly away.

Samuel looked down at Madeline, really looked. Her hair fell softly around her tear stained face, sticking haphazardly to her damp skin. Not a sound escaped her lips, but her golden greens eyes pooled with unshed tears as she watched Jude disappear down the winding road. Right then and there he realized what incredible strength it must've taken for his brother to pull away from the sight before him.

Letting out a shuttered sigh, Madeline looked up at Samuel with uncertain eyes, as if waiting for direction. She looked so fragile, so lost.

Samuel searched his mind. All rational thought seemed to have escaped him as he watched Madeline's lips curve downward at the corners and quiver. He had never felt so helpless. Then an idea struck him. "Uh...Madeline, I know this is probably not the best time to ask this...but I was wondering...would you mind going into town with me. I need some help deciding what kinds of plants to use at the entrance of this new development we're working on. I wouldn't ask, but I'm in a bind. I'm headed to Christenberry's Landscaping, but my friend Michael won't be there. He told me this morning that he and his wife are going to Texas to visit with her father. I need these plants in place by the first of the week. This is a quick decision kinda thing." He put on his best, "I'm in desperate need" kind of face. Offering a distraction for Madeline was the best idea he could come up with to keep her mind off of Jude.

"Okay, Samuel, if you need me. Give me a minute to...uh..." She pointed to her face.

It was hard to think when Madeline was around. Sometimes his mind just went blank, like a doodled on etch-a-sketch that had been vigorously shaken. *What did I just say to her?* He wasn't quite sure, but whatever it was, it accomplished what he wanted, a diversion for Madeline to take her mind off of Jude's departure.

Ten minutes later, a rat-a-tat-tat sounded on the doorframe, "Come in," Madeline called.

"Ready?" Samuel asked, poking his head through the doorway. Looking around he noticed the same candles burning all around the small cottage. "Don't you have electricity, or are you some kind of boarder-line pyromaniac?"

Madeline shrugged. "Call it a quirk, but I don't feel so alone when I have candles burning all around. God called light into existence first you know, even before us."

"You mean as in *Let There be Light?*" he questioned, lightheartedly.

"Uh-huh...so the way I figure it, light must be pretty special. After all, He is called the light of the world?" She cast her eyes to him as if to say, 'Argue with that reasoning.'

Samuel threw his hands up in defeat. "I'm not questioning your reasoning, Madeline. I always say, take comfort where you can...as long as it's not illegal, immoral or fattening. Come on," he reached for her hand, wondering what sort of life this young girl had experienced when a small candle could fill such a hollow void.

They traveled down the road quietly, each lost in their own thoughts. The sky was an eerie shade of purplish gray; it looked heavy with rain. Distant thunder rumbled in the air, vibrating through the seat of the truck.

"Looks like we might be in for it," Samuel observed, breaking the silence with his observation. "But, you never can tell about the weather around here. One minute it looks like the bottom is gonna drop out of the sky, next the sun will be shinning." He reached over to turn on the radio, pressing through the stations until he landed on a weather report.

Lightning flashed, followed by a boom of rattling thunder. Madeline jumped on her seat.

"Hold on...it'll be okay. You're in the safest place you can be," Samuel told her, trying his best to reassure the trembling girl. "Tell you what; let's forget about this little trip to Christenberry's. I'm not in the mood to get all wet and I'm sure you're not either. What'd ya say we find a place in Moss Bay to have lunch and wait for this cloud to pass over?"

Madeline's eyes grew large with fear as she looked at Samuel. He wasn't sure what had caused such a reaction, was it the storm...or the thought of having lunch with him? Narrowing his eyes, he risked another glance at her. Seeing the wild look of fright on her face made him want to comfort her. He noticed her hair as it spilled down her back as she turned to stare out the window. Wishing he knew what she was thinking, he gently pressed. "Storms can be frightening when you're not in a safe place like we are."

"Frightening, but beautiful," she whispered, as she stared out at the storm.

Yeah... just like you, Samuel thought. He tried to reign in his thoughts before they got away from him. Not much ever scared him, but this little slip of a girl was doing a fair job of it.

As they entered town, Samuel slowed, scanning the narrow tree-lined street through the slaps of his windshield wipers. He located a parking space in front of the Blue Plate restaurant. The truck rocked as he hopped out into the steady rain, ran around and opened the door for Madeline. He stood there for what seemed like an eternity, blinking the rain out of his eyes, getting soaked to the skin. She seemed to be contemplating whether or not to get out.

"Madeline. I've had my shower for the day. This second one I'm having isn't all that necessary." He blinked his eyes, squinting through the rivulets of rainwater running down his face. *Should I grab her and make a run for it,* he thought? Before he had a chance to make his move, she eased out of the seat, holding on to his arm for support as her tiny feet hit the wet sidewalk. Samuel felt her hand tremble as he clasped it and began moving toward the restaurant door. *Please Lord, no thunder until we get inside.*

The Blue Plate was known far and wide for having the best Southern cooking around. As for the atmosphere, it was kitschy but comfortable, and nearly everyone in Moss Bay considered it a landmark. Samuel led Madeline into a booth and sat down across from her. He swiped his arm across his forehead to dry his face, noticing an array of colorful Blue Willow plates decorating the wall beside them. Elvis salt and pepper shakers stood guard near the chrome napkin dispenser, reminding Samuel of his younger days and how very little had changed in his favorite eating establishment.

"Good old Southern cooking; stripped of pretense. I've sure missed this place. When I was in South Carolina, I tried out every restaurant, looking for a place like this. Nobody beats their cornbread. I never get tired of it." He smiled at Madeline, trying his best to make eye contact. It frustrated him that he never seemed able to hold her gaze.

After a long stretch of silence, Madeline gave a brief nod and a tight nervous smile.

"So, what sounds good to you? I'll bet you're a chicken liver kinda girl, aren't you?" He was hoping for a reaction and pleased when he received a slight smile.

Shaking her head, she responded, "Uh, no. But I will have a bowl of soup if that's all right."

"No. That's *not* all right. You can have chicken, or meatloaf, or chicken fried steak or just a vegetable plate or all of the above, but I will not stand by while my date orders soup! That's a personal affront...what will these fine people think? They'll think I'm cheap and I'm forcing you to eat bread and water!" he teased.

Grinning widely, Madeline gave in. "Okay, I'll have the chicken plate." Her shoulders dropped slightly and she relaxed a little in Samuel's presence.

"Now, was that so hard?" Closing the menus, he handed them to the pretty little waitress as she stepped up to take their order. "You heard the lady and meatloaf for me with mashed potatoes and field peas."

"Rolls or Cornbread?" the waitress asked, batting her eyes shamelessly at Samuel.

"Cornbread."

"Sure thing, Sweetie. Tea?" Popping her chewing gum between her teeth, the waitress seemed much too preoccupied with Samuel as her eyes roamed his body.

He turned to Madeline for her response. At her nod, he said, "Make that two."

As the waitress stepped away, the restaurant door opened with a clanging of bells to a chattering bunch of young people. Madeline's face dropped immediately upon recognition and she looked down at her hands resting in her lap. Seeing the sudden change in her demeanor, Samuel casually glanced back toward the group that had just entered.

Upon seeing Madeline, one girl pushed her way through the tangle of people so she could get a better look. Her gaze shifted from Samuel to Madeline, then back to Samuel with an incredulous glare. Turning to Madeline, she glowered at her as she passed in front of them slowly. The others in the group followed suit like little brainless ducks. The only male among them whispered in a low voice as he passed, "Hey Madeline."

"Hey Joey," Madeline said, looking up to give him a half-smile.

Samuel sized up the situation, motioned for the waitress then said to Madeline, "If it's all the same to you, would you mind if we get our lunch to go? I need air and this group of magpies," he motioned with his head toward the group that just entered, "looks like they could suck the oxygen right out of a room with all their jabbering."

"Oh no, I don't mind at all. I understand. You've got to have your air…like I've got to have my light. Makes perfect sense to me," she said excitedly. She grabbed her purse off the seat and started for the door.

Samuel clamped down on her arm before she could escape. "Whoa…come here." He hooked her arm, pulling her to the cash register. He winked and squeezed her arm tightly. He had no intention of giving those girls the satisfaction of thinking they'd chased them off. He smiled down at her warmly as he handed the cash to the waitress. Glancing up he saw the group had turned their attention toward them, staring openly. After paying, he lifted the bag off the counter, placed his hand in the small of Madeline's back and led her to the door.

The rain had stopped, leaving behind stifling-hot moist heat that took your breath away. Inhaling deeply as they stepped outside, Samuel replied, "Much better. Now I can breath." He opened the truck door for Madeline and helped her up, placing the bag on her lap. "Hold on tight…we'll go find a picnic table near the bay."

The bay was smooth and tranquil. Sea birds glided silently on wind drafts, circling overhead as the sun sparkled on wet leaves. The fresh air had the mingled fragrance of rain and sea.

Samuel lifted a rain slicker from behind the truck seat as he and Madeline made their way toward a picnic table. Spreading it out on the damp bench, he reached back to guide her to the seat. But, she sidestepped him, gracefully moving around the table arranging the plates, smiling all the while as she placed the utensils in order. *Is she humming?* He was puzzled. Gone was the terrified girl of only moments before, replaced by an almost whimsical creature. He straddled the bench, watching her in childlike fascination. She looked like a water sprite dancing graceful movements all around him. Finally, she seemed to "light" on the edge of the bench and they began to eat.

Halfway through their meal, Samuel wiped his mouth with his napkin and cleared his throat. "I'm guessing you stole all the boys away from that bunch of squawkers back at the Blue Plate."

Madeline shocked him with her sweet reply. "Oh no, nothing like that," she said as she smiled, dabbing the corners of her mouth with a napkin. "One of the girls back there, Robin Chambers…well, I cut her father's ear off with a pair of scissors."

Coughing and nearly choking, Samuel covered his mouth with his fist as he regained some level of composure. "You want to run that by me again?"

Closing the lid on her container, she placed her napkin down, looked up and explained. "One of the girls back there, Robin Chambers, her dad, Beau Chambers made frequent trips to…visit my mother." All Madeline needed to say she implied with her eyes. "Most of the time my mother was in some far off place in her mind. She would call him Alexander, my father's name. Anyway, my mother was not a well woman, emotionally speaking. But one day he happened to catch her on a good day. Good days were days when she was lucid. I still remember her horrified face when he approached her telling her he was Alexander. She screamed and screamed, running up the stairs to her room where she locked herself in. And, that's when he turned to me."

Stunned speechless by her words, the powerful emotions boiling inside of him threatened to choke off his air.

Unaware of the effect her words were having on him, Madeline continued with her story. "I was young, small and scrawny, but I knew I had to do something and quickly or he would overpower me. So, I grabbed the closest thing I could find; a pair of scissors." Taking a deep breath, she hesitated a moment before she continued. "I didn't think of stabbing him at the time, only cutting him. He pushed me to the floor and landed on top of me. I didn't struggle. Something inside of me told me that that was what he wanted. So, I just stayed still. When his face smothered mine I knew he couldn't see what I was doing. I raised the scissors, opening them quietly, and then I pressed down as hard as I could and off came a piece of his ear. He jumped up, yelling profanities, clutching the side of his bloody head. That's when I made my escape. I ran to the pier, ready to jump in Greenberry's boat if he came after me, but he never did. When I was sure he'd gone, I went back to check on my mother. She was still behind the locked door of her room. I found a note on the kitchen table telling me that if I ever told anyone he'd kill me and my mother."

Anger filled Samuel's veins, coursing through his twitching body. He knew Beau Chambers—family man, businessman, deacon in *his* church...*that* Beau Chambers!

How many times had he wondered what heroic act had cause the injury plainly evident to everyone. Gathering all of the composure he could muster, he calmly asked, "Does Jude know about this?"

Sorrow, remorse or some other indefinable emotion shadowed her smooth complexion. "You're the only person I've ever told."

Swallowing the lump that knotted in his throat, Samuel spoke, making a conscious effort to keep his voice low and to react calmly. The admission that he was the first to know startled him. He didn't think she and Jude kept *anything* from each other. "So—is that why you rarely leave home? You're afraid of meeting up with Beau?"

She nodded. "That and the fact that I'm not very well liked around here. People think I'm crazy."

"I see." His mind raced with the implications of her confession. *I'll bet Beau has something to do with that, too. He's covering his tracks...coward,* he thought. *No wonder she never goes to church...especially our church!* He fumed under the surface, not sure how he should handle this new development. *I need to talk to Michael.*

"Madeline." Hesitating, he wasn't all that sure how he needed to proceed. Taking a deep breath, he forged on. "Hear me well. I'll never let anyone or anything harm you... ever. You'll have to trust me." His gray eyes locked on hers possessively.

Shifting her eyes downward, Madeline busied herself clearing off the table when a loud woman's voice drawled from behind them. "Samuel Warren! Well if that don't beat it. Look honey," she said, pushing a small boy forward so he was standing directly in front of Samuel. "This man could have been your father!"

"Whoa now, wait a minute," Samuel jumped up to respond to the accusation quickly, while turning a deep shade of red. Then sudden recognition crossed his face. "Angie? Is that you?"

"Why of course it is you fool. And this here's my son, Jake. Jake this is my old sweetheart, Samuel Warren."

Madeline twisted her lips to keep from grinning. The boisterous woman was as broad as she was tall. She had tinted brassy gold hair with a dark three inch grow-out row running down the center of her head. A very ornate tattoo peeked out from under her T-shirt sleeve on one of her massive arms.

"I thought you'd done run off. Whadya come home for, miss me?" She smiled broadly, displaying a missing tooth.

"You *know* I did Angie. You've haunted my dreams for years!" Samuel laughed, as he grabbed Madeline's hand and pulled her up. "Madeline, this is Angie Mulford...the one true love of my life."

"Pleased to meet you, Angie," Madeline choked out, fearing the woman might back-hand her for being with her man. *I wonder if she lost that tooth in a fight.*

"Same here, honey. Now don't you go gettin all upset, it's just a simple fact of life, some flames don't never die out, they just keep smolderin. I better go now before he turns you loose and comes runnin after me." Her loud piercing laugh echoed around them, sending a flock of birds to flight.

Samuel bent down and hugged Angie's stout frame. "Always the self-sacrificing saint...never ever change, sweetheart."

Angie winked at Samuel before turning around happily, swinging her little boy's hand as she walked away.

Not quite sure what to make of the exchange, Madeline waited for an explanation. When none came, she shrugged and followed him back to the truck.

Chapter 8

Distracted by his thoughts, Samuel stood at the kitchen window, watching as the last rays of the day bathed the sand and Madeline Linville in soft pink. He stood transfixed as he watched her wade about in the shallows, clutching a book in her hand as she gently swiped the water with her toes.

It'd been three weeks since Madeline told him about the incident with Beau Chambers. His patience was running out, especially since he'd had to pretend everything was just fine around Beau when he'd encountered him at church. Michael was due back tomorrow and he was going to make a point to speak to him about the matter before he handled Beau his own way.

"What has so captured your attention that I've been able to sneak up on you?" Bree asked, wrapping her arms around Samuel's waist and peering over his shoulder. "Oh...I see." She dropped her hands and stepped away.

"Bree, what a surprise...I didn't expect you. How about some coffee, I was just going to make a pot." He turned toward the counter, fumbling with the coffee container. "What brings you out?" He waited for her reply.

"Does a girl need a reason to see her boyfriend?" Easing onto a stool, she eyed him warily. "I *was* feeling sorry for you way out here all by your lonesome, but obviously, you have your diversions."

He chose to ignore the insinuation. The stress of his relationship with Bree was beginning to wear on him. Lately, she'd become more of a demand on his time and energy. The workload alone was tough enough without the constant reminders from her of every opportunity to expand and grow. She lived and breathed business, never two inches away from her cell phone, which interrupted almost every conversation they'd ever had.

The business was becoming both physically and emotionally taxing. There seemed to be a huge gash somewhere in the company that was draining the lifeblood right out of it. It was becoming harder and harder to be competitive for new projects. He knew he was partially to blame. Lately, it seemed he'd lost his drive. The business didn't have the hold on him that it once had. Now, he found his thoughts all wrapped up in Bell Bennier. *Maybe I'm just tired.*

"I have to fight to keep from barricading myself out here," Samuel said, taking a seat. "I'm finding I lean strongly in the direction of becoming a farmer." He gave a half-hearted grin.

"What!" Bree exclaimed. "With all the opportunities we have in this area for growth? Now is not the time to rest on your laurels, Samuel. We need to be out there fighting for our place in this environment! We've got to continue our efforts to achieve and not rely on previous accomplishments. We've got to push, push, push!"

Samuel exhaled loudly. "There's more to life, Bree. And, it would do you a whole lot of good to stop and smell the flowers once in awhile."

"Oh…I guess you want me to be like that girl out there, in some kind of dreamland…living off of the kindness of others."

The bar stool scraped across the kitchen floor as Samuel stood up, then leaned forward with his elbows on the counter. Clasping his hands into a tight fist, he looked directly into her eyes. "You have no idea what you're talking about. I suggest you keep quiet about things you don't understand. Stick to topics you're familiar with…like how to make the almighty dollar."

Quickly trying to regain a measure of good will, she reached across the counter for his hand. "Well, I didn't come all the way out here to fight. I came here to find out what time we'll be leaving next week for Charleston. I bought this adorable little night gown at Victoria's Secret."

Biting his bottom lip, he nodded. "I'd forgotten about that. I guess we'll leave at sun up on Saturday. Madeline and I will pick you up around 7:00am."

"Madeline! You didn't tell me *she* was going."

"Actually, Madeline is the *reason* we're going. Jude wants to see her," he informed her bluntly.

"Oh, well that's just perfect. I thought we were going to have a little get-a-way, just the two of us. When are we ever going to be completely alone Samuel? And I think you know what I mean."

His gaze swept her before he turned away to pour his coffee. "I've never misled you about just how far we'll ever go, Bree. You've known from the start. Don't make this little trip into something it's not. I don't plan on having but one honeymoon…from now on."

"Don't be so puritanical, Samuel. This is me you're talking to…not those holier-than-thou church people you associate with. I live in the real world, in this century." Bree stood, walking around the counter to wrap her arms around his neck. She pulled his head down to her lips and kissed him passionately. Pulling away, she said, "That's just a little taste of what's to come."

"All I *want* is a taste." He stepped away, running his hand through his hair in frustration. "I don't seem to be getting through to you, Bree. It's important that we get on the same page here."

"Ha! We're not even reading the same book!" She snatched up her purse from the kitchen table and headed for the door. "Go back to your dream world, Samuel. When you wake up, call me."

As the door slammed, Samuel released a sigh of relief. He walked out onto the veranda, pleased to see Madeline still near the shoreline. Deciding this was as good a time as any to tell her about the trip to Charleston, he stepped off the porch and made his way toward her.

The sky mellowed, it was just before sunset as Samuel approached Madeline. "Mind a distraction? I don't want to break the spell you're under, but I could use some company." Samuel gave her a disarming smile.

"Not at all, I'm just collecting more shells for my soap packages." She held out her hand displaying an assortment of tiny white shells. I have to wait for the tide to go out before I can find the really good ones. I plan on adding the soap I made for Jude to my product list on my website. Hopefully, I'll be swamped with orders."

Samuel looked down at her, taking in her sun-warmed face and smiled. Quickly, she turned away, seemingly disturbed. "Did I do something wrong?" he asked, puzzled at her sudden agitation.

Keeping her eyes diverted from his gaze, she said, "You have a way of making me...uneasy when I'm speaking to you."

Samuel furrowed his brow. "Uneasy? Why?" Concern washed over his features as he waited for an explanation.

"The way you look at me when I'm speaking. You never look away from my face. You watch my lips move...it's disturbing."

"Oh, sorry, I guess I just find you...interesting." The more he thought about what she'd said, the more annoyed he became. "I'm sure I'm not the first person to notice you Madeline," he responded, slightly perturbed.

Dropping her hand into the soft wet sand, she replied, "My mother never looked directly at my face. Her eyes always hovered somewhere over my shoulder."

"What?"

Madeline reached down into the rushing water, snatching up another small white shell as it tumbled in with the surf. "I think I must resemble my father. She never looked directly at me. I believe it caused her pain."

Samuel was quiet for a long moment as they walked along slowly, his mind piecing together bits of Madeline's life. "Well, what about Jude. As much time as you've spent with each other, I'm sure *he* has looked at you."

Madeline shrugged. "Jude and I experience things as one person. We observe things together, we look outward together...does that make sense?" She brushed back a loose piece of hair and tucked it behind her ear.

Samuel straight-eyed her, then spoke sternly, "Well, *I* see you, Madeline and I don't apologize for it. I'm not going to look away from you either…so you'll just have to get use to it!" *Women!* "I just came down here to tell you that I want you up and ready to leave for Charleston by 6:30am next Saturday. Got that?"

Madeline narrowed her eyes at him briefly. "You agitate me, like sand in my bed." She popped her skirt and turned away from him sharply, calling back over her shoulder, "And what makes you think I take orders, 'cause I don't!"

The very sea breeze seemed to taunt him, spraying misty water in his face as he stood there staring after her. Samuel knew he was in over his head with the girl…way over. She was the most complex creature he'd ever encountered. One minute she was soft and kind, and easy to be around; the next, hardheaded and stubborn! He was not the kind of man who was used to having his authority questioned, yet she seemed to question him at every turn. He was beginning to realize that Madeline Linville could not be easily ruled.

After a long time of just staring after her retreating form, he shook his head and reluctantly tugged the cell phone out of his jeans pocket and began dialing Jude. *The only person on the face of the earth that can do anything with that woman! Heaven help us all,* he thought, and the thought unnerved him.

"Jude? Hey, how's it going up there?" Samuel asked, trying to sound cheerful.

"I'm loving it! How's Madeline?"

"Well…that's why I'm calling. I've got a problem. I think I've upset her."

"Upset her…how? Are you trying to boss her already, Samuel?" Jude heaved a laborious sigh.

"Me? Boss somebody? I'm offended."

"Yeah well, just so you'll know, that never works with Madeline. If you want her to do something, just ask her. If that doesn't work, use the "dare tactic", she can't resist it."

Forcing a laugh, Samuel responded, "You make it sound so simple. But, you don't understand how she can be," he continued, rubbing the stubble on his chin, "her...*issues* are way out of my league. I've never felt so at a loss on how to handle a woman. I've always had a way with women, but not *this* particular woman. I never know what she's going to do or what she's going to say. And why is she so blasted nice around you?"

"You don't have to *handle* her man, just be nice. How hard is that? Go over and apologize for bossing her around. She'll forgive you, trust me."

After much thought and deliberation, Samuel decided to take Jude's advice concerning Madeline before he headed back home. He knocked out a hard rat-a-tat-tat on the frame of the screened door of her cottage and took in a deep breath.

Madeline wiped her hands down the front of her soap-stained apron and started toward the door. Samuel came into view through the glass panes. *He's such an impressive man.* She felt her pulse quicken at the sight of him as she barley opened the door. "Do you need something, Samuel? I'm kinda busy here."

When Samuel spoke, it was quietly. "I need to apologize for my earlier behavior," he said, giving her a half-smile. "I'm so used to barking orders; I temporarily forgot that I was speaking to a lady. Will you forgive me?"

"Oh…well, yes. I mean of course. Would you like to come in?" Madeline opened the door wide and stepped back allowing him to enter. She felt dwarfed by his presence. *He's nothing but pure manliness. If it was anyone else, I'd be scared to death.*

The first thing Samuel noticed was a deep sense of relief coming from somewhere inside his gut. It was as if a cork had popped. *Wow…Jude was right! That was easy,* he thought. *She just ushered me right inside. And she's smiling!*

Madeline observed him discreetly; he had an air about him that suggested he was confident, but also caring. Although she believed he had this huge blind spot where women were concerned, she'd always thought he was a good man. Not to mention the best looking thing to ever walk the earth.

Samuel seemed anxious to defend his earlier behavior. Taking a seat on the well-worn and faded couch, he explained, "I'm not here to disturb your life, Madeline." He'd carefully tried to maintain a quiet watchfulness where Madeline was concerned, but lately he was finding it harder and harder to do. "Involving myself in the affairs of others is not what I'm about." Resting his ankle on his knee, he waited for her response.

"That's not what I heard about you," Madeline replied, smiling back at him. Stepping into the kitchen, she called out, "Want something to drink? I have Ginger Ale, or would you prefer coffee?"

"Coffee." Samuel dropped his leg back to the floor and leaned forward with a confused look on his face. "Well, just what have you heard?" he questioned, loud enough that she could hear him from the kitchen.

"I'll get your coffee and we can talk out on the porch," she called back. "I don't want to miss the show." A moment later she returned with their coffee on a tray and a few homemade pralines. "Come on, follow me." She opened the screened door with a bounce of her hip.

They stepped out onto the porch that faced the western sky. The bay was placid and smooth. Hovering just above the water was the most spectacular sunset Samuel had ever witnesses. Colors of intense blue and orange splayed across the sky and mingled in the water, washing everything in its magnificent hue.

"Sit." Madeline placed the tray down on a small metal table that sat between two metal gliders.

The gliders were mostly white with green wearing through on the arms and the seat. A vintage metal settee sat at one end of the ample porch coated with the same wash of white. It held a large green and white striped pillow and an old faded patchwork quilt that draped across the seat, as if someone had just tossed it aside after a nap. Stacked near the pillow side of the settee was a column of worn looking books with a bottle of orange colored nail polish perched on top.

Taking a seat in the chairs, they reached for their coffee simultaneously without looking; only staring straight ahead as they watched in silence as the disk of the sun slowly disappeared into the tranquil waters of the bay.

Madeline's voice whispered, "I usually stay here until dark. It feels like I've been covered by a blanket and tucked into bed for the night."

Saying nothing for a moment as he stared, he broke the silence. "Your blanket has holes." Pointing to the black velvet sky, he indicated the stars.

Lifting her head toward the sky, she smiled. "So it does... looks like pin holes in my blanket, as if the light from the sun was on the other side."

Being crazy is not half-bad, Samuel thought, inhaling deeply of the fresh night air and feeling relaxed all of a sudden. He rested his head on the back of the chair. "I'm a big sky kinda guy. I bet I'd love Texas, all that space where a man can breathe." He rose up slightly and cocked his head. "Hear that? Some field cricket is serenading his sweetheart."

Madeline smiled. "You sound just like your daddy. That's what he used to tell me when he heard crickets or frogs." She grew contemplative for a moment, then asked, "Do you ever wonder why God took our parents the way he did?"

Samuel rested his head back again before he spoke. "I learned a long time ago that it's not wise to argue with God about taking a flower out of his own garden. But," he said, taking a cigar out of his pocket and rolling it around between his fingers, "it has seemed like we've been hit by one life altering blow right after another lately, doesn't it?" He tapped the end of his cigar in the palm of his hand. "We'll weather it though, Maddie...with His help, we'll weather it."

Madeline thought about his words. She admired Samuel's strength of mind, his courage. He seemed to weather times of adversity better than most and that impressed her.

Samuel ran his hand slowly across his scruffy jaw as he gazed up at the night sky. Lifting the fragrant cigar to his mouth he bit down on the end of it, then said through clenched teeth, "This makes me think of a passage from Isaiah I had to memorize in Sunday school years ago, 'Look at the night skies; who do you think made all this? Who marches this army of stars out each night, counts them off, calling each by name...and never overlooks a single one.'"

Madeline reached for her quilt, pulling it across the wooden deck to cover her bare legs. She let out a satisfied breathe as she settled back in her chair, gazing out toward heaven. *And never overlooks a single one.*

Chapter 9

*T*he ground vibrated under Samuel's dusty boots as he made his way around the rumbling backhoe. Michael Christenberry spied him out of the corner of his eye and killed the engine. "You lost?"

"With my keen sense of direction; if I remember correctly, *you* were the one always getting us lost. It didn't matter where we headed, we always ended up at Emily's house."

Michael laughed. "I remember…you were always jealous about that, too. Still are it seems."

Michael and his first wife, Emily, had been together since they were in grade school. Inseparable…until the tragic day an automobile accident took her life and the life of their unborn baby.

"The way that woman affected you…it was down right shameful. I hope you have a better handle on things with this new little wife of yours, it's embarrassing to see you make such a fool of yourself."

Michael threw his head back and laughed. Jumping down from the heavy machine, he dusted off his hands before taking hold of Samuel's shoulders. "You just wait buddy, your day is coming and I pray I'm around to see it. You won't know what hit you."

Samuel dismissed him with a wave of his hand. "There's not a woman alive that'll have that kinda power over me, my friend. Never has been and never will be."

"Famous last words, come on, I feel like a fieldworker hungry for the shade. Let's go find some."

They ambled over to a sprawling oak with thick low hanging branches that blocked out the sun's harsh rays. A wooden plank hung suspended between two cinder blocks, sitting at an angle beneath the shady tree. On the tailgate of Michael's truck there sat an old beat-up looking water cooler. Michael wiped his brow with the back of his hand and let out a long breath as he filled a plastic tumbler with water. Tilting the glass, he gestured to Samuel, offering a drink.

Declining, Samuel sat down, feeling the plank give slightly under his weight. He stretched out his legs in front of him as he stared at his boots. "I've got this situation, Michael, and I'm not sure how to handle it."

Michael eyed Samuel as he gulped down his water. "Ah." Propping his elbows on the side of the truck, he said, "Let's hear it."

Neither man had ever been accused of dancing around an issue. Plain spoken and to the point was the style of both men.

"Beau Chamber's tried to molest Madeline Linville when she was...and I'm guessing here, about ten or eleven years old. She cut off part of his ear in the struggle to defend herself. Apparently he'd gotten mad over Madeline's mother rejecting his advances and...saw an opportunity with Madeline."

Samuel watched as Michael's eyes narrowed, turning a seething green. His countenance was rapidly changing.

Remembering Michael's temper, he decided he'd better say something to simmer him down before he grabbed the rope from the back of his truck and headed toward town.

"Now what I'm wondering...is how this should be handled, *as a believer*? I know how to handle it as a heathen." He indicated with a nod toward the rope.

Michael twitched. He grabbed the side of the truck bed with both hands, pushing back, fighting the urge to ram his fist into it. He turned his head sharply. "Are you sure about this Samuel...Beau Chambers?"

"Yeah, I'm sure. According to Madeline, I'm the only one she's ever told."

A long silence followed as each man thought about what needed to be done. Michael broke the silence. "I think technically we're to bring the accusation to the new pastor." Michael ran a hand through his hair in frustration. "Man, I sure hate to drop all of this on Brother Thad. He's just getting his feet wet here." Shaking his head, he said, "I wish we could handle this some other way, but I don't see how." He swallowed hard, then asked, "She's lived with this secret all of these years? I mean, you just found out about this?"

Samuel nodded. "My gut tells me Beau's tried to intimidate her. She avoids town like the plague and has for years. You should've seen her the other day when I drove her to town. She was shaking all over. I had to practically drag her out of the car when we stopped for lunch."

Michael pushed back from the truck and turned to stare at Samuel, a slow smile turned up the corners of his mouth.

Samuel looked pointedly at his friend. "What are you scheming?"

"Just thinking...what if you were to bring Madeline to church with you on Sunday."

Samuel's blue-gray eyes held a wicked gleam as he thought about his words. "You mean...send a message to Beau?"

Michael gave a quick nod. "Eye him good, make a comment about his ear, let him know in a round-a-bout way that you know what happened." He shrugged. "It can't hurt. If he's guilty he'll have to face it...or leave."

Samuel rubbed the stubble on his chin as he pondered the suggestion. "It just might work." In a flash the glimmer of hope vanished. Blowing out an exaggerated breath, he said, "It'd be easier to herd cats than to get Madeline into that church."

"Get Jude involved. He'll convince her. If I remember correctly, doesn't he have some kinda special powers over her?"

"Yeah, I've never seen anything like the two of them." After a moment, he said, "It's worth a shot."

Two strong bangs on the frame of the door startled Madeline from her thoughts. Busily packaging an order at the kitchen table, she slid out of the chair, brushing loose lavender from her skirt as she moved to unlatch the screened door.

There was no mistaking the steel in Samuel's words as he looked down at her. "Get your things, you're coming with me. There's another storm headed this way and the winds are predicted to get pretty high later tonight. Pack a church dress, too. I've made up my mind; we're all going to church in the morning."

For a moment, Madeline cocked a finely arched brow and looked at him as if meeting the challenge. As she studied his face, she saw a look in his eyes that seemed to dare her. Never one to resist a dare, she stepped back, crossed the room and began packing a few of her belongings into a suitcase.

Fully prepared for a confrontation, Samuel was more than a little surprised at her willingness to comply. *In a million years, I'll never understand that particular woman,* he thought, studying her smooth movements as she placed her clothes in the suitcase.

"All set," she said, standing in front of him, clutching her small night case with both hands. She had the look of a little girl excited to go on her first sleepover.

Lifting the lightweight case away from her, he motioned for the door. "After you," he declared in a soft, low tone that sent shivers down her spine.

It was obvious from a mere glance that Samuel was enjoying himself and that he knew the effect he was having on her. She stiffened slightly, lifted her head and said, "I'm doing this for Jude. He's already called with a weather report."

Even in the early afternoon, the house was lit from within. Warm yellow tones spilled across the shady porches that wrapped around the structure on both levels, lending a soft elegance to the old brick and mortar. Massive moss draped oaks stood securely, flanking the house on each side as if standing guard. Bell Bennier was timeless. Both comfort and elegance seeped from the pores of her graceful structure. Madeline sighed, *Oh, how I love this place.*

"I asked Bree to stay over. She's in the next room. You don't mind chaperoning do you?" Placing her suitcase on the bench at the foot of the four poster rice bed, Samuel added, "Feel free to use my bathrobe if you need to." He winked at her, then turned to leave. Pausing at the door, he asked without turning around, "Has Jude called you again?"

"No," Madeline replied, softly.

With a slight nod, Samuel stated, "I need to speak with you later, in private."

"All right, Samuel."

Madeline moved to the bedside table, fingering a silver mint julep cup that held cuttings of hydrangea blossoms in shades of purple and pale green, echoing the soft colors of the room. Opening the French doors to the second story balcony, she allowed the gauzy white curtains to teasingly obscure the ocean view as they filled and released the trapped ocean air. As she began unpacking her things, she heard a woman's laughter. Parting the sheer fabric she glanced around to find Samuel and Bree engaged in a passionate kiss. She eased her head back inside and quietly closed the doors.

Samuel heard the sound of the doors closing and pulled away from Bree. *She must have seen us,* Samuel thought. And why that bothered him, he didn't quite know. Lately, thoughts of Madeline seemed to pick the absolute worst times to haunt him. Bree looked up at him with hooded eyes, hungry for more as she reached behind his head and tightly grasped his hair. Her cell phone rang before their lips met. Letting go, Bree stepped back to retrieve her phone from the wicker table.

"Hello, this is Bree."

A prospective buyer, Samuel thought. That alone could cause the excitement in her voice and the giddy way she expressed herself, gesturing wildly with her hands as she spoke. He watched her a moment, then caught a glimpse of Madeline on the lawn below and the contrast struck him. Bree tapped on his shoulder indicating that she was going inside to talk. He leaned his frame against the porch post in a casual position, sticking his hands into his pockets as he observed Madeline's trek across the lawn. *Out to her secret place among the wild ferns,* he supposed. Why they'd always called that spot Madeline's secret place, he didn't know. It was certainly no secret. She'd been going there most of her life. Everyone knew that if you needed to find her, you'd look there first. She held a book in her hand, no shoes, same white skirt she was fond of wearing with the same lavender T- shirt. If at that very moment she began walking on air it would not have surprised Samuel. She seemed ethereal, half woman, half fairy with her long honey colored hair lifting in the wild wind.

Madeline's mind headed in a direction she was unprepared for. Appalled by her feelings, she sought out an escape from her wayward thoughts. Books had always been a means of escape for Madeline. As she approached the familiar clearing with its circling row of sheltering trees, she sat down on a bed of soft pine needles, pushing her back against a tree.

In years past, monk hands had built a small bridge at the foot of the hillside to span the brook that trickled down from somewhere in Bell Forest. It meandered its way to the bay, singing as it tumbled over rocks and smooth stones. Long forgotten now, the crumbling structure hadn't been used for anything except a landing for birds and a place where squirrels could eat their seeds and nuts. Still, the familiar old bridge brought comfort to Madeline, showing her that anything, no matter how worn and battered could still be useful...beautiful even, with a purpose in this life.

Before she could open her book, she felt the air stir behind her, carrying with it the scent of lemons. Slowly, Madeline turned her head to peer over her shoulder. There, sitting on the ground with a trowel in her hand, stabbing at the dirt around a wild fern was a small woman. The determined look on the woman's face amused Madeline. She watched as her golden hair fell across her eyes time and again, noticing how the woman kept blowing it off of her face, but never once did she stop what she was doing to brush it away. Biting her bottom lip to keep from laughing, Madeline slowly reached down and picked up a pinecone, tossing it in the woman's direction.

The pinecone landed on the woman's shoulder, starling her. Madeline smiled at the surprised eyes and sharp intake of breath as the woman zeroed in on Madeline.

"Did I scare you?" Madeline asked, as her face broke into a huge grin at the possibility.

"Yes, you did," the woman said, with a shaky voice. "I once threw a pinecone at a monk...I thought this was my day for pay back." She dropped the trowel and placed her hand on her heart, hoping to slow its rapid beat. "For a minute there I thought I was seeing a ghost! But, it serves me right. I knew the day would come when my thieving ways would catch up with me." She stood up, slapping the dirt from her hands as she walked toward Madeline, extending her hand. "I'm Telie Christenberry, monk assaulter and thief extraordinaire."

"Michael's new wife?" Madeline questioned, as she stood to take the woman's hand.

"One and the same...we're living here at Bell Forest now, most of the time, if I can help it." Telie smiled, taking in Madeline's face. "I've seen you from time to time...up here or on the tractor in the fields over there." She waved in the direction of the hayfield. "I take it you're Madeline. When I described you to Michael, he said that sounded like you."

Madeline looked through the trees, noticing for the first time how easy it would be to observe her from the cottage at Bell Forest. "Yes, I'm Madeline Linville."

The hillside tumbled downward from the knoll and ran unfettered with its tangle of brambles until it leveled off at the lawn of Saint Thomas Monastery. The cottage, known simply as Bell Forest, was located just on the other side of the monastery and could be viewed across the open expanse of green lawn that splayed out in front of the medieval looking stone structure. Only small animals lived among the thorns and brambles of the slope, but, somehow Telie had managed to breach the security of the hill. Madeline had once thought that the rough terrain would be the only defense she would ever need to keep trespassers out, but not anymore. Not since this small woman with golden hair and dirt on her face seemed to navigate the hillside undaunted and unscathed.

"I've seen you, too, mostly with that dark haired monk from the monastery. I've even heard you a few times," Madeline responded, finding it hard to pull her attention away from the sparkle in Telie's golden eyes.

"That's Brother Raphael. We're partners in crime." Telie said, teasingly. "Oh and sorry for digging up your property," she apologized. "I thought I could slip one out without notice and without disturbing the land. I should have asked permission."

Madeline saw kindness in Telie's face. She practically glowed; even with dirt caked on her cheeks. "Don't be silly, you can have all you want. I don't mind at all." Madeline smiled with pleasure. She was not used to being met with such consideration and she found she liked it. "I have to say...I'm impressed that you've been able to scale this hillside. Those thorns are pretty nasty."

"Yeah...well, I'm an explorer at heart, drives my husband crazy, too. I think he would prefer that I'd stay put where he could see me every single minute of the day." Telie grinned, "He's kinda over protective that way."

"Sometimes that's nice. At least you know he cares."

"What's your favorite flower, Madeline?" Telie asked, changing the subject. She walked over and plopped down on the ground in front of her. "I promise to replace the wild fern with whatever plant you choose. I have an inside connection with the owner of Christenberry's," she said, winking.

"Oh, that's not nes...."

Lifting her hand as if blocking the protest, Telie said, "I insist. It's the only way I'll ever learn to keep my hands out of other people's gardens. I've been known to even rob a few cemeteries," she confessed. "They have some of the most beautiful old roses."

Madeline smoothed her skirt under her and sat down, enjoying the light-hearted conversation more than she'd realized. She missed having a woman to talk to. "I'd have to say...lavender-blue hydrangeas."

"Nice choice," Telie added. "I only wish they had scent and not just color. If they did, I guess they would be just about perfect."

"I like that scent you're wearing...lemon something... maybe sage?"

"Wow, now that's impressive. How did you guess... about the sage I mean?"

Scents are kinda my specialty. I make soaps and lotions, even a few shower gels. That's how I make my living."

"What!" Telie leaned forward, excitedly. "Do you make gardener soap, you know, the kind of soap with a scrub built-in?"

"Well no, not yet, but that would be pretty simple to make. I'll try my hand at a few bars and let you sample them. How does that sound?"

"Wonderful! I've been looking for gardener's soap for months! Must be divine intervention! Oh, look!" Telie exclaimed, pointing to a wave of yellow butterflies coming up from the clearing and fluttering all around them. "School butterflies!"

"School butterflies?" Madeline looked at Telie, waiting for clarification.

Telie laughed. "According to my mother, when you see yellow butterflies, you know that school is just about to start. They're sent out to announce it, you know. Don't they look excited?"

"Oh, she was good. I'll have to remember that if I ever have children." Madeline grinned, leaning back on her arms.

"Tell me about it. She'd have me so excited about school starting that I'd almost wet my pants! I couldn't wait for summer to end so I could see the first school butterfly. My mother should've been reported. That has to be some form of child abuse." Telie laughed, and the sound of her laughter warmed Madeline's soul.

Madeline grinned, then dropped her eyes. What she would have given to have a mother like that; one that took her shopping for school clothes, or waited expectantly for her to return home from school to find out about her day. Or even one who would make up some silly story just to get her daughter excited about school. Instead, she came home to a cold empty kitchen with her mother locked away in her room. No joy in her mother's house, only the harsh bite of cold reality…a joyless and bitterly cold reality.

The girls stood up and dusted off the backs of their clothing. "I'm sure glad we've met, Madeline. I can't wait to see what you come up with. I have such a weakness for bath products. I'm such a girl," Telie said, tilting her head.

"Don't forget your contraband." Madeline pointed to the wild fern in the loose soil. Seeing her new friend all covered in dirt, she thought it funny that Telie enjoyed bathing. *Hmm,* Madeline thought, *I might just have to create something extra special for my friend, Telie. Something to remove all kinds of natural things she might get into.*

"Don't tell my husband I said this, but there's really no reason to buy plants at a nursery if you want a simple and natural look to your landscape. Wild ferns are perfect for that," Telie stated, blowing the hair off of her forehead.

"So that's your secret. I love what you've done to Bell Forest."

"No secret to it. All you need is a good shovel and a willingness to get dirty, other than that, there's nothing to it." Telie smiled, flashing sparkling white teeth. "You know, come to think of it, since I discovered your secret spot, it's only fair that I show you mine. Come on." Telie grabbed Madeline's hand and pulled her toward the woods.

"Where are we going? There's nothing that way but swamp." Madeline couldn't help but laugh as she was being dragged along behind Telie. Her spirits began to soar as a new sense of adventure took control of her.

"This slope just screams for winter jasmine. It looks so good tumbling down a hillside and it grows fast, too. Those little yellow blooms always make me smile. Of course, my monks would benefit the most from all that color." She stopped dead in her tracks, appraising the area as if lining up the hillside so it could be easily viewed from the monastery windows. "But, you could come down here and clip all you want." She continued on her way, chattering the whole time as she stepped over fallen logs, pulling back limbs to allow them to pass underneath. "It'd be like bringing sunshine into your house in the dead of winter."

As they came near the bayou, Madeline scanned the olive green surface of the water, cautiously stepping around a limb sticking halfway out of the swamp. Ever mindful of water moccasins and gators, she pressed her foot lightly on the soggy swamp floor.

Trudging up ahead through the dense brush was Telie. Madeline was somewhat amazed as she watched her friend maneuver, stealth like around vines and undergrowth. Every now and then she would see her break off a branch or toss a limb as she cleared the path.

"I wish I had my machete," Telie called out, as she yanked down a twisted vine. "You'd think we were in the Amazon jungle the way these vines cover over everything."

Madeline wiped her forehead with the back of her hand, then swatted at a mosquito that had been circling her head. "How much farther until we get to your spot?"

Telie stopped and pointed up ahead. "That's where we're going. Hang on, we're almost there."

Quickening her pace, Madeline caught up with Telie as they stepped into the clearing at the same time. The fresh smell of sea air filled their senses. The small secluded area curved, forming a crescent, which allowed the sea to gently roll up onto a pristine swath of sugar white sand. The thick maritime forest and mangrove trees provided shelter on three sides, closing in the private little beach. A large flat rock sat near the shoreline, a perfect perch with the promise of warmth from the heat of the sun.

Making her way to the rock, with its scent of sea brine and slick, pungent green underside, Madeline suddenly came to a halt. There on top of the rock was a large carved heart, cut deeply into the surface of the stone with the words, 'Michael loves Emily'. She glanced back at Telie. She knew Telie must've discovered the carving, if so, why had she continued to come to this spot. Did it not bring her pain to see evidence that her husband had loved another?

Telie lifted her golden eyes to the horizon and smiled before turning to Madeline. Her countenance held gentleness, with its own good sweetness that spoke of a peace that had settled somewhere deep within her being. "They loved each other very much," Telie responded, reading the question in Madeline's eyes. She tucked her hair behind her ears and continued, "This must've been their spot, too."

Madeline looked at Telie with confusion in her eyes. "And, that doesn't bother you?"

"I owe a great deal to Emily. She taught my Michael how to love."

With the soothing voice of a hushed whisper, Madeline responded, "Yes—I see that now." After a long moment, she asked, "Does Michael ever come here with you?"

"Oh, no…I would never ask him to come here with me. This was their place and it holds memories for him, special memories that I'll never tread upon. Emily deserves that…even now. Love is eternal, you know. Even though she is no longer bound here by time, her love, *their* love will last forever…just as our love will last forever. And, I get the feeling that Emily doesn't mind sharing this place with me at all. We're nothing alike, she and I, but we do have a few things in common. One is our faith in Christ, the other…we both love Michael."

Madeline sighed deeply, wishing that one day she'd find someone that she could share a love like that.

Chapter 10

Samuel stared at Madeline as she walked up the brick path between the boxwoods. He watched her sunlit hair blow across her face, and how she moved her hand to gently brush it away as she hesitantly faced him. *Why does my heart flop around like a beached sunfish every time I see that girl?*

"We were just going for a walk, want to come along?" Samuel asked Madeline, as he watched Bree gingerly walk down the front steps in her high heels, clutching her cell phone in her hand as if her very lifeblood depended on it. "Bree, why do you insist on wearing high heels, you'll break your neck out here."

"Madeline is the one more comfortable barefoot, darling, not me. I prefer heels," Bree added, as she patted Samuel's face.

Samuel turned back to study Madeline, noticing her muddy bare feet. "Well, Maddie, whatcha say? Want to join us?"

"Oh no, thanks, you two go on. I'll just go in and find Willa...see if I can help with supper." Samuel's piercing blue-gray eyes made her want to squirm under their scrutiny.

The repeated buzz of Bree's cell phone halted any further discussion as Samuel turned toward Bree watching the now familiar animation play out in front of him. She closed the phone, disregarding Madeline's presence completely as she moved past her to Samuel. "Rain check on the walk, sweetheart. This is really big. It could mean the difference between a six-month project and a three-year project. I'll fill you in on the details later, I've got to run." Bree lifted up on her tiptoes and pecked Samuel on the cheek before turning to go. "Call me later," she called back, waving.

"Well, there you have it...story of my life." Samuel shook his head, playing for sympathy.

"You look like somebody licked the red off your candy. Let me go wash my feet and get my sandals...*I'll* go with you." Something about the dejected look on Samuel's face was too much for Madeline to overlook.

Brilliant clouds tinged with colors of sherbet hung over their heads as they walked silently down the overgrown path, both aware of where they were headed. As they neared, they saw old and crumbling bricks, waist high and sitting askew in the roughly outlined barrier of Bennier cemetery. An old and rusted iron gate hung from a single hinge at the opening to the graveyard. Scattered debris cluttered the ground with bits of faded plastic flowers tangled in the collection. Dead branches lay around, like the bones of fallen soldiers. Madeline shuttered, moving to stand under the enormous live oak that stood sentinel outside the opening to the cemetery.

"Looks like I've got my work cut out for me," Samuel said, eyeing all of the wreckage of fallen limbs and debris. He reached for Madeline's hand. Come on; let's see what's inside. Some of this must've happened when that storm came through the other night. It looks like we might be in for another round of storms later tonight. I must admit," he added, glancing around, "it didn't look much better the day of Dad's funeral." He cleared the debris from the path with his foot, carefully leading Madeline over the fallen limbs.

What a tiny soft hand, he thought. "I can tell you make lotion for a living, your hands are so soft."

"Thanks. That's the best part of my job, getting to try out the products." Gathering her hair over her shoulder with her free hand, she tried to hide the sudden redness easing up her neck.

"Well, if you ever need a testimonial, I'm your man." Samuel squeezed her hand once before letting go.

Spying fresh dirt on a new grave, they approached the site reverently, looking down at the double headstone with the name "Warren" in bold lettering across the face of the marble. Samuel kissed his fingers, placing them tenderly against his mother's name. He wiped the mud splatter from his father's name before stepping back. "Is there anything as final as the dates on a tombstone?"

A melancholy feeling washed over Madeline as she thought about the man, James Warren, and all that he had meant to her. "I miss him." Her voice melted away, smooth. She wiped a tear away with the crook of her finger and sniffed, starring down at the grave of the only father she'd ever known, even if he had been a borrowed one.

"Life can change so abruptly and leave you with nothing but questions." Samuel patted her back, the way you would a child. "I'd forgotten how much my father meant to you, Maddie."

"I owe him so much...I can never repay him for all he's done for me. It's because of him that the Spirit of God lives inside me...like water to my soul."

Samuel steady eyed her, as if questioning what she'd professed. Not sure how to respond to that revelation, he remained silent.

Suddenly, a wind out of nowhere rose up, causing a low resonating bell sound behind them. Turning toward the tone, they looked near the cemetery wall. Caught on a limb and hanging from a fallen branch was a bell. Samuel looked at Madeline with the same question on his face. He stepped near and reached down, twisting the bell from the clutches of the limb. "Well, well, what about that. I haven't seen this old elephant bell since I was a child." Samuel searched his mind, vaguely recalling having had the bell in his hand the day they buried his mother. *I must've dropped it at the gravesite,* he thought. Turning to Madeline, he stretched out his hand, displaying the object.

A weighty piece, the bell was a little bigger than an orange with a surprisingly deep chime. Made entirely of cast bronze with cloisonné etchings of blue and red around the upper half; the bell was in splendid form with tight tines bending inward like a claw.

"Did you say 'elephant bell?'" Madeline asked, as she closely examined the bell.

Samuel nodded, smiling. "It's a 17th century bell from Burma, India. They use bells like these to help locate their elephants. But, Mother used it to call the cook from the kitchen. I always remember seeing it on the table near my mother."

Madeline grinned. "You'd think it would be hard to loose an elephant. Seems like it'd be better used to know when one was sneaking up on you."

"Look at this." Samuel leaned near her, turning the bell on its side. "Can you read the inscription?"

Not being able to resist the scent of him, Madeline inhaled deeply, then read, "Great men are not always wise, nor do the aged always understand justice. Job 32:9." Looking up into his eyes, she waited for an explanation.

Samuel shrugged. "It's a mystery. I'd love to find out where it came from and whom it was given to. But, all I know is that my mother found the bell in the attic in an old trunk filled with clothes and letters...that sort of thing. She always kept it on the table in the dining room. Michael and I used to sneak it out of the house once in awhile and ring it under Mrs. Christenberry's bedroom window at night. You remember the legend of Bayou Bell, don't you?"

"Who could forget? I still have nightmares about it. How could Mr. Bennier do that to that poor slave girl...have tied her up and thrown into the bayou like that...and all for simply destroying his wife's silver bell?" Madeline shook her head. "And you should be ashamed of yourself for scaring Michael's mom like that. I don't know anyone who lives around here who doesn't halfway listen for that stupid bell, expecting the ghost of that poor girl to materialize in front of them at any given moment." Madeline shivered. "Don't get me started. I've lost a lot of sleep over the years because of that story!"

"We were some rowdy boys. But, Michael's dad fixed us good. He'd apparently had enough of our pranks, called my dad and the two of them devised an evil plan."

Madeline's eyes widened. "What did they do?" She stepped backward, smoothing her skirt under her as she sat down on an old iron bench near the cemetery wall. Her eyes riveted to his face.

Samuel hid his grin at her wide eyes. "Well, our dads decided to teach us a lesson. They got together and planned a campout on the back property, in the deep woods." Samuel propped his foot on the bench as he leaned his arm across his thigh. "Michael and I were so pumped! We'd worked all afternoon cutting wood for the fire and pitching our tent...begging them to leave us alone so we could rough it all by ourselves. As night fell and the fire blazed before us, Mr. Christenberry asked my dad a question."

"Ever see Rabbit anymore?" he asked.

"Well, curiosity got the best of us and we asked, 'Who's Rabbit?'"

"Oh, just some crazy man that used to ride his bike through the woods at night, playing his harmonica," Mr. Christenberry answered.

"We laughed. Then I asked, 'So why is he called Rabbit?'"

"Mike Christenberry grew serious. 'Rabbit had the strangest compulsion. When he rode through the wood at night, he liked to scare up rabbits. If he ever found one, he'd jump off his bike, grab the rabbit by the ears and stab it over and over until there was nothing left but a bloody heap of fur and bones. He always liked to sneak up on things, so it was always better when you could hear his harmonica, but once it stopped....'"

Madeline was sitting on the edge of her seat with her chin in the palm of her hand. "Then what happened?"

"Well, our dad's looked at each other across the campfire and decided that they would give in and let us campout by ourselves. Long story short...it took us about five minutes to pack up...put out the campfire and hightail it on home. The lecture came the next morning. Needless to say, we never tried to frighten Michael's mother again." He shook his head, remembering. "I hope I'm as wise as those two old men when I have boys one day." He picked up a branch and tossed it over the cemetery wall.

"What if you have girls?" Madeline teased, standing up to face him with her hands on her hips.

He studied her, reaching into his front pocket for a cigar before replying, "Well, then I pray they take after their mother."

"Bree?" Madeline questioned.

He cocked his head, giving her a sidelong stare, then answered back, "What makes you think the mother of my children is going to be Bree?" Lighting his cigar, he gave it a couple of quick puffs, squinting at her through the smoke.

Stepping gingerly over a grave, she added, "Isn't that why you date—to find a potential mate?"

"There are other reasons," he said, picking up another limb and giving it a toss. He was anxious to let the subject drop.

"Oh yeah, I forgot…like finding a great salesperson or a good kisser with long legs."

Something about Madeline seemed to keep him off balance. Annoyed now, he shot back, "You'd be a better judge of dating if you actually had a date every once in awhile, Maddie."

One eyebrow rose slightly as she looked at him. "You may be right." She brushed by him, walking out of the cemetery and down the path toward home.

Samuel stood frozen. Madeline's casual words tossed back over her shoulder knocked the breath out of him as successfully as any blow to his chest.

Warmed by the evening sun, the colors on the porch wall mellowed into saffron and the palest pink as cicadas sounded from the nearby oak trees. Climbing the steps, Samuel spoke from behind Madeline. "We need to talk before you go in, Madeline."

"What about?"

Samuel swallowed hard. Inwardly apprehensive, but outwardly calm, he extinguished his cigar carefully on the railing. "Please, sit down." He indicated two rocking chairs, then caught a glimpse of Willa stepping around the corner, carrying glasses of tea with orange wedges stuck to the sides.

"Thought you two could use a little refreshment... dinner's in an hour," Willa stated briefly, before turning to leave.

As they sipped their tea, both seemed uncomfortable with the silence. Samuel spoke first. "Madeline, tomorrow...after church, we're going to talk to Pastor Thad about what Beau did to you."

"No," she responded, with a shake of her head.

"I've carefully thought this out. This is the only way."

"He said he'd kill me if I ever spoke of it." Madeline put her tea glass down and reached around her knees, bending like an un-watered zinnia in too small a pot.

"The man's a coward. It's no great achievement to frighten a little girl, Madeline. But you're not that little girl anymore."

"I'm not like you, Samuel. I step lightly through this world...you run at it head long. Besides, I'm all by myself."

The thought suddenly hit him. Jude's words rushed at him from out of nowhere. *Dare her.* "You know...I've always admired a woman who'd let someone run them out of town."

Straightening her back, she defended, "No one has run me out of town!"

"In that case, I dare you to confront this man. You won't be alone; we'll face it together. And, after we talk to the pastor, it's probably not in your best interest to stay at Bay Cottage for a while, at least not until this blows over. You'll stay here. And," he emphasized. "You're not all by yourself. You have me and Greenberry. I'd appreciate it if you'd remember that."

Madeline rested her cheek on her knees, thinking about his words for a long time before she spoke. "I'll face this tomorrow and talk to the pastor. But, I'll go home afterward. I can take care of myself; I am not your concern." She lifted her head up defiantly.

"I've made you my concern," he stated flatly, narrowing his steely gray eyes as he dared her to challenge him. "You have a tendency to persist in an opinion, Maddie girl, and usually with more stubbornness than reason."

"Well, your refusal to accept facts makes discussion impossible!" she yelled, surprised at the intensity of her words. "You are not responsible for me. No one is. "

Compassion swept over him as he looked upon the girl, reminding him that she had not been abused as much as neglected. The disregard by her mother and the failure of her other family members had left the poor girl at the mercy of strangers. Thankfully, with the Lord's providence, that job fell to a couple of old rough farmers; Jim Warren and Greenberry White as well as one glass eyed African American cook with enough love in her heart to share with a motherless child.

Samuel took a slow sip of his tea, then cleared his throat. "Maddie, I care very deeply about you. You are family to us and you belong under my roof, with me for protection. Now, I'll not hear another word about it. Come on." He reached down and clasped her hand. "Let's go in before Willa takes a hickory stick to both of us."

Hesitating briefly, she reached for his strong hand and allowed him to pull her to her feet. Her readiness to respond to his command startled him, pleasantly.

Chapter 11

*T*he wind was steady from the west and the sun shone down gloriously on the day as Madeline peered out the French doors of her room. The only evidence of the previous night's storm was an Adirondack chair lying on its side in the grass near the flagpole.

Grabbing a hair clasp from the nightstand, Madeline arranged her hair as she made her way down the stairs. Following the aroma of fresh coffee and the hushed tones of low voices, she found Samuel, along with Bree and Willa casually sipping coffee around the kitchen table.

The kitchen had that farmhouse feel that made you want to linger too long over your coffee around the table. The morning sun crept across the dark wooden floors warming the room.

"Good morning, Maddie." Samuel said, eyeing her over the rim of his coffee cup.

Holding her gathered hair, she took the hair clasp out of her mouth with her free hand and quickly fastened her hair behind her neck. "Good morning. I hope I haven't made y'all wait too long. I've had a time with my hair this morning."

"Ah, but it was worth the wait. You look beautiful, doesn't she girls?"

Bree raked her eyes over Madeline. "Yes, she does. I've thought that each and every time I've seen her wear that outfit. What's it made of?" Bree reached over and fingered the material. "That's *some* material to hold up to so much constant use. NASA needs to know about that fabric."

Madeline stiffened at the insult, but kept smiling.

Willa quickly responded, "You're a vision, Madeline. And truth be told, you'd be a vision in a paper sack." Willa signaled Bree with her eyes, as she must've done a million times with her own daughters when they got snippy. "Beauty *is* as beauty *does*," Willa chided.

"Hear, hear." Samuel finished swigging down his coffee and placed the cup in the sink. "Come on. Let's get rollin." He held out his hand for Bree.

"Uh, Samuel...I'm not going with you, remember? I'm going to church in Mobile."

"Surly you can make an exception and go with us this once. I'm taking all of us out to the White Grape for lunch after service." Samuel smiled, charm oozing out of him.

"I'm afraid not. The Lawson's are expecting me. You know...that's the firm I've been telling you about...the three-year project? Jay Lawson wants to discuss his vision over lunch." Bree raised her eyebrows. "This could be big for us and for the company. And, goodness knows the company can use more business."

Inhaling deeply as his chest expanded, Samuel pushed out the words. "Let's talk about this outside." He strode from the kitchen and out the door.

Once outside, Samuel turned on Bree, accusingly. "Your real motivation for joining that huge church was not for worship, but to meet potential clients! I can't believe you

Bree! Where do you ever draw the line where business is concerned?"

Resting her hand on Samuel's chest she replied, "I'm only thinking of us, Samuel. And what will it hurt to profit a little while worshipping the Lord all at the same time. I think you should help support other believers and vice versa...don't you?"

Samuel ran his hand down his face, he knew what he had to do and he dreaded the face off. "We'll talk later. We've got to go." He walked away from Bree and headed toward the truck where the girls were waiting.

Willa scanned the lawn as she and Madeline waited on Samuel. "Is Greenberry going to church with us this morning?"

Samuel hesitated. "Well, I'm sure if a certain pretty lady would ask him he'd be delighted to go. But to answer your question, no, he never goes...not to my knowledge anyway."

"Oh. I see." Disappointed, Willa stepped up into the back seat.

"Shall we?" Samuel waved his hand out in front of Madeline.

Reluctantly Madeline moved forward, then stopped suddenly and turned to face him. "You *are* going to be with me aren't you? I mean, you're not going to leave me, right?" She felt her throat tighten, and the all too familiar pressure closing in around her.

Samuel put his finger under her chin and raised her head up so she could look him straight in the eye. "Trust me."

Madeline's palms grew sweaty and her throat became dry as they reached the church house doors. Fidgeting with the material of her skirt, she nervously chewed on her bottom lip as they walked down the aisle. People turned to stare as they walked by and Madeline could feel her throat closing up. Relief flooded her at the sight of Telie's friendly smile and enthusiastic wave, motioning them forward.

"Sit here, by me," Telie said, patting the seat beside her.

Willa and Madeline moved into the pew, passing Michael to take their seat on the other side of Telie. Samuel sat down near the aisle next to Michael.

"You always manage to have a harem with you, even at church," Michael spoke under his breath.

Samuel glanced at Michael, flashing his signature wicked smile. "I've got my reputation to think of, Michael. So, are we ready for this?"

"Ready as we'll ever be. And by the way, what are you doing here early? Did you get struck by lightning last night?" Michael waited for an explanation. It wasn't like a Warren to be early for church.

"I didn't want to miss all the excitement."

After a few panic-stricken moments upon entering the church, Madeline settled down, feeling safe nestled between Telie and Willa. The presence of the two strong women comforted her in a way she didn't think possible.

Madeline observed a gorgeous woman with long wavy chestnut hair standing in front of them. The woman paused and turned her head slightly, giving them another angle to observe her beauty. Madeline remarked softly to Telie, "Moss Bay has some of the most beautiful women I've ever seen."

Telie leaned over, whispering, "That's Mary Grace Adams. She's been after Michael for years. From the show she's putting on this morning, my guess is she now has her sights set on Samuel."

Without missing a beat, Madeline responded, "She looks shallow."

Telie laughed out, causing Michael and Samuel to bend their heads in her direction.

"Am I going to have to separate you two?" Samuel warned, trying to look stern. He didn't know why, but he enjoyed seeing Madeline and Telie so comfortable around each other.

"Is that you, Samuel?" Mary Grace moved into the pew squeezing between Samuel and Michael. Facing Samuel, she flipped her hair, hitting Michael across the cheek. "It's so good to see you! I heard you were moving back." Mary Grace embraced Samuel a little *too* long. "We'll have to get together soon and catch up, talk about old times." She patted his leg, a frozen beauty pageant smile on her face.

"Uh, Mary Grace, do you mind?" Michael shifted his leg to keep her from crowding him. She was practically sitting on his lap.

"Am I bothering you, Michael?" she asked, looking over her shoulder seductively.

Taking about all of Mary Grace she could stand, Madeline leaned forward and whispered, "What he's trying to say, Sweetie, is that your rump is cutting off the circulation in his leg." She eased back in the pew, pleasantly staring ahead as if she'd simply explained the situation.

Stunned, no one said a word. All faces stared blankly ahead. Mary Grace stood, reached down and whispered to

Samuel, "Call me." Sensing a competitor, she turned toward Madeline and sweetly said, "I don't believe I've had the pleasure." Mary Grace extended her hand. "I'm Mary Grace Adams and you are?"

"Madeline Linville." Madeline grasped Mary Grace's hand in a quick shake.

Recognition registered on Mary Grace's face. "No! Well I never would have known you. You certainly have changed...isn't that funny. Well, that explains a lot." She turned dismissing Madeline as effectively as tossing unwanted junk mail in the trash can.

"Charming isn't she?" Telie said to Madeline, grinning.

"Lovely."

Not sure what had just transpired, Samuel leaned forward and cocked a questioning eyebrow in Madeline's direction. The amused glint in his eyes made it almost impossible for her to pull away from his penetrating stare. She flushed under the scrutiny, feeling suddenly exposed. Madeline smiled sweetly in return, trying to convince herself that she meant nothing by the comment, really. It had merely been an observation.

Throughout service, Madeline waited and watched for a sign of Beau Chambers. She began to relax, thinking it was evident that he was not present...until the offering. An arm presented itself directly in front of her, hesitating. She glanced up meeting the cold dead stare of Beau Chambers.

Samuel's knuckles grew white, understanding all too well the message Beau was conveying to Madeline. He saw Madeline press her back into the seat, then cast her eyes downward, to avoid his gaze. Samuel's face was devoid of expression as his anger mounted. Reaching across Michael, he took hold of Beau's elbow, gripping it painfully. "Hey buddy, how's that ear?"

The color changed on Beau's face and he swallowed hard, telling both Samuel and Michael that he'd hit the mark. Beau meant to deliver a warning to Madeline, but instead, Samuel threw down the gauntlet. The next move was Beau's.

Once Madeline's heart stopped pounding, she turned her full attention to the sermon. Pastor Thad's words rang true in her ears as he quoted the twenty third psalm. She recalled the many times Mr. Jim sat with her and comforted her when she was frightened, reciting the very same psalm. She could still hear his low resonate voice in her head. Having committed the psalm to memory, she often quoted it when she was afraid or simply lonely. Transfixed by the sermon, she listened intently as Pastor Thad began expounding on the meaning of the passage.

After the final hymn, the congregation began filing out of the church, slowly. Gathering her purse, Madeline waited for Willa to collect her things before turning to go. Glancing over her shoulder, she took a sharp intake of breath. There, standing in the back of the church was Beau, dead eyeing her.

Samuel noticed the expression on Madeline's face and followed her gaze to where it ended. He extended his hand to her, never taking his eyes off Beau. A muscle tightened in Samuel's jaw as he challenged him with his expression. "Come with me, Madeline." He turned to speak with Michael. "We'll talk later."

"You bet we will. Telie and I will be waiting to hear from you."

Madeline squared her shoulders and lifted her chin. "Let's get this over with."

Turning to Willa, Samuel said, "I've called Greenberry and he's going to pick you up out front. You're gonna drive on over to the White Grape and save us a seat. We'll be along in a little while."

With an understanding nod of her head, Willa slid by them, patting Madeline on the arm.

Telie squeezed Madeline's arm as she passed and whispered in her ear, "You're in His hands now, Madeline. God has you covered."

Pastor Thad's office was cluttered with books and papers and every kind of literature imaginable. Clearing off stacks of books from the chairs, Thad directed Samuel and Madeline to the seating.

"Pardon my mess. This is the only place my wife allows me to trash so I guess I've gone a little overboard." Thad's smile seemed to wrap around his entire face. Deep groves lined his cheeks; the telltale sign of a person who laughed often. Walking around to his desk, he rolled his chair around to face them without the obstruction of the heavily piled desk getting in the way of his line of sight. "You know, I've often said that when settling a conflict I'd rather have something horrible to deal with than something trivial. For the record, I've reconsidered my thoughts about that. If this accusation is true, then it's wicked and will be handled in the correct way to bring about healing and restoration for all parties involved." He hesitated a moment before continuing. "Our elders, Brother Bill and Brother Nathan will be joining us shortly, along with my wife, Ann. I thought the presence of a woman might ease the situation for you. We have a daughter not much older than you." He shrugged in a casual way. "Madeline, I'm old school so bear with me."

Madeline looked into Pastor Thad's eyes, grateful for what she saw there. *This man is kind.* She thought how very blessed his family must be to have such a man.

There was a slight knock on the office door as a tall woman eased inside followed by two rather large men. Samuel stood up and faced them, shaking hands with each one, greeting them all by name. The woman had fine wispy blond hair and marble like clear blue eyes. Her rosebud mouth seemed permanently fixed in a pout. The younger of the two men was attractive with an outdoorsy air about him, like he'd be more comfortable up in a deer stand or out on a fishing boat than in a pastor's study. The other man was middle aged with graying hair at the temple. He looked suited for the role of elder, dignified but with a sense of meekness, like power under control. Each one smiled at Madeline, then quietly moved to the back of the study and took their places as witness.

"You see, Madeline, whenever a matter like this is brought before the church, it's important to have our elders here as witnesses. That's all they're to do is witness our conversation. Forget they're there. Are you comfortable? Would you like something to drink?"

"No, thank you," she replied softly.

"All right then." He cleared his throat. "I see no need in having you repeat everything Samuel has already told us. It would only be upsetting to you...so I took the liberty of having it typed up so you could read over it. Just let me know if you agree with this accusation." Pastor Thad handed Madeline the document. "Take your time."

Madeline took the paper and began reading. After a moment, she handed it back. "Yes, that is correct."

"Would you like to add anything?" Pastor Thad raised his brow as he waited for a response.

"No." She shook her head, then looked down at her hands, folded in her lap.

"Well…I must tell you that Beau Chambers has vehemently denied everything. That leaves us without proof. It basically comes down to your word against his." An odd expression crossed his face, something between compassion and helplessness as he rubbed a wrinkle on his forehead. "Is there anything else you wish to say?"

"Would the letter he wrote me, the one telling me that he was going to kill me if I said anything, help?" Madeline asked, innocently. "I have it with me." She reached in her purse and pulled out the letter.

The sound of chairs scraping the floor from the back of the room broke the silence. "Let me have a look at that," Pastor Thad said, anxiously. His head bent over the letter reading it over and over again. Handing it to his wife he said, "Ann, make a copy of this and give it to Nathan. Nathan, you and Bill compare this to Beau's handwriting. Beau's been deacon here long enough that you shouldn't have any trouble finding papers with his handwriting. His penmanship is unusual enough that identifying it should be relatively easy."

"I have some right here," Nathan interjected, surprising them as he slapped the papers in his hand. Nathan and Bill took the letter and began to compare. They passed the papers to Ann for her inspection. Lifting their heads in unison, they all nodded in agreement. "It's the same handwriting. Without a doubt," Nathan said.

Drawing a deep breath, Pastor Thad turned back to face Madeline. He spoke softly as he gathered her hands in his large rough one. "This is a brave thing you've done. We can't find wholeness until we face our fears and confront them courageously and honestly. You coming forward may also save someone else from going through the same nightmare you have. God knows you've been hurt. It's not how it's supposed to be…this man should have been there to protect you instead of harm you. I'm telling you that it matters; it matters to me and most importantly, it matters to God. *You* matter to God." He released her hand and nodded to Samuel.

Samuel placed his arm around Madeline's shoulders, pulling her into his chest as she softly cried tears of relief.

After all the years of living in fear, finally someone knows and is going to speak on her behalf. *It's over, it's over,* she kept repeating to herself.

"Well, gentlemen," Thad announced, "I'll go to Beau with this information and seek his repentance and restoration…and his resignation." He turned once again to Madeline. "And you, young lady, I'll expect to see you in church again next Sunday." He smiled down at her as he stood up and began shaking hands with Samuel.

Pastor Thad watched as Samuel and Madeline walked out of the church. His attention was drawn to a woman with an unnatural shade of red hair, sharply dressed and walking briskly down the aisle, her head held high. Annoyance seemed to emanate from her whole body. Her cool aloofness and high maintenance style took him by surprise. He'd never seen the woman at any of the services. He made a mental note to get together with his deacons very soon to find out more about them *and* their wives.

Following closely on her heels was Beau Chambers. Brushing by the pastor, they stepped into his office and took a seat before his desk.

"I assume you're Mrs. Chambers." Pastor Thad extended his warm hand toward her. "I'm pleased to finally meet you." He turned a questioning eye to Beau.

"Please, call me Brittle...my nickname stuck." She shifted on her seat, impatient to get on with it.

"I hope you don't mind my wife joining us, Pastor. You see, we hold no secrets from one another." Beau lifted his wife's hand to his lips, kissing it softly.

"Not at all, that is completely your choice." Pastor Thad gestured to Brother Nathan. "I've asked Brother Nathan to sit in on our discussion. I see no reason for anyone else to remain. He's here as a witness only. I'm sure you're both quite comfortable with your former pastor."

Brittle nodded. "Can we just get on with this if you don't mind? I've got a million things to do today." She forced a smile.

"Of course," he said, clearing his throat. "My position here is to listen to all sides without prejudging. It's the truth of the matter we need to discover."

Beau stated calmly, "My visits to the Linville's were well-intentioned, I assure you. The purpose was to see after the needs of two very troubled people who, frankly, had no one else." Beau turned his eyes soulfully to his wife. "The unfortunate circumstances of the Linville's greatly troubled our daughter, Robin. You see, Madeline was in her class at school. So, I took it upon myself to keep a check on them from time to time to reassure my daughter that they were doing well and that their needs were being met. My only mistake was not involving my wife. I should have been smarter about it, the world being what is today." He reached over and squeezed his wife's knee. "Forgive me honey for being so careless. You were just so busy with your projects...I didn't want to take you away."

Brother Thad witnessed the exchange and then calmly unfolded the threatening note and placed it on the desk in front of the couple.

Leaning forward in their seats, Beau and his wife each read the note.

"This is an outrage!" Beau shouted, turning a deep shade of red. He snatched up the paper and tore it to pieces. "This is some kind of conspiracy to ruin my good name. I'll not allow this smear campaign from a half crazy girl to ruin my reputation in the community. Everyone knows she's crazy. Just ask anyone, they'll tell you. But, I do know one thing. We'll never set foot in this church again!" Standing, Beau reached out to take his wife's hand, "Come on sweetheart, let's get out of here."

Brittle made no attempt to move. "That was your handwriting, Beau. I'd know it anywhere. Don't treat me like I'm stupid. I won't be humiliated— get your resume together, we're moving to Jackson."

Chapter 12

Samuel nudged Madeline with his shoulder as they walked down the sidewalk outside the White Grape Restaurant. "You did big today."

"Thanks to you," she shot back. "I never would have done that if you hadn't bullied me into it." A slow smile spread across her face as she pushed him back playfully.

Samuel noticed Greenberry signaling him from the courtyard of the restaurant. "There they are, come on, let's get through this line." Samuel took hold of Madeline's hand and led her through the crowd.

The courtyard was arranged with small wrought iron tables covered in crisp white table linens. A small votive candle flickered in the center of a dish of water surrounded by fresh and floating flowers tops. A nearby willow tree danced gracefully in the blowing breeze. Soft jazz music floated around them, emanating from some hidden place in the landscaping.

"This place is beautiful," Madeline whispered, as they sat down with Greenberry and Willa. "I've never seen anything like it." She glanced all around, taking in the scenery.

"Just wait until you try their chocolate cheesecake." Samuel gave a wicked grin. "It's better than...*almost* anything."

"Mind your manners boy, there are ladies present," Greenberry grumbled.

Noticing Greenberry for the first time since arriving, Madeline was struck by the difference in his appearance. Gone were the dusty boots and dirty shirt, replaced by an unbelievably attractive man wearing a light blue collared shirt tucked into a nice pair of fitted jeans. His tanned and weathered face seemed older than his sparkling blue eyes. For a man his age, he was surprisingly fit. Willa seemed to be very relaxed around him, but Madeline had a sneaking suspicion their arrival had interrupted a very deep conversation.

"How stupid of me to forget my manners, thanks for reminding me, Greenberry." Amused at the situation, Samuel tried to suppress a grin. Turning to Madeline, he said, "So, I take it this is the first time you've been here?" Looking into Madeline's pale green eyes he thought for a moment about all she would have missed because of the selfish bullying of Beau Chambers.

Madeline nodded, looking around. "It's really beautiful...so relaxing." She closed her eyes, listening to the sound of water splashing from the fountain near a vine covered brick wall. Sensing Samuel's eyes on her, she looked up, feeling a blush cross her cheeks. "It's been a long time since I've been out to eat...not counting that day at the Blue Plate. It's nice."

Willa broke the awkward silence by saying; "I really enjoyed the church service today. I like Pastor Thad. He's a very compelling speaker. Greenberry and I were just discussing the importance of being a part of a body of believers."

Samuel cut his eyes to Greenberry. "You're absolutely right. That's one act of obedience I intend to follow. Dad used to say that once you find your way, stay the course."

Madeline shifted in her chair as the waitress walked up to take their order.

Samuel noticed Madeline seemed to be at a loss over her menu choices. "Do you trust me to order for you?" More than anything it mattered to him that she trusted him. Why? He hadn't figured that out yet.

Relieved, Madeline nodded her agreement.

"She'll have the Creole chicken with raspberry tea *and* for dessert, chocolate cheesecake." Closing the menu, he motioned to Willa.

"Oh that sounds good…I'll have the same," Willa said, licking her lips.

Greenberry smiled at the gesture, then said to the waitress, "Steak, well done with steak fries." Handing back his menu, he turned an admiring eye to Willa as he watched her smooth her hair.

"Same here, only with a baked potato, loaded." Samuel winked at the waitress, causing her to drop the menus. As she bent to retrieve them, the extra linen napkins that were stuffed in her apron pocket fell out onto the ground.

Flustered, the young waitress quickly began picking up the scattered items.

"Here, let me help." Samuel bent down and grabbed a few napkins, handing them back to her with a dazzling smile.

She took the proffered napkins and smiled back with shaky lips before turning away.

"You should be ashamed of yourself, Samuel James Warren. I think you do that on purpose," Willa reprimanded lightly.

"What?" Samuel raised his eyebrows, questioning innocently.

"Don't you "what" me, Samuel. You know perfectly well what you're doing. I haven't forgotten all of those waitresses back in Charleston or how they would fight over who would get to serve you." She leveled her gaze. "I've never seen such a commotion. Especially with that...oh what was her name...Zolotta?"

"Whole lotta Zolotta," Samuel rhymed, then grinned. "She was such a healthy child."

Willa rolled her eyes.

Madeline and Greenberry listened to the banter back and forth, enjoying it. Speaking up, Madeline added, "You do seem to enjoy flirting, Samuel. How has that worked out for you so far?" she inquired, softly.

Leaning forward on the table, he answered in a husky whisper to her ear, "I'll let you know...later."

Goosebumps covered her flesh, giving her a shiver. Covering her arms, she wasn't about to let him know how her own body responded to his appeal. "You do that."

It was one of those afternoons when you just wanted to sit and drink up the beauty around you. After an enjoyable lunch, Greenberry and Willa decided to stay in town and window shop before going home. Saying their goodbyes,

Madeline and Samuel headed for the truck and back to Bell Bennier.

The truck sank onto the dirt and sand packed road that ran along the edge of the property of Bell Bennier. Towering trees linked overhead to form a light canopy as sunshine filtered through the branches, flashing brightly as they passed beneath. Bumping along the road with Blue's from Muddy Waters playing on the radio, Madeline spoke up. "Don't turn to Bell Bennier...I'm going home."

Samuel reached for the volume, turning it down. He cocked an eye at her.

She gave a half-laugh. "That look doesn't bother me. I'm going home."

He could see the stubborn set of her jaw and knew there would be no talking her out of it.

The truck eased to a stop in front of Madeline's house. Turning to her, Samuel quietly said, "I'm very proud of you, Madeline. What you did today...it took guts."

"Thanks, Samuel...and thanks for lunch. I really had a nice time."

He reached for the door handle, but she stopped him.

"No need to get out, I'll see you later."

As Madeline hopped out of the truck, Samuel watched as she made her way up the back steps to her door. A movement from inside the house caught his attention as a shadow crossed in front of the kitchen window. Reacting quickly, he jumped out of the truck and yelled, "Maddie, don't go inside!"

Confused, Madeline held on to the doorknob as she peered back at him with a puzzled look. "What is it, Samuel?"

Quickly mounting the steps, he pulled her away from the door. "Wait in the truck and lock it, there's someone inside the house."

Stunned, Madeline blinked once as Samuel's words registered, then she eased down the steps toward the truck.

He waited until she was safely inside the truck, then turned the knob and rushed inside the house. Moments later he came back outside and motioned for her.

Hopping out of the truck, she rushed to his side. "What was it, what did you find; anything?"

"Looks like whoever it was...wanted you to know that they'd been here." Samuel held a lit cigarette in his hand. "I found this in the kitchen sink."

Madeline gasped as she looked down at the gray smoke swirling from the cigarette.

"Get your things, Maddie. It's not safe here anymore; you need to come with me." He pulled out his cell phone and began dialing Greenberry. "I want to know where this guy came from. Maybe we can find some tire tracks or something. You just can't vanish into thin air like that."

That night, Madeline awoke to the sound of voices on the lawn down below as Samuel and Greenberry returned from the woods. It was well past midnight. Her questions would have to wait until tomorrow.

An impatient breeze ran through the curtains followed by the sound of distant thunder. Bright flashes of lightning illuminated the bedroom, casting eerie shadows along the floor and walls. Madeline rolled over onto her side, hugging her pillow close as she waited for the thunder. Her mind drifted to Jude. Oh, how she missed him. Swallowing down the sadness, she pulled up from the bed and eased onto the floor, tiptoeing to the far side of the room.

Listening at the door, she quietly pulled it open and peered down the long darkened hall toward Samuel's room. *Good, he must be asleep.* Carefully, she navigated the hallway, avoiding loose boards that squeaked, and knowing exactly where to place her foot. Once downstairs, she silently slipped outside into the cool darkness, down the steps and out onto the grass. The wet dew tickled her bare feet as she relished the feel of the blades running between her toes.

A low voice reached her ears. "Have you decided to surrender to the enemy?"

Frozen in fear, her heart pounded in her throat as she slowly turned around in the direction of the voice. There in the shadows, leaning against a tree was the strong frame of Samuel Warren. Relief flooded her as she stepped toward him.

"Mind telling me where you're off to?" he asked, pushing off the tree with his back.

"Mind telling me what *you're* doing out here in the middle of the night?"

"I asked first," he responded, in a singsong voice.

Madeline sighed, "I needed air," she said, using the same excuse she'd heard him use countless times before.

Suddenly, a forceful gust of wind banged the plantation shutters against the house, howling through the trees.

Startled by the unexpected noise, Madeline flung herself into Samuel's arms, burying her head into his chest.

A strange feeling of protectiveness came over Samuel as he stroked her hair, breathing in the fresh lilac scent. Placing his finger under her chin he lifted her head. "It's only the wind."

Pale green eyes stared up at Samuel, pulling him toward them. Moved by Madeline's reluctance to pull away, he lowered his head, pressing his lips into hers as his arms encircled her waist. Madeline's slender arms reached around his neck as she returned the all-consuming kiss. He pulled back, looking into her passion filled eyes. He was not prepared for the rush of emotions he felt. Thoughts assaulted him from every angle. He felt like someone had doused him with lighter fluid and tossed a match.

"I...I'm sorry about that, Samuel." Madeline said, embarrassed by her behavior and misreading the startled expression on his face. "I was wrong to...to act so...so *trashy*," she spit the word out as if getting rid of a bad taste.

"Trashy—for kissing me...oh no you don't; call it rash, impulsive or even crazy, but don't ever call it trashy. Look here, I'm the one that should be apologizing. You did nothing wrong so get that out of your head." Uncomfortable with the awkwardness of the situation, Samuel was suddenly unsure of what to do with his hands. Shoving them into his jeans pocket, he said, "But I'll have to say this...that was probably the best kiss *I've* ever had." He winked at her, happy to lighten the mood and ease the seriousness of the moment.

"Yeah, for me, too," Madeline added softly, then looked down at her hands.

Samuel smiled, then turned serious all of a sudden. "But you don't have to worry about me, Madeline. I'm here to help and not become part of the problem. I'm sorry about what happened and it won't happen again, I promise you that."

Trying to hide her disappointment, she smiled. "As long as you promise; when you tell Bree, let her know it was my fault and that I'm sorry."

"We'll leave Bree out of this...we can handle our own affairs."Samuel looked up feeling rain on the wind. A loud clap of thunder sounded, followed by a dazzling display of lightning charged against the night sky. "We'd better head inside. Whatever's coming, it promises to be a force to be reckoned with."

Morning light darted across the surface of the dark and marred kitchen table as Samuel and Madeline sat facing each other. Lifting his coffee cup slowly to his lips, he studied her.

Not at all comfortable with the scrutiny of his intense gaze, Madeline began shifting in her chair and tugging on the collar of her white blouse. "Are you going to stare at me much longer, or am I free to leave?"

Samuel cocked an eye at the coolness of her tone. "Just thinking...I'm having difficulty trying to determine why someone would be stalking you. Last night, we found evidence in the woods that someone has been watching you for some time. We came across old cigarette butts in this one area, the same brand as the one found in the kitchen sink. Whoever it is seems to be more interested in you than your stuff. We couldn't find anything disturbed in the house...but, of course, you'd be the better judge of that." He tried to sound nonchalant, but failed. "Can you shed some light on this for me? Is there some guy out there that may be interested in you?"

"No, not that I know of." She gathered her hair in one hand and lifted it away from her neck. "I feel like it's safe for me to go back home now, Samuel. Whoever it was is long gone and I've got work to do."

"What possessed you to wander around outside last night?" he questioned, suspiciously.

"It felt safe," she shrugged, dismissing his concern.

Letting out a frustrated sigh, he responded, "I don't know how to deal with your 'if it feels *right* it is *right*' approach to everything. It's ridiculous to judge a situation based on your feelings."

"Listen to you! You judge women the same way...except it's more 'If it looks *good* it is *good*!*'* Madeline raised her chin defiantly.

Shock registered on Samuel's face, then quickly turned to aggravation. "Miss Behrends happens to be a very capable woman. What do you know about her value?"

"Are we discussing your business now...or Miss Be-hrends. I sometimes get the two mixed up."

Having said her peace, Samuel eyed her steadily. She could irritate him like no other woman, throwing him all out of sorts. He wasn't used to being out of control and no one *ever* challenged him. But, once he decided on something he stayed his course. He wasn't a man to change direction easily once his mind settled on an action.

Silence came between them. Samuel ran his hand down his face, taking a deep breath. "Jude told me that y'all had plans to move your business to the old servants' quarters sometime this year. Now's a good time to do it, so, with your permission, I'll have your business moved there while we're gone to Charleston. All we need is for someone to vandalize your place while we're gone and there goes your business. I'll arrange to have all you need, including Internet and plumbing. Meanwhile, I'll inform the authorities and some of the neighbors, like Michael and Telie, to be on the lookout." Samuel leaned back in his chair, crossing his arms over his chest. "Greenberry is going to stay behind until we head back from Charleston, then he'll drive Willa up and help her move her things down. Willa's decided to stay here… I'm happy about that. I'm driving you and Bree up to Charleston, then y'all can drive my car back and I'll follow in the truck—how does all of that sound to you?"

What Madeline once thought to be arrogance, she now believed to be confidence. His self-assurance both annoyed and comforted her. "Thanks for informing me of your plans, Samuel. I'll get back to you if I'm interested in being a part of them. I guess because of last night, you seem to have the idea that I'm free for the taking…but I'm not, I assure you."

Samuel didn't like the tone of her voice. And it further aggravated him for her to bring up what had happened between them the night before. "Look, I wasn't the only one out there in the dark; seems I remember there being two people out in the storm last night." He watched as she narrowed her eyes. It promised to be a good one. Although he enjoyed seeing her eyes flash when she was angry, he intervened. "Madeline, I'm appealing to your good reason. Don't make me call Jude. Remember, he has his first exam this week and I don't think he needs the distraction. You know as well as I do that he'll be on the first flight home if he gets wind of this."

"You wouldn't." She lifted one eyebrow at his threat.

"Try me." The kitchen chair scraped across the floor as Samuel stood up. "I'm going to work." He gulped down the rest of his coffee, and placed the cup back on the table with a bang. "We live to fight another day, Miss Maddie."

The smell of chicken frying greeted Samuel as he walked through the front door at the end of the long hard day. The aroma seemed to fill the entire house. Stepping into the kitchen, he found Madeline busy over the stove, barefoot with his mother's apron tied around her skirted waist.

"What's this?" Samuel asked, as he tossed his keys on the counter.

Looking over her shoulder, Madeline replied, "Oh, I thought you might like supper early for a change. I gave Willa the afternoon off. She and Greenberry are out on a date."

Samuel made it to the stove in two steps. Reaching around her, he began lifting the lids on the pots where he discovered mashed potatoes, field peas, fried squash and okra along with an iron skillet full of cornbread. Overcome with delight, he grasped her shoulders and moved her aside as he opened the oven door. "Don't tell me that's blackberry cobbler." The steaming hot cobbler bubbled in the pan as Madeline bumped him out of the way with her hip.

"You're in my way. Let me get that out of the oven."

Samuel's eyes danced with delight, making him look boyishly handsome. "Let's eat outside on the veranda," he said, rubbing his hands together as was his habit when something excited him. "Oh, wait." He narrowed his eyes at her. "You're not going to poison me, are you?"

"Why on earth would you ask that? Do you think I'm crazy or something?" Madeline twisted her lips to keep from smiling.

"Well, we didn't exactly see eye to eye on everything this morning."

Madeline waved her hand, dismissing his comment. "That was this morning, this is now. Besides, you're Jude's brother and I would *never* do *anything* to hurt Jude." A warm smile slowly spread across her face. "You'll just have to trust me," she said, using the all too familiar words on him for a change.

Their relationship was changing, as if they'd crossed some invisible line. Like rocks in a tumbler, they'd knocked off a few of the rough places on each other.

Shortly after they'd finished the last bite of cobbler, Madeline went inside to pour two cups of coffee. Upon returning, she found Samuel stretched back in his seat with his feet propped up on the table and his hands behind his head, clenching a cigar between his teeth.

"You know, for someone with such an aversion to alcohol, tobacco sure doesn't seem to bother you." She smiled sweetly, taking the edge off her words.

Rolling the cigar over to lodge in his cheek, he stated, "That blasted Greenberry got us started. And now, he doesn't even smoke."

"Us?"

"Yeah…me and Michael. Back in the day, when we were mean old boys, we'd asked Greenberry for his lighter so we could light some fireworks on the fourth of July. He told us there was no way he would ever give the likes of us a lighter 'cause we'd probably burn down the whole plantation.

Instead, he gave us his lit cigar. Needless to say, we found every excuse in the book to shoot fireworks that year." He pursed his lips into a soundless whistle, blowing out a steady breath of smoke. "Michael's almost kicked the habit. He mostly chews on them now. I'm the last hold out. But, I do enjoy a good cigar and a pipe on occasion."

Her face grew thoughtful. "You love Michael, don't you?"

"Like a brother. We've been through a lot together. He'd give his life for me, and I'd do the same." Pausing, he added, "I guess I've always treated Jude more like a son than a brother...the age difference and all. But...he always had you." A shadow of sadness moved over his eyes.

"We had each other." Madeline smoothed her skirt over her knees. "I don't remember you being around much...except for the time when I got my leg stuck in that mud-hole near the bayou."

He squinted from the smoke encircling his head. "I remember that. You were all covered with mud and crying. You kept saying that the alligator was going to come and eat you. It took me forever to convince you that that old log floating in the bayou wasn't a gator."

"I was so glad you saved me. I remember having the biggest crush on you after that. You were my knight in shining armor and I dreamed of you off and on for about a month," she added softly, remembering some of her childhood fantasies. "It was during that time that I found every excuse in the world to fall down whenever you were around just so you'd pick me up and carry me inside."

Samuel grinned. "Always at your service, milady," he mocked, bowing his head slightly. "And you were the dirtiest and clumsiest little princess I've ever had the pleasure of rescuing. Same goes for that animal you called a French poodle."

Bree came out onto the veranda, holding Madeline in a piercing stare as she moved toward Samuel. "Hello sweetheart. I came by to see what I needed to do before we head to Charleston."

"Bree!" Samuel sounded surprised as he leaned forward in his seat. "I didn't hear you pull up."

"I came around the back way."

"Oh, I didn't know you knew about the back way. You almost have to get lost to find that old road." Samuel watched her face, as if looking for a sign of deception.

"Want some coffee, Bree?" Madeline inquired, as she stood and began collecting plates from the table.

"Yes, cream and sugar and I'll take some of whatever that is in the dessert bowl." Bree sat down in Samuel's lap, wrapping her arms around his neck as she leaned in for a kiss.

Madeline wasn't one to wallow in self-pity; she'd learned long ago to make the best of her circumstances. And, since coming to know the Lord, she was beginning to recognize His hand in her life, leading and guiding her through the sometimes hidden paths. *So what if Bree treated her like a servant. She is Samuel's girlfriend and she has every right to be where he is.* Still, she wasn't looking forward to a long road trip with the charming, Miss Breanna Behrends.

Chapter 13

*T*he cool vapors of morning filtered through the pecan orchard as Madeline made her way down the dirt road toward town.

Deciding to head out early had seemed the wise thing to do to avoid the heat of the day. But, as the early morning mist began to enshroud her, she began to have second thoughts. Shaking her head to clear it, she observed low hanging fog in the meadow. "Those aren't confederate soldiers in the field, only shapes in the mist, nothing more. You've just heard too many stories about this place, that's all," she told herself, shivering as she spied one particular form leaning against a tree with what appeared to be a rifle in his hand. She was just about to turn back toward Bell Bennier and make a run for it when she heard tires rolling over the packed sand and shell drive. As it neared, Madeline moved to the side of the road without glancing back. Catching a glimpse of the sleek black body of Samuel's truck, she secretly released a breath as it pulled beside her.

"Mind telling me where you're going?" Samuel's deep voice vibrated through the damp air.

"To town," Madeline answered simply, continuing to walk straight ahead. The courage she'd lost moments before suddenly returned with Samuel's presence.

The truck eased forward, keeping pace with her steps. Leaning out the window, Samuel said, "It's dangerous out on the road, Maddie," he cautioned. "Anything could happen to you. Get in, I'm going that way."

Madeline stopped in her tracks and faced him. "Thanks, but I'm fine. I enjoy walking."

Samuel flinched. "What part of everything I've just said were you not listening too? Was it the part about 'the roadways being dangerous', or the 'anything could happen to you'?"

She hesitated.

"Madeline, get in the truck." When she didn't respond, he added, "Get in the truck or I'll put you in the truck."

"You're bluffing."

"Let's find out," he threatened, grinning broadly.

Something about the wicked look on Samuel's face caused Madeline to change her mind. She crossed in front of the truck and hopped in. Settling into the seat, she felt small. Not wanting to meet his gaze, she turned her attention to the misty fields where all the ghosts seemed to have vanished away like a wispy vapor.

They drove along in silence, each one not sure about the other. He adjusted and measured the airflow, making sure the air from the vent reached her. The simple act caused Madeline's throat to tighten.

"You cool enough?" he asked.

"Yes," she choked out. She was on the verge of tears and didn't know why.

"Where were you headed?" Samuel took his eyes off the road momentarily as he waited for her reply.

"To see Telie, at Christenberry's. I have a few samples to drop by." She indicated the small bag in her hand.

He reached over to the glove compartment and pulled out a pack of gum, offering her a stick before taking one himself. "Don't worry, it's not spearmint," Samuel said, eyeing her steadily. "What's wrong with your car?"

Madeline shrugged. "It won't start."

"I'll look at it when we get back. It may be the battery."

"I'm not your responsibility, Samuel. I'll have it looked at when I...later."

Samuel glanced at her, noticing her chin lift up a notch. "Never said you were my responsibility...I just like looking at cars, do you mind?"

"Guess not." Madeline relaxed a little at his tone. Seeing the hint of playfulness on his face caused her to lighten up.

They pulled off the county road and onto the long dirt road that stretched out to Christenberry's Landscaping Company. The compound before them was massive with low-lying buildings scattered all around the sprawling landscape. As they pulled up in front of the building, Madeline spotted a colorful display of bright yellow mums and pumpkins perched on top of hay bales. A scarecrow stood guard over the scene with hay sticking out of his straw hat. The sleeves of his shirt and pants were stuffed, causing him to lean slightly from the heaviness.

"Oh, how cute!" Madeline beamed. "It's been a long time since I've seen a scarecrow!"

"We need to work on getting you out more, Maddie girl." Secretly, it delighted Samuel that simple things brought her such joy. She was childlike in that way.

Hopping out of the truck, Madeline heard a deep commanding voice. It was a woman's voice, but she couldn't see the woman over the hood of the truck. Samuel was smiling, looking down toward the ground as Madeline stepped around the truck. There, in front of her, was a pixie of a woman with a deep booming voice. She wrapped both arms around Samuel's waist, twisting back and forth.

"Boy, if you aren't a sight for sore eyes! You get better looking everyday! Now, give old Martha a kiss."

Samuel planted one on the old woman enthusiastically, then reached down and picked her up, swinging her around.

The woman slapped his shoulder. "Put me down, Samuel before I get dizzy."

Placing her back down on the ground, he looked up to see Madeline staring at them, with a stunned look on her face. "Madeline, this is Martha, the one true love of my life."

I've heard that before, Madeline thought.

Martha slapped his arm. "Oh, stop it," she said, turning to greet Madeline. "Nice to meet you, Madeline; I feel like I already know you. Telie's so excited about the gardener's soap your making that she's had me rearrange a whole corner of the shop just to make room. I think she expects a whole shipment."

"Well, that's why I'm here. I brought some samples for her to try."

"Oh good, she's over there helping that man load corn stalks."

Samuel raised his hand over his eyes, shielding them from the hot Alabama sun. "What man?"

Martha waved in the direction of the tractor shed. "That man," she repeated. "The one that looks like he jumped out of a Dr. Seuss book; guess he won't need a scarecrow to go along with those corn stalks now will he?" Martha chuckled as she stepped away, waving her hand in the air as she went back inside the office.

Not quiet sure what to make of Martha, Madeline twisted her lips to keep from smiling at the comical little woman with the big booming voice. Her gray hair, bobbed at the shoulders, swished as she walked back inside the shop. Madeline imagined her gait would look more at home on a cowboy than on a petite little woman somewhere in her sixties.

"Martha runs the place. She's Michael's right arm," Samuel informed Madeline as they headed toward Telie. "She can be quite descriptive. When I was here the other day, this man walked up wearing a white puffy jacket. He was rail thin. Martha said he looked like a marshmallow on a roasting stick!" Samuel shook his head. "That's my Martha."

Rounding the corner, dodging an assortment of potted shrubs, they spotted Telie, finishing up with the customer Martha had so accurately described.

As the man drove off, Telie turned her attention to Samuel and Madeline. "I hope that's what I think it is,' Telie said, pointing to the small sack in Madeline's hand.

Madeline smiled, "I hope you like them. I've come up with three different varieties so far and I want you to test them for me." Reaching into the bag, she pulled out a bar of soap. "This one I've named after you, it's called 'Telie's

Sunrise.' I've also included a bath gel with the same fragrance."

Telie gasped, widening her eyes. She took the bar and inhaled the lemony scent, running her fingers over the smooth surface. "You named it after me?"

"Yeah, I notice the fragrance of everything and I happened to notice the citrus on you. This bar is made with lemongrass and grapefruit with a little hint of palmarosa. The base is olive oil and shea butter with cornmeal. I use cornmeal instead of pumice. It's really gentle on the skin but strong enough to remove sap from your hands...even from oleander. "

Telie threw her arms around Madeline's neck, surprising her. "Thank you, thank you! I can't wait to try this out!" Telie said, excitedly.

"What's going on out here? Are you disrupting the hired help, Samuel?" Michael called out as he walked up on the commotion.

Turning, Samuel replied dryly, "Oh, it's just your wife again. She gets all worked up like this whenever she sees me. It's embarrassing, really."

"Telie, I thought I told you to steer clear of Samuel. He's nothing but trouble."

Ignoring the banter, Telie placed the bar under Michael's nose. "What does this remind you of?"

Michael sniffed the soap, then slid his arm around Telie's waist, forcefully pulling her to himself. "You."

Seemingly unaware of the presence of anyone else, Michael and Telie held each other in a deep gaze before breaking the connection and turning their attention back to Samuel and Madeline.

"Oh, get a room for Pete's sakes. How long have y'all been married anyway, two or three months...enough already?" Samuel smiled, seeing the slight blush staining Telie's cheeks.

"One blissful year, technically, we're still on our honeymoon," Michael said, smiling down at his wife.

An idea formed in Samuel's mind as he heard Michael's answer. "Well my friend, that's what I needed to see you about. We're heading up to Charleston this weekend to see Jude, but when we return, I'd like to have you and Telie over to celebrate your marriage. You slid the ceremony right by me, but I'll not stand by and let my best friend get married without a celebration. Invite anyone you want...the more the better."

"It's been a long time since I've been to one of your shindigs, Samuel. I can't wait." Turning to Telie, Michael stated, "You haven't lived 'till you've been entertained by Samuel."

"Yeah, that's what all the girls say," Samuel teased. "But, there's one more thing I need to tell you about, my friend." Samuel gripped Michael's shoulder. "When I dropped Madeline off after church the other day, someone was in her house. They'd left a lit cigarette in the kitchen sink."

Michael reached into his shirt pocket and took out a skinny cigar, lodging it in his cheek as he bit down. "You think it was Beau?" he asked, squinting as he appraised his friend.

"Don't know. I've never known Beau to smoke, but I've also never known him to molest a child either. But, whoever it was has been watching her for a while. Greenberry and I found old cigarette butts scattered around some of the undergrowth in the woods with a birds-eye view through the cottage window. Looks like he parks near the bayou and walks up. We found tire tracks near Miss Theda's drive as well, but that could be from some of the construction workers building her house."

Michael raked his hand through his hair. "It would be a good idea for you girls to stay close to the house for a few days. We need to catch this guy. It sounds like he's wandering around the property, up to no good."

Both girls nodded their agreement.

Samuel clasped Michael's hand in a firm handshake. "I'll drop by the monastery and see if any of the monks have seen anything suspicious. I'm headed over to see Sheriff Kyle now. Keep me posted on any news and I'll do the same."

"You got it."

Smiling his signature bad boy grin, Samuel gently reminded his friend, "And, don't forget about the party. Just so you'll know; I plan to kiss the Bride."

Chapter 14

*R*ain dimpled the dry dust at Madeline's sandaled feet as the energy from the approaching storm hung on the air.

Lifting her mother's old beaten and faded suitcase from the ground, Madeline approached the back of the truck where Samuel was busy loading the designer luggage set of one very polished Bree Behrends. Bree was a striking and cruel woman. She'd insisted on staying at Bell Bennier the night she found out that Madeline had been installed there on a somewhat permanent basis. Madeline avoided her whenever possible, which was easy to do considering Bree spent most of her time working. But, the thought of spending the next ten hours trapped in a vehicle with Bree made her physically ill. *Maybe she'll ignore me. I can only hope.*

Madeline was used to being overlooked. Her school days had conditioned her well for that. Being invisible had its advantages, though. She could lose herself in books with ease and without interruption. Reflecting back on her childhood days, books were one of the few pleasures she'd truly enjoyed. At night, after the light went out in her mother's room, she would curl up on her window-seat bed and travel within the pages of a book to some distant land. She preferred stories about families, large ones with brothers and sisters and lots of cousins. She wanted a husband and many children someday. And, if the Lord saw fit, maybe she would have just that.

Taking the suitcase from Madeline's hand, Samuel hoisted it up onto the back of the truck. "Is that all for you?" Samuel asked, as he looked around the ground at Madeline's feet.

"Yeah, I have my books and a few pralines; I'm all set." She picked up a tote bag and her purse and climbed into the backseat of the truck.

Samuel tossed a pillow to her. "I never travel without my pillow. You're welcome to use it."

As soon as he was distracted, Madeline pressed the pillow to her face, inhaling Samuel's scent. *I could get drunk off that*, she thought.

Bree stepped into the passenger seat and buckled up without a word. As soon as Samuel hopped in, she turned toward him and smiled. "You look well rested. Did you have an enjoyable night?"

"Slept good for a change, now, are we ready?" He adjusted his rearview mirror until he had Madeline in his line of sight.

Clicking the seat belt around her waist, Madeline shrugged off the shoulder harness and pulled out a book from her tote bag, settling in for the long drive.

Thankfully, Samuel and Bree kept their conversation to themselves and allowed her to remain absorbed in her book. Occasionally she would look up and catch Samuel's eyes on her. He'd wink then turn his attention back to the road.

"So what's *your* favorite all-time movie, Madeline?" Samuel asked, adjusting the mirror so he could see her face.

"Bree happens to like "Dirty Dancing"...can you believe that?"

Madeline straightened in her seat, closing her book as she contemplated her answer. "It's a toss-up. It's either "The Quiet Man" or "The Horse Soldiers". I'm a John Wayne fan."

"Now that's more like it. Who doesn't like the Duke? Why...that'd be un-American," Samuel said with force. "Now, Rio Bravo with John Wayne and Dean Martin is right up there. Do you happen to know that Dean Martin has the greatest voice known to mankind?" he stressed. "He sings that cowboy song in the movie...what is it?" Samuel snapped his fingers as he tried to think.

"My Rifle, Pony and Me," Madeline blurted out, smiling.

"That's it. Dad used to sing that song to us when he'd put us to bed. Course, Dad's voice was always a little scratchy, but Dean...he has that rich, bluesy sound I like."

Bree made a face of utter disgust. "You've got to be kidding me, Dean Martin and John Wayne? I detest them both, *especially* John Wayne."

Madeline looked shocked. *What kind of a person hates John Wayne?*

"Slip on your shoes, girls. We're stopping for lunch," Samuel said, over the noise from the highway.

As they got out, Bree hurried around the truck and slid her arm around Samuel's waist possessively.

Looking around, Samuel spotted Madeline behind them. *She doesn't walk, she sashays,* he thought, as he stopped to wait on her. "Why are you always bringing up the drag? Walk beside me."

"Sorry, I guess I'm still in another world. Books have that effect on me." Madeline pulled her hair back and secured it so it fell softly in loose waves down her back.

"I admire you, Madeline," Bree said, curtly. "You couldn't care less about your appearance. How freeing that must be." Bree raked her eyes over Madeline's crumpled skirt, then looked away.

"The simplest styles are the most beautiful...to me," Samuel said, with tension in his voice. "Beauty is in the woman, not the clothing. Now, let's go in and have some lunch, shall we?"

Once they were seated, it was only moments until the lunch they ordered arrived. Madeline toyed with her food, not really having an appetite while sitting across from Bree. She decided to leave them alone. "I'm going to look around in the gift shop. This is for my lunch in case I miss the ticket." She handed Samuel a ten-dollar bill.

"Don't insult me, Madeline. Put that away." He narrowed his eyes, daring a confrontation.

The look on his face confused her. He looked as if he'd been slapped! "Well...thank you for lunch."

"Oh, Madeline," Bree said sweetly, as she looked up from her phone where she'd been texting. "Samuel told me you like candles. This place has some of the best. You should pick up a few."

Madeline nodded, surprised at the odd, almost pleasant tone to Bree's voice. "I will."

Intent on separating herself from her traveling companions, Madeline walked into the gift shop and headed straight for the candle and soap bins. Sniffing each one, she selected a few of each and then made her way over to a shelf lined with Jude's favorite candy bar, the Goo Goo.

After making her purchases, Madeline headed for the door, anxious to get back in the truck and on the road again. But, the thought of climbing back into the truck with Bree caused her stomach to tighten. So, she wandered around outside to wait and breath in some fresh air to calm her body.

Seeing a line of rocking chairs along the porch of the restaurant, Madeline plopped down in the first one she came to and began rocking, allowing the gentle rhythm to sooth her. Her reservoir of energy had dried up a few miles back, and now her body and mind needed a recharge to get her through the last leg of the journey. Resting her head against the back of the rocker, she closed her eyes.

"You sure look mighty sweet just resting there all relaxed and comfortable. I'm tempted to sit right down and join you."

Madeline's eyes flew open at the sound of the unfamiliar twang of the stranger's voice. There, standing in front of her, leaning against a post, was a ruggedly handsome man with sandy colored hair and a lopsided grin. He wore a cowboy hat, jeans and a white buttoned down shirt, opened at the collar just far enough down to reveal a bronzed hairless chest. He smiled, showing a perfect set of white teeth against his tanned skin.

"Are you with someone? I'd hate to be shot by some jealous husband before I even get the chance to know your name." The stranger looked down, watching as his booted foot made a line on the ground.

Madeline smiled. It had been a long time since anyone flirted with her. Shaking her head, she replied, "No…I'm traveling with friends to visit a friend in Charleston. I'm not married."

Encouraged by her words, he stepped closer and asked, "Well then…in that case, do you mind if I sit down?"

"Not at all," she replied. The thought of sharing a few minutes with the handsome cowboy brought a smile to her face, instantly reviving her.

"The name's Clayton. Clayton Holt. And you are?" he asked, as he leaned forward in the rocker.

"Madeline Linville, it's nice to meet you." She stuck out her hand, feeling the warmth of his grip as he pressed his hand into hers.

He stared down the road, making a gesture with his head. "I'm headed down the coast of Georgia, then cutting over to Mobile for one last show before going back to Texas. I'm a roper on tour with a Rodeo."

"Oh! I don't live far from Mobile. I live in Moss Bay," Madeline said, excitedly.

Clayton stared at her with such intensity that she had to divert her eyes. "Well, then." A slow smile spread across his face. "You plan on being back home by next Thursday?" he asked, taking off his hat and tossing it back and forth in his hands.

"Yes, I should be."

"Mind if I get your number. I'd love to take you out while I'm in town."

Without warning, Samuel's words popped in her head. *You'd be a better judge of dating if you actually had a date every once in awhile, Maddie.*

"I'd love to go out with you." Her pulse raced as she reached into her purse to pull out paper and a pen to jot down her number. Handing it to him, she said, "I've never been to a Rodeo."

"I can't wait to...take you." He grinned widely. "Next Thursday, then," he said, as he sauntered off toward his truck, flipping his hat in the air and catching it. He glanced back one last time before getting into his truck.

"Who was that?" Samuel questioned, as he held the restaurant door open for Bree. His investigator eyes scanned the area, as if searching for clues.

"Clayton Holt."

"You know him?" Samuel asked. He hesitated at the door, waiting for a reply as he watched the guy get in his truck and pull away.

Madeline cast an admiring glance in the direction of the truck now pulling onto the highway. "Not yet, but I sure hope to. He asked me out next Thursday. Clayton ropes for a Rodeo that will be coming to town."

Bree and Samuel snapped their heads simultaneously in her direction.

A certain feeling of satisfaction welled up within her. Suddenly she felt much better about herself.

"What about Jude?" Samuel questioned, a confused look crossing his face. He drew in a quick breath and held it, waiting for her answer.

"What about him?" Madeline blinked, then narrowed her eyes as she looked up at Samuel.

"Well, won't you break his heart? I mean, isn't that the whole point of this trip, for Jude to see you?" Samuel asked, more than a little annoyed.

"When will you ever understand, Samuel? It's not like that between us. Actually, I'm going on this trip to meet his new girlfriend, Jenny." For the first time, Madeline detected from Samuel a slight sense of being caught off guard.

Stunned, it took Samuel a moment to find his voice. "What? What new girlfriend? I didn't know about a girlfriend!"

"Relax Samuel, Jude wanted to surprise you. From the sound of it, he's pretty serious about this girl, Jenny."

Samuel ran his hand down his face before reaching into his pocket for a cigar. "And all this time..." he let his voice trail off.

"And all this time, what?" Bree demanded.

Lighting his cigar, Samuel tossed his match. "It doesn't matter." His purposeful stride was steadfast as he walked toward his truck with only one backward glance toward Madeline.

Chapter 15

*L*ow- hanging clouds held a fine mist causing Madeline to shiver. Standing before the stately and aged red brick home, she held her breath. The haunting presence of the place took her by surprise. She slowly let out her breath as she took in her surroundings. It was a picture she knew would most likely stay fixed in her mind for a long time. The sight of moisture dripping from the eaves as if the very house itself were crying chilled her body as she stepped closer to the entrance.

The home sat on a diagonal to the path of the sun so that in the South Carolina heat it created its own shade. The piazzas, or deep porches, block out much of the light allowing breezes to blow across the house from the tidal creeks and salt marshes that surround the property.

Madeline's senses began to awaken to the unusual smells that assaulted her. *What is that smell?* She looked around, trying to determine the source of the unidentified pungent smell.

Seeing Madeline's interest, Samuel explained, "This house belonged to my mother's family. It's one of only a few homes in this area that withstood the war. And, that fact alone is still spoken of with a certain amount of pride by the locals. Seems my mother's family was a fierce bunch. Even the Yankees gave them a wide berth." He winked at her as he reached for their luggage.

The place held secrets. You could feel it in the very air moving around you. A dragonfly crossed Madeline's path, zigzagging in an erratic pattern up and down her body, as if taking her measurement before allowing her to pass.

Suddenly, the front door flew open and Jude ran out and down the stairs, lifting Madeline in a joyful embrace. "Madeline! You're a sight for sore eyes! Just let me look at you!"

Madeline laughed at his exuberance. Looking over his shoulder she saw a pretty petite girl standing in the shadows of the doorway. "This must be Jenny," she said, sliding down the length of Jude as her feet touched the ground again. She stepped past Jude, making her way up the steps to the seemingly shy girl.

Jenny had a quiet reserve about her. With straight, fawn colored brown hair and warm brown eyes, Jenny had the wide-eyed look of an innocent young girl; Madeline knew instantly that she was going to like her. Reaching out, Madeline extended her hand. "Jude has told me so much about you, Jenny. I feel as though I already know you."

Jenny smiled sweetly. "I feel the same way about you. Hardly a day goes by that your name is not mentioned."

Samuel walked toward the steps with suitcases in hand. "It's nice to meet you, Jenny. I'm Samuel, Jude's brother. Good to see you too, Jude."

Jude spoke up, slapping Samuel on the back as he passed, "Oh...hey Samuel. I forgot all about you being here," he joked.

Samuel smiled. "Mind giving a man a hand with these?" He indicated the truck and the rest of the luggage. Bree placed her hand on Samuel's back as she waited for him to continue on into the house.

"Hi Bree, that's Jenny," Jude said as Bree slipped by him.

Bree gave a tight smile. "Pleasure."

"Same here," Jenny responded softly, as they stepped by her.

The home was furnished tastefully with richly carved mahogany pieces, giving it more of a Caribbean feel than one of an old southern mansion. The relaxed elegance felt less like a home and more like a get-a-way. Comfortable seating along with pillows and throws peppered the large gathering room. A fireplace filled one wall and was made entirely of stacked stone. French doors stood open to the back porch with a view of the tidal creeks and marshes beyond. From nearly every corner of the room you could hear a symphony of crickets and frogs filling the air, as if you were somehow apart of their world and not the other way around.

Seeing the wistfulness on Madeline's face, Samuel smiled, wishing he could stay and show her around. "I'm taking Bree to her house in town and then I'm going to stop by our office and check in with Bart. I'll be back later." He tossed his keys in his hand, waiting as Bree stepped from the bathroom. "If you look around outside, Maddie, stay close to the house until one of us can go with you." He reached for Bree's hand and pulled her to the door.

"All right," Jude said. "Take your time. I've got the girls." He smiled wickedly, as if sensing Samuel's disappointment at having to leave so soon.

Madeline kicked off her shoes and headed for the back door. "I'm going to look around."

"Wait, I'll go with you," Jude called out, running over to join her at the door.

Madeline stuck out her hand, halting him. "No, you stay here with Jenny. I'll be back in a minute." She lifted up on her toes, then caught herself before she kissed Jude's forehead, mindful of Jenny's presence and the concerned look on her innocent face. She knew she had to distance herself from Jude, no matter how hard that might be. Their relationship had to take a back seat to the new and budding relationship he was forming with Jenny.

"Oh okay, just be careful. An estuary is one of the most biologically productive ecosystems on Earth, so watch your step out there."

"I'll remember that," she smirked. Jude had always existed in a world apart from her, a world of marine biology where everything that mattered had its beginning in the sea.

Jude watched anxiously from the porch as Madeline made her way along the bank, following a footpath of sand and crushed shell.

Later that evening, Samuel returned home just as the muted light of day began to fade into grayish pink on the horizon. He plopped down on the couch, seeking rest from the long days drive. "Where's Madeline," he asked, to no one in particular. He looked around the room, finding everyone there but her.

"The last time I checked, she was out on the pier," Jude said, as he slowly slid a checker across the board. His attention was fixed on the game he and Jenny were playing and he never once looked up at Samuel.

"I'll go check on her." Samuel stood, biting back a comment about how anybody could be so casual about Madeline's whereabouts, especially when she was so unfamiliar with the area.

He rounded the bend toward the pier, then stopped as he heard the sound of Madeline's voice carried on the wind, calling out for help. Without hesitation he bolted forward, coming to a halt at the foot of the pier. Madeline was leaning over in an awkward position with her hands pressed flat against the boards, supporting her weight. Assessing the situation, he casually stepped onto the pier.

"Some days it just doesn't pay to chew through the straps, does it Maddie girl?"

She shook her head. "My foot went through a board and it's stuck. I'm afraid I'll shred my leg if I try and pull it out. The wood is jagged." She glanced at the sky noticing the dark clouds brooding overhead, gathering, it seemed, for a torrential downpour.

"Something seems oddly familiar about this..." Samuel fought back a grin. He shifted his weight from one foot to the other, as he seemed to contemplate the situation.

Madeline twisted, lifting the weight of her body with her hands. Seeing she was on the verge of tears, Samuel stopped teasing and knelt down beside her.

Swallowing hard, Madeline took her free hand and slowly lifted her skirt to just a few inches above her knees, then wrapped the fabric tightly against her legs. On her left thigh was the transparent skin of an old burn. Noticing Samuel's eyes on the fleshy scar, Madeline remarked, "It must be hard for a "leg man" to see such a gruesome sight. I turned over a skillet of hot grease on my leg when I was little," she explained, embarrassed by the disclosure.

He leveled his gaze at her. "There is nothing gruesome about you, Maddie. Nothing! Now hold still, let me do this." The feather light feel of her loose hair brushed against his arm as he reached inside the tight space and clasped her slender ankle, gently but firmly guiding it through the splintered wood.

"Thank you, Samuel." She breathed out a sigh of relief, as her trapped leg was set free. "I just knew there had to be an alligator somewhere under this pier looking at my leg and licking its chops."

"Well, if I was a gator…that's exactly what I'd be doing," Samuel said, with a leering grin. He made a wide sweeping gesture with his hand. "As always, it's my pleasure to come to the aid of a damsel in distress. Are you gonna dream about me again?" he teased.

A smirk played on her full lips. "Do nightmares count?" she teased.

Samuel tilted his head, observing her leg. "Not even a scratch, would you look at that? I should have been a surgeon," he said, proudly. "Come on," he grabbed her hand. "We better head back."

The next morning, Madeline stood on the pier, leaning against the rail as she watched Samuel work to repair the wooden deck. There was something so intoxicating about watching a man work, some deep enjoyment watching his strong masculine hands work to repair something fallen down and broken.

"I think you have a gift," Madeline said quietly, as she observed his rough hand running smoothly down the lumber. The new wood looked oddly out of place next to the old and weathered gray boards of the pier.

Looking up, Samuel remarked, "You better try this out before coming to any quick conclusions about my carpentry skills." He hammered in the last nail. "By the way, why didn't you go with the girls in to town? Don't you like to shop?"

"I wasn't invited...not that I'd go if I had been," she added, softly.

"Where's Jude?" Samuel stopped what he was doing and looked her in the eyes.

"He went to the library to get a book about tidal creeks and oyster reefs. I made the mistake of asking about them. Guess I know what I'll be listening to all night." Madeline picked up a stone and tossed it into the creek, watching it as it plopped into the water, rippling out in all directions.

It bothered Samuel that the girls left Madeline out of their plans. "I'm sorry the girls didn't invite you to go with them. It's their loss."

Madeline's pale green eyes confronted his without wavering.

His voice was lower, rougher. "I'm impressed. You're actually looking straight at me...for once."

Blushing, she turned away from his penetrating stare.

The air stirred, scattering loose sand across the boards as it whipped around her skirt, pulling the hair around her face in different directions all at once. "What *is* that smell? I can't identify it?" Madeline said, wrinkling her nose.

"Aaahhh, pluff mud! It's as Lowcountry as boiled peanuts. Makes me wish I was crabbing out here instead of working." Seeing the confused look on her face, Samuel explained. "Things wash into the tidal swamps and never completely wash out. Over time, this sediment creates pluff mud. The tide recedes twice every 24 hours on a cycle, and the exposed mud releases a smell like none other...anywhere. It's worse in the heat of summer after it's been baking in the sun all day. But trust me, to most folks around here, it smells like home. As a matter of fact, you could smear some on you and save yourself about three hundred dollars! That's what the finest Charleston spas charge to slather it on you, and look...all this for free." He stretched his hand out over the bank then smiled a wicked smile before adding, "I'd be happy to demonstrate."

Madeline rolled her eyes at his comment. "Oh, I just bet you would." She got down on her knees and stretched over to touch some of the mud. Rubbing it between her fingers, she remarked, "This would make a good facial mask. I'd need to do something with the smell, though." Leaning forward again, she wiggled her fingers in the water, trying to remove the sediment. Slinging her hand back, some of the mud landed across Samuel's square jaw. Looking back, she sucked in a quick breath. The mud and water mix ran along his jaw and dripped off his chin. A light shone from his steel gray eyes. His wicked, deadly smile seemed to grow in intensity as he watched her. Before she could react, he lunged forward and grabbed her up, dangling her over the side of the pier.

"You wouldn't!" She kicked her feet trying to squirm out of his arms but he held her firmly.

"Wouldn't I?" Taking a few steps back, he jumped off the pier, drenching them as he landed in the water. Moving over to the bank he deposited her on the mud, trapping her between his legs. "Oh, this is going to be fun. He scraped up a handful of mud. With his finger, he began applying a thick swipe of mud across the bridge of her nose."

Madeline fell back on the bank, limp.

Seeing the sudden change in her countenance, Samuel grew concerned. Leaning over her, he asked, "Maddie! Are you all right? I didn't mean…"

Once he was within striking distance, Madeline took aim with a fist full of the thick mud, hitting the target squarely on the jaw. Seeing the surprised look on his face from the ambush, she rolled over on her side, laughing until she was gasping for breath."

Not to be outsmarted by the little wisp of a girl, Samuel pinned her struggling body down, forcing her to look up at him. "Now Maddie, is that anyway for a young lady to behave? I think you owe me an apology." He was enjoying the resistance she was giving him in her struggle to be free, however weak.

Madeline looked up at him with her pale green eyes sparkling. He saw something there that he'd never seen in a woman's eyes before. It was joy…pure, undiluted joy.

Before Samuel could respond, a voice called from the direction of the house. "Madeline, Samuel, where are you?" Jude's steady voice pierced the air.

Looking down once more at Maddie pinned beneath him, he hesitated, wanting to hold on to the memory. He stepped back, pulling her to her feet. "Let me do the talking."

Dragging up from the marsh, all wet and dripping, Samuel and Madeline walked toward Jude. He rushed toward them with a concerned look on his face. "What happened?"

"Brother," Samuel stated flatly, "don't even ask."

Jude could only stare after them as they made their way back to the house, dragging their waterlogged bodies across the lawn.

As they reached the house, Madeline removed her shoes and gathered her dripping skirt in one hand as she tiptoed toward the bedroom. She stopped at the bedroom door and looked over at Samuel. He winked, then flashed a devastatingly handsome grin before disappearing into his room.

The sky was tinged grayish black. It was disturbing in its stillness. All natural sounds had quieted around them; even the nearby marsh grasses that pressed against the water in surrender to the wind remained quiet, without a rustle.

Jude, Jenny and Madeline settled into chairs on the porch to watch as the coming storm gathered strength.

"I heard on the news this morning that a tropical storm is headed our way," Jude said. "Hope it passes through pretty quickly. I don't want y'all driving back in all of that rain, it's dangerous." Jude patted Madeline's leg. "We're heading back to school late tomorrow, all this bad weather should move on out by then."

Madeline saw Jenny stiffen. This was going to be hard. How could she explain to Jude that the little ways they showed affection to each other had to end now that Jenny was in the picture? Resting her head back on the chair, she watched as the storm clouds approached, wondering what lay ahead for them and praying she'd be able to weather all of the changes that were sure to come.

Chapter 16

Madeline leaned forward on the steering wheel of Samuel's black Lexis, staring out the windshield between the slaps of the wipers. Blinded by the driving rain and bright flashes of lightning, she strained to see the highway before her. An explosive boom reverberated through the air followed by torrential rains that threatened to sweep the car from the road.

She made her way off the interstate, not sure where she was going, but deciding it was best to wait it out. Through silver sheets of rain, she made out the blurred image of a Hotel sign. Making a break for it, she drove slowly toward the familiar welcoming sign.

Once inside her hotel room, Madeline shed her damp clothes and stepped into a hot shower. She felt her muscles relax as hot water pounded her tense shoulders. Lathering up, she worked the stiffness out of her cramped arms and fingers where she'd gripped the steering wheel tightly. After drying off, she lifted a T-shirt from her suitcase and pulled it over her head, then fell across the bed, exhausted. Never in her life had she felt so completely exhausted or so completely alone.

The rain continued to fall into the night with a steady patter against the window, lulling her to sleep. She curled up on the soft bed, listening to the distant thunder of the storm far away as she drifted off to sleep.

A persistent knock sounded on the door, jarring her awake. Startled, she shot up and out of bed with her heart pounding in her chest. Making her way to the door, she peered cautiously through the peephole. "Samuel," she whispered, before unlocking the door.

As an after-thought she remembered her appearance. Clothed in nothing more than a T-shirt, she stepped back and grabbed the sheet off of the bed, wrapping it around her.

Samuel faced her, a mixture of relief and aggravation played across his features. "What possessed you to leave, Madeline? What is so important that you had to run away? Is it that cowboy, Holt...whatever his name is?"

Stunned, Madeline's wide eyes were fixed on Samuel's face. His steel gray eyes flashed dangerously as he rubbed his scruffy chin. He smelled strongly of cigar and she got a heady whiff of it each time he passed in front of her. He paced the room like a caged panther, never taking his eyes off of her. She felt as if his glare would penetrate through to the very core of her being.

Samuel stopped, then said in a measured voice, "I'm in the next room. In the morning, I'm taking you back home, to Bell Bennier." He leveled his gaze at her. "Don't even think about running away from me again." He held out an open hand. "I'll have your keys."

Madeline arched her left brow.

"That look doesn't frighten me, Maddie. If I'm to get any sleep at all tonight, I'll have your...*my* keys," he corrected, in a firm but controlled tone.

Seeing the determination on his face, she thought it best not to provoke him. Reaching beside the bed, she lifted her purse from the floor and retrieved the keys, handing them over.

"Thank you. Now...we'll both sleep better." Samuel's face softened somewhat, like a fleeting shadow, compassion crossed his features. Patting her head, the way you would a child, he gave her one last long look before turning to leave.

Back in his room, Samuel tried to settle down. The image of Madeline's startled eyes fixed on him and her slender form draped in a sheet burned in his mind. Shaking his head to clear it, he tried to erase the vision. *What caused her to bolt and run like that?* Picking up his cell phone, he dialed Jude.

After giving Jude the run down on their whereabouts, he asked his brother, "Can you shed some light on what I'm dealing with here, Jude? Is Madeline prone to these...these...irrational responses?"

There was silence on the other end of the phone, then Jude quietly responded, "Yeah Samuel, I think I can." He inhaled deeply. "Jenny told me about a conversation she and Bree had earlier. Jenny said that Bree had been reassuring her how she didn't need to worry about Madeline and her relationship with me. Bree told her that Madeline was nothing more than the family charity case and would probably always be around, but not to let the lunatic girl trouble her, that every good Southern family had either a ghost or a crazy person on the property. That that was the southern way of things and Madeline was just a pitiful tag-a-long living off the mercy of the Warrens."

"What!" Samuel yelled out. "You've got to be kidding...Bree said that?"

"Jenny was upset with Bree's comments, Samuel. She left the room and that's when she saw Madeline in the kitchen where she was sure she'd overheard the conversation." Jude sighed. "Jenny is blaming herself. She told me she was jealous of Madeline because of our relationship, but that she never meant to hurt her. I believe her. She's been crying all night." Jude let out a heavy breath of air. "But Madeline *is* hurt...and I'm hurt. She won't return my calls...she's never ignored me like this before. I'm coming down there. Where are you again?"

"We're in Savannah and you're not coming down! It's bad out and there's no reason for you to make the drive. I have things under control on this end, you handle your end and we'll all be fine. Drive Bree down to pick up the truck tomorrow, we're taking the Lexis to Bell Bennier. There's an extra set of keys on my dresser. We're at the Hampton near the Cove. Madeline will call you tomorrow. Don't worry; it's going to be all right."

A gray mist shrouded the parking lot as Samuel opened the car door for Madeline. As she settled into the seat, he noticed her slow movements. "Not feeling well?"

"No...I'm a little chilled...I just don't feel very well," she whispered, resting her head against the back of the seat.

"Think you might be coming down with something?"

"No...it's nothing like that." Madeline's voice was barley audible.

Concern registered on Samuel's face as he walked around the car and slid into the car seat. He hit a button on the dash and reached behind the seat, pulling out a small blanket. "Stretch out and relax, the seat will warm up in a minute."

Madeline eyed the blanket suspiciously. It smelled faintly of perfume. Reading the question on her mind, he said, "I keep it for Bree. She's cold blooded."

Aren't all reptiles? She thought, then felt guilty for thinking that way. After all, Samuel loved Bree. She must have *some* redeeming qualities, even if she hid them extremely well.

Samuel pulled into a gas station and got out to fill the tank. Whistling, he got back into the car and handed Madeline an Advil and a bottle of water. "Thought this might help, but if that doesn't..." With the other hand, he reached into the pocket of his jacket and pulled out a homemade praline. "Maybe this will."

Madeline's eyes lit up. "Thank you." She took a bite of the praline, gestured with it as she chewed and swallowed before she asked, "How did you find me last night?"

"There's a tracking device in the car," he stated, before taking a swig of ice-cold Coke. He cut his eyes playfully toward her. "Did you think I had some kinda magical powers?"

She rolled her eyes at his question. "So...you can locate your car anywhere?"

"Yep, all my vehicles have them...except my old truck back home." He winked at her. "And that old truck happens to be my favorite. It's priceless...to me. Fortunately, no one else understands the true value of her or she would've been stolen away from me a long time ago."

They pulled back onto the interstate as he popped in a blue's CD, keeping the volume low to soothe her.

"This is a really nice car. I've never been in a car with leather seats like this before. They're so soft, and the seat gets warm." She leaned back against the headrest, relaxing as she breathed in the smell of leather, listening to the soothing sounds of Samuel's music.

"Yeah…well I've always felt more at home on the stiff leather seat of my old rattling pick-up. But, my clients and my women seem to prefer a little luxury."

Madeline raised her head and looked at him. "Your women…as in plural?"

He remained focused on the road in front of him. "In case you haven't noticed…I'm single, Madeline." He lifted his left hand indicating his bare ring finger by wiggling it.

She stared at him for a moment longer, then rested her head back on the seat again. Her voice was low and filled with the soft consonants of a Lower Alabama accent as she said, "I'm beginning to understand the benefit of that particular way of life."

He turned sharply toward her, but she had already closed her eyes. He watched for a long moment as her head rocked gently with the rhythm of the road. *Why do I suddenly feel like ramming my fist through the windshield?*

Chapter 17

Samuel and Madeline arrived at Bell Bennier later that evening with dark leaden skies pressing close above the house. There was a damp chill in the air that sent shivers through Madeline. She went straight to her room to take a hot bath, feeling as if she needed to wash the whole Charleston experience away and watch it swirl down the drain.

Samuel had insisted she not return to Bay Cottage until he'd had a chance to get with Michael and see what he'd discovered while they'd been away. Someone was prowling around the property, that was certain, but until they caught the guy, he wouldn't rest easy. He'd also informed her, as they drove home from Charleston, that he was having an alarm system installed in the cottage for his own peace of mind. Madeline reluctantly agreed, then told him that as soon as it was installed, she was returning home.

Sinking slowly into the hot bath, Madeline let out an exaggerated sigh. *When did everything get so complicated, Father? I need direction,* she silently prayed. Ensconced in the warmth of the fragrant soapy water, Madeline moaned in delight as the hot steamy liquid covered her shoulders. She eased down into the tub. Closing her eyes, she let the rising steam caress her face as she soaked her tired and stiff muscles. Picking up a bar of lilac soap, she scrubbed her body hard, working the soap into a creamy lather, bent on scrubbing away all the memories associated with Bree before hate could find its way through her skin and into her heart.

Lifting her head, she caught a whiff of burning wood on the air. Stepping out of the tub she patted herself dry, donned her pajamas and wrapped up in Samuel's blue bathrobe and eased into the hallway. Stepping near the top of the staircase, she noticed a pulsating glow on the walls, turning them soft amber. The crackle of a fire with its pops and hisses became more obvious as she descended the stairs and neared the study.

Samuel's back was to her as she entered the study. With his socked feet propped up on an ottoman, he stretched out filling the chair perfectly. On the floor next to him was a basket with a blue linen napkin draped over the top of it.

"Which got to you first, the smell of the fire or the smell of this *fine* cobbler," Samuel asked, lifting the napkin from the basket, not even turning around. "Nothing sparks my Southerness quite like sweet bubbling cobbler-right out of the oven...puts a smile on my face every time. Oh, almost forgot, we have vanilla ice cream." He lifted the container with the ice cream scoop still stuck in the frozen cream.

"You made this?" Madeline asked, as she crossed the room to his chair.

"Um, well, no." He cleared his throat. "One of the ladies from church dropped it by while you were taking a bath."

Madeline's brow lifted. "Mary Grace?" she asked innocently, while taking a seat on the ottoman at his feet. She lifted the last bowl out of the basket, noticing how there were only two, a matching set, the one she had in her hand and the one Samuel just placed on the floor beside his chair.

"Uh huh," he mumbled, as he swallowed down the last bite of cobbler and tossed his spoon into the empty bowl beside his chair. "Someone must've told her that blackberry cobbler was my favorite."

Madeline scooped up a spoonful of cobbler into her bowl, then reached into the ice cream container and placed a rather large dollop right on top of the warm mixture. She turned toward the fire as she took a bite of the dessert. "This is really good. Why is she not enjoying this with you? If I went to all this trouble for a man, I'd at least want to share his company."

"Is that so? Well, I think when Miss Mary Grace saw your purse and sweater on the bottom step of the staircase, she got the impression I wasn't alone."

A red heat began to creep up Madeline's neck as she realized for the first time that they were actually alone in the house, and not only in the house, but on the property as well. Greenberry and Willa had left for South Carolina shortly after they had arrived home.

Seeing the embarrassment on her face, Samuel tried to ease her mind. "I think Mary Grace assumed those things belonged to Bree. Michael told me that she cornered him after church one day asking if I was seeing anyone. That's when Michael told her about Bree."

Madeline was relieved. It was hard enough to face the folks of Moss Bay when they just thought she was crazy, but loose *and* crazy would be pretty hard to overcome. "Good. I, I mean...well, it's just good...that's all," she stammered out, twisting the robe tightly around her neck.

"I understand." Samuel's mouth softened into a lazy smile at her words, he was amused by how uncomfortable she seemed to be getting around him all of a sudden. *Is she blushing? Innocence, how refreshing,* he thought.

Seeing Samuel so cocky and self assured aggravated Madeline. She was determined to show him that she wasn't some naïve' little school girl but a full grown and mature woman. She stood, dropping her empty bowl on top of his with a clang as she leaned over and placed a soft lingering kiss on his cheek. "Thanks for sharing your dessert, Samuel," she whispered, in the sexiest voice she could muster.

Samuel touched his cheek, a boyish grin spread across his face. With confused delight he watched as she sauntered out of the room, casually swinging the belt of his robe and swinging her hips to the sound of soft blues in the background.

"That woman is going to be the death of me."

Morning arrived on Bell Bennier with shafts of light filtering through the live oaks. A few men began pulling up in front of the house joined by their yapping dogs that eagerly hopped out of the backs of their trucks even before they'd rolled to a stop. The policy on Bell Bennier had always been; bring your wife or your dog, which ever suits you. Funny, but Madeline never once remembered seeing anyone with their wife in tow at harvest.

She gathered her hair in one hand and wrapped a band around it, allowing it to fall across her shoulder. Hearing boots hit the porch boards behind her; she turned to find Samuel approaching.

"Thanks for breakfast, Maddie. The guys thought they'd have to do without since Willa's away."Samuel smiled as he reached in his pocket for a cigar.

"You're welcome. I hope they liked my biscuits. I like them almost fried in butter and golden brown. A little molasses and...shut your mouth!" she teased, then began walking down the steps and out toward the field.

"Where you goin?" Samuel asked, noticing she was headed for the barn.

"Didn't you say you wanted to bring in the hay today? It's nice and dry...perfect day for it." Starting out across the field, Madeline could feel the soft dirt give slightly under her shoes. "Rain's supposed to move in next week," she said, looking back at him over her shoulder at his dumbfounded expression.

"Maddie, don't think for one minute that I'm going to sit back and let you mow a hayfield!"

"Relax, Samuel. Greenberry always wants me to cut the north field. He says the other guys just butcher it. He likes the way I take the corners. Call him. He'll tell you."

"Well, you just hold up there a minute." He pulled out his cell phone, clamping down on his cigar with his teeth as he walked around the corner of the house. A few minutes later he returned, eyeing her carefully. She stood in front of him with her head tilted and a hand on her hip, her skirt flapping in the breeze around her slender legs.

A few of Samuel's men, new to Bell Bennier, rounded the corner. They stopped in their tracks and just stood there gawking at Madeline in wide-eyed wonder, as if it was the first time they'd ever laid eyes on a woman.

Samuel cleared his throat. "Josiah, I'd like to introduce you to Madeline Linville. She owns the property to the west and some of the land we'll be working on today. Madeline, Josiah is my right hand man. He can do just about anything I need him to. We have a lull on our development site, so I thought we could use the extra hands to bring in the harvest."

Josiah reached up to place his coffee cup down on the rail of the porch before turning to offer his hand. "Pleasure to meet you, Miss Linville."

"Thank you, Josiah, and please call me Madeline. If you have Samuel's stamp of approval, you must be a very capable man."

Josiah smiled at the compliment and nodded his head. "Sounds like you know him pretty well. He's never had much patience for slackers…that's for sure."

Josiah was a rugged man. His deep blue eyes crinkled around the corners. His face was tanned, proof that he was a man accustomed to working out in the elements. Easy laughter and kindness shone through his eyes, but there was grief in them also. It was hard to determine his age. He could fall anywhere between twenty and forty.

"Tell me Josiah," Samuel inquired. "When's the big day?"

Taking a deep breath, Josiah pushed out the words, "There's not going to be one."

The men that had walked up behind Josiah seemed restless all of a sudden and started shifting around like spooked cattle. Some even ambled off.

"I'm sorry to hear that, I didn't know."

"I reckon it's for the best." Josiah picked up his coffee cup and slung the remaining contents on the ground before walking off.

After watching Josiah head off toward the barn, Samuel wheeled around to Madeline, abruptly. Aggravated at the attention she seemed to be getting from his men, he pointed to her skirt. "Is that some sort of religious practice?"

"My skirt?" she asked, bewildered. "Is there a problem with my skirt?"

Madeline had him all out of sorts. Samuel struggled with his words. "Yeah, it has a way of flying up over your head at every puff of wind!" he exaggerated. "With all of these men around, I'd suggest you find some blue jeans, or better yet, stay in the house!"

Madeline's foot tapped out a warning. "I don't own a pair of blue jeans!" It took every bit of self-restraint to keep her voice level.

"Well, hook some fishing tackle to your hem or find a pair of jeans. But, you're not getting on that tractor in a skirt! End of discussion."

He pushed by her, heading for the barn.

Madeline fumed as she called out after him. "Somewhere in the Warren bloodline is a pure strain of stubbornness!"

"And, somewhere in the Linville bloodline is a pure strain of craziness!" As the words left Samuel's mouth he knew they'd struck there mark, right between the eyes. He'd crossed that dreaded line. But it was too late to take the words back now. He didn't have the guts to turn around and face her. If he'd hurt her with his careless words, he couldn't stand to see it on her face.

Madeline felt as if the air had been knocked right out of her. Regaining her composure, she straightened and walked up the stairs and into the house. A lump formed in her throat, but she swallowed it down and mustered up all the courage she could find. Walking into the laundry room, she spied a pair of Willa's nicely folded jeans on top of the laundry basket. Seeing one of Jude's old denim shirts hanging on a rack, she grabbed it and put it on along with the jeans. Surprisingly, the jeans fit well, really well.

Not one to be pushed aside, Madeline muttered under her breath, "I'll work the field today...and your words, Samuel James Warren, aren't going to stop me." From the corner of her eye she spotted a pair of Willa's boots. She eased her foot into one, then the other. They were slightly large in size, but close enough that it gave her toes a little more wiggle room. She crossed the mudroom, her boots hitting the floor hard as she headed out the door toward the barn.

The sun warmed hay smelled grassy and sweet as Madeline started out across the field. Ground wasps dipped and circled in wide loops, hovering over the earth in the early morning sun. Field crickets chirped from the sagebrush, it was the beginning of a fresh new day.

The sudden flight of quail from the field caught Samuel's attention as he turned his head, watching Madeline's approach. The sunrays gave her hair a golden sheen. She was breathtaking. He swallowed hard as his gaze traveled down the length of her. What had just been hinted at before was now fully disclosed. *I'm such an idiot. If these guys get a look at her now, they won't be worth shooting!*

Madeline drew in her breath and stiffened her back, ready for a confrontation as she walked toward Samuel.

"Greenberry tells me you cut a mean hayfield, Maddie." Samuel lightened his voice; aware of the pain he'd caused her with his misspoken words. "If that's the case, and you can maneuver the edges the way he says you can, I'll let you handle the north end. The rest of the guys will be down on the south end harvesting. I've gotcha all set to go." He paused, looking sheepish. "And, by the way, I'm sorry about the little outburst back there. You just frustrate the devil out of me sometimes, Maddie. Will you forgive me for being such an idiot? Those words just slipped out. I don't feel that way about you...I don't think you're crazy."

She hesitated before answering. "Well, your daddy always said, 'what's down in the well comes out in the bucket.' Anybody ever tell you that you're a hardheaded man, Samuel Warren?"

He shrugged, "Seems I may have heard that a time or two."

"Well, it's true. I'll think about forgiving you, but just this once."

"Just once...I guess that means you don't believe the whole seventy times seven thing, or the command to forgive or you won't be forgiven. I thought my dad *surly* must've taught you that lesson."

"Nope, but I did happen to read it for myself. It's hard to do sometimes...but I guess the good Lord knows what's best. "

"Amen." Samuel smiled his knee-weakening smile before turning back to the barn.

Madeline called after him. "Are you mad at me for calling you...what was it?"

"Stubborn, hardheaded...probably several more things once you were inside the house," Samuel stated bluntly, blowing the dirt off his sunglasses. "Mad? No...I'll never be mad at you for speaking your mind. I've always respected your frankness, even when it's down right insulting. I like that about you. I always know how you see things. It's refreshing and, I might add, rare among the fairer sex."

"Yeah, well…sometimes I hurt people without meaning to. I hate that about myself. It's just better not to ask me what I think."

He turned to face her, narrowing his steel gray eyes. "Didn't your mother ever tell you it's not polite to be so blunt? You know, if you can't say something nice…"

A slow grin spread across her face. "No…she didn't."

Samuel gave a half-grin, sliding on his sunglasses. "Well then, seems to me that you've got an excuse. Come on, we're burning daylight. Oh and Maddie, Greenberry said the price is the same as usual. I'll have your check by days end."

"No. The price is one alarm system for my cottage. Warrens aren't the only people who can be stubborn."

Samuel shifted, looking down as if he regretted what he was about to say. "Bree will be back sometime tonight."

Thanks for the warning, she thought, but replied, "Good. I'm sure you're happy about that."

Chapter 18

"Sometimes I just hate people," Madeline announced, as she stepped through the kitchen door, making her way to the coffee pot.

"Want to tell me about it, or should I just go get my gun?" Samuel folded down his morning paper and waited for an explanation.

"You'd shoot your girlfriend...for me?" Madeline looked hopeful, as she finished pouring her coffee and turned to face him.

"Bree...what has she done now?"

"She dumped all of her dirty clothes at my door with a sweet little note that said, 'since you don't do anything all day long, I thought you wouldn't mind washing a few clothes for me.'"

Samuel smiled. "I guess she hasn't seen you handle a tractor yet, has she?"

Looking around, she asked, "Is she here, or is the broom missing and she's flown off to work already?"

Samuel gave a half-hearted laugh. "Don't hold back, Maddie. Tell me what you *really* think of Bree."

"All right then, I will. I think she's a very cold and calculating person who just so happens to be blessed with an incredible body and good hair." Madeline paused, then noted, "Why do we treat the beautiful differently?" She propped her back against the counter, holding her coffee mug with both hands. She contemplated the subject. "I mean…we cherish some bugs and try to annihilate others. We admire the butterfly and the dragonfly, but what do we do to the plain old housefly? We swat at it!"

Samuel scrutinized her. "You're not comparing yourself to a housefly are you? And, to quote Eleanor Roosevelt, 'No one can make you feel inferior without your consent'."

"I don't feel inferior…I feel disregarded; there's a difference." She took a sip of coffee, then asked, "What do you get out of the relationship, Samuel…I'm just curious? I mean; she must treat *you* well."

He tapped his fingers on the table. "I suppose I'm in the presence of an expert when it comes to relationships." Samuel scowled."

"I'll bet you scare little children with that face, but I'm not a little kid. And to answer your question, no, I'm not an expert on relationships. I just happen to think you have this huge blind spot when it comes to women!"

Samuel calmly took a sip of his coffee. "Why's that?"

Madeline topped off her coffee cup with another splash of coffee, then moved over to the table, sitting down across from him. "All you see is a pair of long tan legs without one thought to character."

"Is that so?"

"That's your pattern." She took a small sip of coffee before reaching for a pastry.

"Well, tell me then Miss Madeline, what do you look for in a man; any guy that tells you he's a cowboy?"

"Do you enjoy making me angry?" Her eyes flashed as she regarded him, chewing slowly on a bite of pastry.

"Give me a second to consider that. Any chance you're going to do some more of that foot tapping?" He locked his hands behind his head smugly. More than once he'd had to talk himself out of picking a fight with her just to get a reaction. He enjoyed stirring her blood.

"And, by the way, I'm not looking for a man." She swallowed down the pastry almost choking. Immediately she felt guilty for lying and it showed. Everything she thought and felt was as plain on her face as if someone had taken a red marker and written it across her forehead in bold lettering.

"You're lying to me, Maddie. I can read it on your face." Samuel grinned; enjoying the little contest of wills more than he knew he should.

Flustered, Madeline looked hard into his face. "Well...you're so flint faced it's hard to know *what* you're thinking!"

"Did you just call me flint faced?" Samuel cocked his head slightly.

"I did," she said, lifting her chin defiantly.

"Do you remember what I said you needed, oh, about eight years ago?"

"You wouldn't."

His chair scraped across the floor as he pushed it out from the table. "I would."

"You're bluffing."

"I'll let you in on a little something...if I said it, I meant it, and that's exactly what I'll do." A wicked grin spread across his face.

Madeline eased out of her chair, taking a cautious step backward before swinging around, hoping to get a running start ahead of him. All too quickly, she felt Samuel's strong arms clamp around her waist, pulling her backward against his chest. She felt his warm breath on her cheek, smelled the spicy scent of his skin and shivered, his voice was deep and resonated in her ear. "I'm not in the habit of showing mercy, but...for you, I might make an exception...if."

"If what?" Her voice sounded weak and shaky.

"If you promise to show your elders a little more respect and...be nice."

Madeline nodded once and he reluctantly loosened his grip.

Turning around to face him, still trapped within the circle of his arms, she looked up into his eyes. "I can be nice," she said, her voice low and smooth.

Samuel's heart lodged in his throat. Without thinking only reacting, he bent down and covered her lips with his, savoring the warm sweetness of her mouth. Madeline's small hands slid up and around his neck. He moaned, as she pressed closer. As the passion built between them, Samuel pulled free of the embrace, shocked by his response to her.

Out of breath and gasping, Madeline could only stare up at him. He ran his hand through his hair as he caught his breath. Searching his mind to come up with the proper words to explain what had just happened, he knew it was up to him to explain...trouble was; he had no idea what had just happened. He'd never experienced anything quite like that before, except once when he'd gotten too close to a lightning strike. Their dynamic seemed to be getting stronger, dangerously stronger.

Madeline broke the awkward silence. "You sure don't kiss like your brother."

"I'll take that as a compliment since I don't see you gagging and spitting on the ground."

She smiled a nervous smile.

"Listen...Maddie. I'm not sure what just happened here, but one thing's for sure, I'm going to be more careful before I ever grab you up again. I guess I lied about the 'never kissing you again' part. Maybe we're just too close here, in this house I mean. Seems we're always bumping up against each other. I'm just sorry it happened and I'm sorry about the kiss."

"You're sorry you kissed me?" Hurt reflected in Madeline's green eyes as they pooled with tears.

"Not on your life. I'm just sorry that I got so carried away. Remember, I have a girlfriend. I shouldn't be kissing anyone."

"I guess I blocked that part out. I owe her an apology."

"Nah...we'll keep this between us, once again. No since upsetting her over something so minor."

His words struck her, as if he'd slapped her face. That kiss was anything but minor. She'd felt the earth shake. Mustering up as much dignity as she could gather, she calmly turned from him and walked out of the room without a second glance.

For the rest of the day, they seemed to dance around each other, as if getting too close might prove fatal. They kept their words few and to the point trying hard not to make eye contact. Madeline was cool toward Samuel. His words had hurt her pride and her feelings, but she was determined to not let it show. She didn't want Samuel to know how much his words bothered her.

"Greenberry and Willa will be coming in today," Samuel commented, as he stuck his head in the door of the old servants' quarters where Madeline now made her soap.

Madeline wiped her hands down the front of her apron. "Good, I've missed them. I owe Willa a new pair of blue jeans." She looked down at her legs, noticing how well they fit and how comfortable the soft and worn denim felt against her legs.

Samuel followed the path of her eyes, then shaking his head as if clearing it said, "Just thought you'd like to know." He paused briefly, then asked, "Tonight's when you're going out with that cowboy, isn't it?"

"Yeah, he's coming by to pick me up around 7:00. Why, did you need something?"

Caught off-guard, he stammered, "No, no, just wondering. Where's he taking you?"

She shrugged, "He didn't say, only that we'd go out to dinner and then see what happens."

"See what happens? What did he mean by that?" A scowl darkened his face.

"I guess he meant we'll play it by ear...you know, see what we want to do next. He's not from here, Samuel and I'm sure he doesn't know what we can do."

"That's right." Samuel nodded. "Well, have a good time."

"Will do." Madeline turned back to her soap molds and began cutting around the edges of the bars, a little *too* firmly. A glass of water on the table shook as the sliced lemon plopped into the glass, catching the attention of Madeline. Sounding a little frustrated, she asked, "Is there anything else, Samuel?" She looked up, noticing he was still lingering in the doorway.

"I was just wondering if you like the set-up." He looked around the cabin, eyeing all of the changes. There was a sense of order about the place. It had a clean soapy smell. Samuel glanced around, noticing bins and baskets full of soaps in muted colors all properly labeled. "I know it's kinda primitive, but I tried to have everything out here that you would need."

"I love it; I have so much more room. I especially like the windows across the back. I get to see all kinds of wildlife out here. There's even a family of fox over by the old smoke house." Madeline raised her eyebrows as she looked up at Samuel.

"I'm surprised you haven't seen deer. The woods are full of them."

"Maybe I have...maybe I haven't," she teased. "I know how you like to bow hunt. You're the last person I'd ever tell if I saw a deer."

He cocked his eye. "You've seen some good ones then, a few bucks maybe?"

"Quit licking your chops, I'll never tell." She again looked up from her work and smiled at him.

Stepping near, drawn by her smile, Samuel asked, "So, how's my soap coming along. Have you settled on a fragrance to capture my masculine essence; maybe something that says, 'Great and mighty hunter'."

Before she could answer, Bree stepped through the door. "I thought I heard voices." Bree eyed Madeline like a warrior eyeing an opponent. Turning her attention to Samuel, she asked, "Where are you taking me tonight, darling? I need to know how to dress." Bree pouted, then leaned into Samuel as she wrapped her arms around him, kissing him thoroughly before turning her attention to Madeline. "I've been looking for you. Where are my clothes?"

"Clothes?" Madeline asked, trying her best to look confused.

"Yes. The ones I left for you to wash." Bree answered, seemingly exasperated at the question.

"Oh *those* clothes...well you left before I could explain. I don't take in laundry. I'm too busy with my cottage industry here to work another job, but thanks for the offer. If I ever get in a bind and need the extra cash, I may consider it." Madeline enjoyed, maybe a little too much, the shocked look on Bree's face. "And, I dumped," she shook her head, then clarified, "I mean I *put* your clothes in the bathtub to soak."

"You what!" Bree yelled. "Unbelievable! Why on earth would you do such a stupid thing? Now I won't have anything to wear out tonight!"

Madeline shrugged, "I'm just crazy I guess." Biting her cheek to keep from smiling, she turned her attention back to her task.

"*Now* what am I going to wear? Oh, come on Samuel, let's get out of here." She reached back and grabbed Samuel's hand, trying to pull him toward the door.

Without moving a step, Samuel faced Madeline and said, "Have fun tonight, Maddie, and be safe."

Madeline shook her head as she watched Samuel walk out with Bree on his arm. Madeline muttered under her breath, "I don't see it. I just don't see it." She listened intently, wanting to hear the sounds of Bree being thoroughly scolded, or better yet, beaten, but all she heard was Bree's whiny attempts to gain sympathy.

Headlights flashed across the distant trees as the sound of Greenberry's old rattling pickup truck reached Samuel's ears. He stood and waited in the darkness of the porch.

The truck door slammed and Samuel saw a figure slowly make its way down the brick sidewalk in-between the boxwoods. He rubbed his chin, his eyes felt gritty from lack of sleep but he continued to watch the progression of the figure with interest. Running a finger around the rim of his glass, he waited for Madeline to reach the porch. Samuel raised his hand in acknowledgement to Greenberry, signaling him, then watched as his truck slowly pulled away.

Madeline peered up into the darkened porch. Seeing a form take shape out of the shadows, she froze in her tracks until she realized it was Samuel. He wore jeans and a white T-shirt, was barefoot holding a half empty glass. The ice tinkled as he swished the glass around in his hand. "Well...I see you made it back home, finally."

Madeline felt the resistance in her body, like trying to walk through water. Stumbling back, she said, "They're too heavy. My legs, they're...heavy. I can't walk."

Samuel eyed her suspiciously, then stepped down to get a closer look. Bending near her face, he smelled alcohol on her breath. "You've been drinking." It was a statement, not a question.

"Nooo." She waved her hands in protest, drawing out the word "no" into two syllables. "I had chocolate milk *and*...I don't drink."

Narrowing his eyes, not quite sure what to think at this point, he began questioning her. "So...this cowboy, he was a nice guy?" he asked, positive now that Madeline was plastered as he watched her teeter back and forth in front of him.

"Uh huh...real nice." She looked up at Samuel and started to fall backward.

He caught her before she fell and put his arm around her waist, helping her up the stairs. "Chocolate milk you say. That must've tasted really good."

"Yep...Cowboy Clayton asked me what I liked to drink...sweet of him wasn't it? Do you like chocolate milk?"

"I think what you had was a Black Russian, Maddie."

"Huh? I don't know any Russians," she shook her head, "I only know one Filipino; she buys my hand salve for her little husband." Madeline brought her hand up to her chest, indicating the size of the Filipino husband.

"How many chocolate milk drinks did you have?"

"Just three...Clayton ordered four, but a fly landed in the last one. They were little bitty." Madeline measured a small amount with her thumb and forefinger. "That's why I needed so many...Clayton said that. Mr. Fly must've liked chocolate milk, too. Poor fly, people always swattin at him." Opening her eyes wide, trying to focus on Samuel, she said, "You sure know how to kiss. Who taught you how to do that anyway, Jennifer Crosswhite?" Changing the subject as fast as changing channels on the T.V., she said, "We saw Greenberry."

"Oh?"

"Yeah...he took Clayton away...and came back to get me. Clayton had to go somewhere. Good thing Greenberry was there. I love Greenberry," she sighed. "He taught me how to shoot a gun...said I might need to shoot a man someday...oops...I forgot...I wasn't 'posed to tell you...sorry," she whispered, as an afterthought.

Making it into the house, Samuel eyed the staircase. "Come on, I'll give you a ride to your room." Reaching down he lifted her limber body into his arms and cradled her closely. Surprising him, she quickly wrapped her arms around his neck and pressed her warm face under his chin.

Madeline inhaled deeply. "You smell sooo good...like something sandalwood," she whispered, her warm breath tickling his skin. "That's it...I got my finger on it this time, sandalwood." She nuzzled his neck.

Samuel's temperature was rising rapidly with every thump of his heart. A bead of sweat trickled down his jaw-line. Looking up, he noticed Willa standing at the top of the stairs in her lightweight robe, rubbing her hands up and down her arms anxiously as she waited for them to climb the stairs.

"Is she okay?" Willa asked, concern showing on her face.

Samuel nodded, "Better than I am at the moment. Did Greenberry call you?"

Willa nodded a response. Stepping back, she moved down the hall behind them, following them into Madeline's room. Reaching the bed, she turned down the covers. "Put her here." She tapped the mattress. "I'll take care of her."

Some combination of relief and disappointment crossed his face as he placed her on the bed. "Thank you, Willa. And...*this* was not her fault."

"I know. But even if it was, I'd still love her." Willa tenderly brushed the hair out of Madeline's eyes. "I'll go get a wash cloth."

Still shaken, Samuel waited for Willa to return before he left the room to find Greenberry.

Returning home at sunrise, Samuel walked across the floor of his bedroom and tossed his keys on the dresser. The only visible sign of his anger was the tick in his jaw. He wearily eased his weight down on the bed, running a hand through his hair as he thought back on the night. Earlier, as he'd set out to find Greenberry, he'd found him waiting for him on the porch.

"I told that boy if he valued his life, he'd better clear out of South Alabama," Greenberry confessed, as he watched the muscle flex in Samuel's jaw.

"Pap's Cove?" Samuel asked.

With Greenberry's nod, Samuel headed for his truck.

He'd had no problem tracking down the so- called cowboy. *I bet he's never even been to Texas!* Samuel thought. But little did he know all that he would uncover that night, sitting at the bar next to a terrified and badly bruised Clayton Holt.

As he thought about Madeline in the next room, he got up and walked down the hall, stopping momentarily in front of her door. Easing it open, he could see her form under the crumpled bed sheets. Gently, he shut the door and headed again for his room. Tossing the covers back on his bed, he fell into it, silently hoping he could quiet the troubling thoughts in his head long enough to sleep. With the steady hum of the ceiling fan circling lazily overhead, he closed his eyes with a prayer on his lips, "God, help me."

Chapter 19

*W*aking up to shafts of golden light seeping through the louvered slats of the window blinds, Madeline knew that it was well into the day. She lifted her eyes to the washcloth still draped across her forehead and moaned, remembering the night before. Too fatigued to move, she forced herself to focus on what she could recall from the previous night.

Clayton took me to dinner...but we never ate, only drank. Okay...what did I drink? Chocolate something...it must've been spiked. Then Greenberry appeared and Clayton disappeared. "I might not be the sharpest crayon in the box, but even I get this one," she said out loud, wincing from the pain shooting through her head.

She turned her head into her pillow rocking it listlessly, suddenly feeling very stupid and humiliated. *I don't even have enough sense to know a loser when I meet one. Maybe Bree was right...I am the Warren's special charity case.* The more she dwelled on it, the more determined she became. "Well, not anymore! I'm going home with or without Samuel Warren's permission."

In the days that followed Madeline's return to Bay Cottage, she had felt a growing determination and a sense of ownership that she'd never experienced before. Thankfully,

Greenberry was the only one she needed to convince that her move back to Bay Cottage was the right thing to do. She'd always been able to convince Greenberry to go along with her plans. And, with a few more shooting lessons under her belt, he'd been easy to win over to her way of thinking. Come what may, Greenberry would always stick-up for her right to live her life as she saw fit, with-in limits, of course.

Samuel had flown to Charleston for an important business matter. That left her decision to move back to the cottage unchallenged, just the way she liked it. Bay Cottage and twelve acres of pristine coastal property belonged to her. It was her home, where she'd build her life if God saw fit, with or without a husband.

Opening the mailbox, Madeline retrieved yet another letter with the now familiar stationary of Mason and Clark, Attorneys At Law. The day after her mother's burial and each month since, she'd received an inquiry about the purchase of her land. "I guess you have to admire their tenacity, whoever they are," she said, speaking the words out loud. The action of talking to herself caused her some brief concern, but she quickly dismissed it and began sorting through the mail.

Hearing the sound of muffled hoof beats fast approaching, she looked up, seeing Samuel astride his horse. He reined in as his hands gripped the saddle horn.

"Nice day for a ride," Madeline said, smiling up at Samuel.

"You know what they say; the best thing for the inside of a man is the outside of a horse. Reagan, Churchill, some great mind said that and it's true. Horses are natures Prozac." Samuel smiled down at her, seeing light in her eyes once again. "But, I'm just checking on you...my friend at

Shoreline Security called and told me she'd fixed you up with a system yesterday. Did you sleep better last night?"

Madeline nodded. "I did. It doesn't feel so creepy when I'm in the shower anymore." Shielding her eyes with her hand, she looked up into his face, seeing his smile widened. Her heart slammed into her chest. His tousled dark hair and scruffy face sent chills over her body as she remembered the feel of the warm spot just under his chin. "What brings you out this way?"

"My friend here possesses this uncanny ability," he said, patting his horse, "no matter what direction we head, he always finds his way to a pretty lady."

"Uh huh...so your horse led you here." She quirked the corner of her mouth but managed not to smile.

"Yep, it was all him." Samuel reached down and patted the side of the gelding once more. "You know, all this riding sure does make a man thirsty." He grinned, waiting for an invitation.

Taking the bait, Madeline extended warm hospitality. "Please come in for a drink. You're certainly welcome in my home." That simple statement seemed to inspire a sense of pride of ownership. Exactly when she began taking possession of Bay Cottage emotionally, she didn't really know. But, it belonged to her and she knew without a doubt that the One who formed her was with her always, even as she drew her very last breath. That thought alone brought more peace of mind than any security measures ever could.

"If you insist," Samuel stated formally, as he stepped off his horse. He secured the horse loosely before following Madeline up the back steps. "Say, you wouldn't happen to have any chocolate milk would ya?"

Madeline glared at him unappreciatively, then pushed at his chest. "Don't remind me."

"I promise...I'll behave," he said, grinning.

A swarm of gnats encircled Madeline's head. Waving them away, she said, "I wish these pesky *Georgia State Birds* would fly away home. They've been pestering me all day long."

Samuel held open the screen door for her and with a smirk said, "I can certainly tell Greenberry's had an influence on your opinion of the fine state of Georgia. With him, everything negative seems to have originated in that state...never understood why."

Madeline shrugged, "Who knows with Greenberry. I've always thought some girl from Georgia must've broken his heart sometime or another."

"Never thought of that, you may be right." Samuel stepped through the door and looked around the cottage, taking in all of the changes since he'd last been there. The room was charming with a very French Country feel. Light pieces of eclectic furnishings stood out against the Robin's egg blue walls. The color seemed to invoke a relaxed comfortable atmosphere that made you want to kick off your shoes and stretch out on the couch. "Looks different from the last time I was here."

"I've been busy playing decorator," Madeline said, sheepishly. "I've found most of these pieces at Miss Wren's antique shop out from town. Can you believe she still calls us her chilluns? She asks about you and Jude every time I go in there."

Samuel tossed his head back and laughed. "There was a time when I thought my father just might pursue that woman.

I wish he had. Something tells me she would've been good for him."

"I've always liked her eyes, black as coal but they sparkle like diamonds." Madeline pressed against the wall, smiling as she took in the rainbow colors splashed all around the room. "She gave me a box full of prisms, told me they are guaranteed to catch all of the colors of the sun. It's been fun, like treasure hunting. I think people too often make the mistake of confusing value with cost. Sometimes a keepsake can be a simple thing, like something as sweet and lovely as a light-catcher prism."

"The overall effect is…very nice."

Smiling at his words, she motioned with her hand. "Sit down. What's your pleasure, tea or coffee? I think I may even have some ginger ale."

"Coffee's fine." Taking a seat, he commented, "It's gotta be quiet out here, compared to all that racket and commotion going on up at the big house."

"That's the worst part of this time of year; it's so melancholy and noiseless, except for the ocean, of course. I love the summer sounds, you don't feel so alone when there's so much noise going on outside. I like the sound of cicadas and tree frogs." She busied herself making the coffee, feeling cheerful all of a sudden.

"Yeah, well when you get ready to come ho…back," he caught the word, correcting it, "you come on. Willa is feeling lost without you. I don't understand why you force yourself into this exile. Do you really prefer solitude to my charming company?"

Madeline poured their coffee, placing the cups on a tray along with a few brownies. "I do miss y'all, but this is where I belong," she said, gracefully moving toward him.

Samuel reached over and took hold of his cup. "I'm here for two things, really." He took a long sip of his coffee before continuing. "First, you were right about Bree."

Madeline smoothed her skirt before taking a seat across from him. "Oh?" she questioned. He'd suddenly captured her full attention.

Reluctantly, Samuel disclosed the information. "Clayton was hired by Bree to get you drunk, basically." He let his words sink in before continuing. "We're not sure about the motive yet, but we do have some theories. For the past several months, Bart and I have tried to figure out what's been happening to our company. We've lost some pretty big accounts and taken a few unexpected hits in the business. The job we're working on here has been held up due to some major problems. There's no way some of the information that's been leaked could have been obtained without the help of someone from the inside. Now, with this recent development, things are all pointing in one direction...Bree."

Madeline kept quiet, trying to read his reaction to the revelation about his girlfriend. Personally, she'd never trusted the woman, but still, Samuel had to be brokenhearted. *Why are men such fools when it comes to women*, she thought, as she gazed into her coffee cup, as if the answer might suddenly appear on the surface of the golden brew.

A frown wrinkled Samuel's brow. It seemed odd to him that upon hearing the news about his girlfriend, all he could manage was a feeling of relief. Shouldn't he feel devastated? He'd never been possessive of a woman...or even jealous, for that matter. Long ago he'd learned to accept the fact that he was missing something vital in the relationship department...and it troubled him. "We think there's someone above her, someone calling the shots. Bart overheard a conversation she was having over the phone the other day and it raised a red flag. After I...ascertained my information from Clayton, we put two and two together." He rubbed his chin. "Clayton said that Bree paid him to take you out and get you drunk. He said he was supposed to drop you off at Bay Cottage once you were pretty well plastered." Samuel shuddered at the thought of how that might have ended. "We've thought of every conceivable reason as to why she would want you drunk and we haven't come up with anything, yet. It may be unrelated to the whole business issue...or not, we're just not sure at this point. This makes her a suspect in the break-in as well...but, we just don't know."

Madeline looked at him for a long time, not sure how to respond. Finally, she said, "If it's any consolation, I'm glad to never have to look at that woman again. I didn't trust her the moment she told me she hated John Wayne. Something's bad wrong with a person who doesn't like the Duke."

Samuel shifted in his chair. "Well, that's not exactly how this whole thing is going to play out. Bart and I need to catch whoever is behind this and the only way to do that is to pretend that all is well...for a little while anyway." He heaved a heavy sigh. "My acting is lousy, but I've got to carry on like nothing is wrong so Bree won't get suspicious and leave before we know who we're dealing with. Whoever it is, they're trying their level best to force us under, not to mention whatever it is they're trying to do to you. Rest assured; we've got our eye on her. That's why when Greenberry called and told me that you'd moved back to the cottage, I got on the phone and called in a marker from a friend and got your system installed as soon as possible. The security company is to contact me first if you have an alarm, then Greenberry and after that the Sherriff. We can get to you much faster."

The house fell silent; all that could be heard was the sound of the ocean through the open door. Madeline shivered. Her dislike of Bree had been from the start. Seldom, if ever had she had such an adverse reaction to someone she barely knew, but there it was, some vibe Bree gave off that told Madeline she was not to be trusted.

"You said two things…that you were here for two things." Madeline waited; not at all sure she wanted to know what else he had to tell her.

"Yeah…well, I'm kinda in a bind. There's this woman from church…."

Madeline twisted her lips and rolled her eyes.

"No…it's not what you think, let me finish. Anyway, she's a single mother. She has a boy, Trey, who is about twelve. He's in the Sunday school class I teach. I promised him that we'd go fishing tomorrow. His dad's out of the picture and it bothers him. Something else is troubling the boy and I need to see if I can find out what it is. He needs a little male guidance." He hesitated before adding, "Trey has a little sister, Bitsy. She's maybe six or seven; I'm not sure. Anyway, when she found out about the fishing trip she pitched a fit to go. With the world being what it is today, I don't feel comfortable taking a little girl out on a fishing trip. I was wondering if you'd come along with us and help me out with the little girl." Samuel's eyes held hope as he waited for her answer.

"Sure," Madeline responded. "I'll even pack a lunch for us." Secretly, she was thrilled. Nothing excited her as much as being outdoors, especially on the bayou. She hadn't been fishing since Jude left home.

Chapter 20

*T*he gentle lap of the bayou waters against the boat caused a smile to cross Madeline's face. The sound, as familiar as her own beating heart, eased the tension of the last days from her body.

Samuel fumbled around in the tackle box as he explained to Trey the importance of finding the right kind of lure to fish properly. Bitsy seemed content to sit still with both hands gripped tightly to her fishing pole as she watched her bobber dance to the rhythm of the slow but steady current. A cooling October breeze stirred, turning the boat slowly in the direction of the wind. Madeline turned her face to catch it, noticing how silver the leaves looked in the light as they trembled on the trees that hung over the water. One leaf let go, gracefully falling as if on purpose to reach the water and float lazily down the creek.

Turning her attention back to Samuel, Madeline studied him while he was distracted, teaching the boy how to cast a line. She watched as his muscles played beneath his white T-shirt. This was a side of Samuel she'd never seen. She was having trouble reconciling his bad boy image with the one now before her. He was good with children...patient and attentive. He cared enough to help out a single mom, giving her a break while giving her kids an experience they might not ever have. He was so much like his father, Jim. Why he seemed to resent that, she didn't quite know.

"Does God know me, Mr. Samuel?" Trey asked, as he slowly reeled in his line. "I mean...really know me?"

Samuel reached for a canned drink, popping the top; he took a swig before answering. "God says that *before* he shaped you in your mother's womb, He knew you. He knew you previously. God is always previous, Trey...remember that. He knows you so well that he's counted the hairs on your head."

Trey seemed to ponder the words. Scratching his head under the brim of his baseball cap, he looked troubled. "What happens if He thinks you're a hopeless case? Do you just get ready to burn in hell one day?"

Without missing a beat, Samuel replied, "I've never met a hopeless case, Trey. God says all men have sinned and come up short. But, He's made a way of escape from hell. Jesus is that escape. Trust in Him, not in yourself. It's all about what He has done for you by dying for you; in your place...understand?"

Trey nodded and got quiet, lost in thought.

Samuel leaned forward and took the fishing-pole out of Bitsy's hand. "Let's see what's going on here." He whistled softly while he pulled the line out of the water.

"Okay, but after that can we go back to your house," Bitsy asked, wiping damp hair out of her eyes.

Samuel gave a half laugh. "Why would you want to do that?"

"'Cause Mama told Miss Becky she'd give *anything* to get inside your house. It must be *something* for Mama to want to get in there so bad."

Clearing his throat and eager to change the subject, he asked, "What's the matter here? Let's take a look at that worm on your line."

"It don't work," Bitsy stated matter-of-factly.

"What doesn't work?"

"My worm…it don't work." She looked up into his face, swatting at a gnat. Samuel noticed a pink tinge to her nose and cheeks. The way her hair stuck to her face around her eyes told him she was getting too hot.

Reading his concern and grateful for the distraction, Madeline reached into her purse and pulled out a wipe and some sunscreen. Twisting her lips to hold back a smile, she said, "Come here, Bitsy. You're getting too hot. Samuel, I think we could use a drink."

"*You* know don't cha Mr. Samuel." Bitsy held still, pulling her lips in tight while Madeline rubbed sunscreen over her face.

"Know what, Bitsy?" He held his breath, never knowing what might tumble out of the little girl's mouth.

"What it's like bein hot. Mama said you was a hottie."

Biting her lip, Madeline turned her face away from Bitsy to keep from laughing.

"I'm beginning to see the problem here," Samuel stated, studying the hook between his fingers, as if he were referring to the worm.

Risking a glance at Madeline, he noticed how she tilted her face toward the sun; holding her eyes shut. He watched her, forgetting the worm in his hand, admiring the way she seemed to become a part of all she experienced. The wind gently blew her hair across her forehead, but she didn't brush it away, simply let it play over her face. A smile gradually touched her lips. He could just imagine what she was amused by.

"Mr. Samuel...you gonna sit there and stare at Miss Maddie some more, or can I go back to fishin." Bitsy heaved a sigh as she slumped over impatiently, waiting on an answer.

Madeline turned to find Samuel's brow furrowed as he studied the hook in his hand without comment.

The unusual heat of the day diminished slightly by the long shadows of the mighty oaks on Bell Bennier. A breeze picked up, catching an empty can and clanging it down the road in front of Madeline as she walked toward the Warren home. She reached down and picked it up, thinking it must've been left by one of the harvest workers not accustomed to working on the farm...especially under Warren supervision. A Warren could never abide such laziness as littering. She could still hear Mr. Jim's voice in her head, 'Poor is one thing; but there's no excuse for pure laziness'.

Guests began arriving, pulling onto the pebbled drive. Their laughter could be heard over the sound of slamming car doors and the hushed whispers of the nearby sea.

Samuel Warren was a laid-back host. Not even the threat of rain could dampen his spirits when his friends gathered.

He loved having friends around, filling the rooms of the sprawling plantation.

His stress-free style and low maintenance handling of his guests was legendary in South Carolina, gaining him the reputation of a much sought after host. Most folks would never even think of missing one of the coveted events, but most folks were nothing like Madeline Linville.

The half-mile drive that leads up to the stately home from the main road offers the visitor panoramic views of gentle slopes where cattle graze; dotting the landscape. Pecan groves with their symmetrical lines all in form can be glimpsed through the moss covered trees along the road. Occasionally, when the terrain will allow it, you can see the ocean as it stretches out in sparkling array in frothy blues and greens. As you come near the house, a long alley of giant oaks usher you forward to a circle, where old boxwoods lead you to the brick steps of Bell Bennier.

Madeline neared the house and lost her nerve. Turning from the well-worn path, she headed back toward Bay Cottage, taking a different route through the woods. She had not gotten very far before she heard someone running toward her from behind.

"The party is in the other direction," Samuel stated, out of breath and smiling. She mumbled a response but the wind swallowed her words. He bent his head near her lips, intent on hearing her reply.

"I'm not good with crowds." She shrugged. "I think I've spent too much time alone." She offered the excuse and kept walking.

"Things can change…if you want them to." Samuel kept pace with her, aware of the struggle going on inside of her by the emotions playing across her face.

"It's just...I'm uncomfortable around people, as a general rule." Madeline blew the hair out of her face and kept walking.

"Who set the rule...you?"

She stopped and turned to him. Surprise crossed her features. "Yes...I guess I did."

"Well then, you can just set a new rule can't you? One that says, 'I'm comfortable around people.'"

"You make it sound so easy." She looked at him as if doubting his words.

"I'm not saying you shouldn't avoid some people, but not *all* people. Some people are worth knowing...like Michael's wife for example. From what Michael tells me, she's pretty much a recluse by nature. He probably had to drag her here kicking and screaming." Samuel was rewarded with her soft laughter. "So...I'd imagine she might need you around, for support."

Madeline considered his words. "Oh...all right then. Let's get this over with."

Samuel threw his head back and laughed. He was completely taken back by her reluctance to attend his party. That had never happened before. "Is the thought of enjoying my hospitality so bad?"

Madeline didn't respond, but squared her shoulders instead; she had the look of one facing down an enemy. "I can't make any promises, but I'll last as long as I can."

"Fair enough," Samuel said, biting back a grin.

As they approached the house, the flickering glow of the gas lanterns that flanked the front door lent an old world charm to the atmosphere. Two large black wrought iron fleur-de-lis sculptures sat perched on either side of the massive door as if anchoring the house to the spot. Bree stepped through the door, eyeing them warily as they walked up from the yard. Madeline's eyes locked with Samuel's as if questioning the wisdom of her presence there.

"The good Lord has never taken me into His confidence, Maddie girl," he whispered, low. "But I've given this over to Him, so I'm guessing He's got it all worked out." He winked at her before taking the front steps quickly, reaching Bree.

Madeline sighed deeply, then wandered off toward the back of the house.

Samuel turned back around and watched Madeline walk away. A mixture of emotions coursed through him; Madeline's innocent reluctance and bold forthrightness was an irresistible, albeit odd combination. She was soft and kind, but with an unconquerable faith that stood no matter what life seemed to toss her way. She was unconventional, yes...but definitely unforgettable.

Bree moved in front of Samuel and lifted up on tiptoes as she kissed him, then slid her hand over the front of his shirt. "Miss me?"

"Now how can you even ask that question?" Samuel led her through the front door and disappeared into the crowd.

Madeline managed to hide out from the crowd most of the night, side stepping guests by helping Willa in the kitchen. Walking outside to get some air, she heard a woman's voice call from the darkened veranda. "Care to join me? I'm really enjoying the peace and quiet on this side of the house."

Boisterous laughter spilled out of the French doors as if on cue. Adjusting her eyes to the darkness, Madeline could make out the tiny silhouette of Telie, sitting quietly in a rocking chair, starring out across the lawn.

"I'd love to." Madeline said, moving toward the rocking chair.

The relief in Madeline's voice caused a laugh from Telie as she watched her settle into a rocking chair beside her. "It's nice out here,' Telie observed. "I'm pretending I've traveled back through time and I'm living here just after the war." Glancing over at Madeline, she asked, "Do you come to a lot of Samuel's parties?"

Telie got the answer she wanted when the deep voice of Samuel came through the French door. He seemed to be searching for someone as he kept up a conversation with a man following closely on his heels. Madeline pressed back into the rocking chair, moving further into the shadows. Once Samuel was out of earshot, Madeline shook her head, and answered, "No."

"Ah...another anti-socialite!" Telie raised her glass. "Hear, hear!" She caught a glimpse of two darkened figures walking toward them. Both girls looked up simultaneously into the faces of Samuel and Michael.

"Michael...seems to me we have a couple of...what's the opposite of party crasher?"

"Party pooper," Michael added, folding his arms over his chest.

"Well," Samuel shook his head in disgust. "We certainly can't allow that. I've spent way too many years perfecting my hosting skills to allow that to happen. What do you suggest we do with them?" Samuel asked, turning to Michael. Seeing the glint in Michael's eyes made him wish he'd never asked the question. "Tell you what, you tell us what you've been scheming out here and we'll think about forgiving you." Samuel's clear gray eyes missed nothing; even in the dimly lit night he could see the glow on Madeline's light olive skin as her lips spread into a slow smile.

The quiet reserve of Madeline's manner spoke of maturity well beyond her years as she replied, "My friend Telie and I were simply recounting our experiences during those horrible days of the Northern aggression. When those Yankee invaders trampled over everything around here, even our muscadine vines!" Madeline drawled, batting her lashes as she turned to Telie for reinforcement.

"You know, *that's* what I taste when I sip this muscadine juice, pure Yankee!" Telie spit out the words in disgust, indicating her glass.

Michael took the glass out of her hand and tossed the contents over the porch rail before pulling Telie to her feet.

"Come here." Michael demanded playfully. "I'll get that taste of Yankee off your lips." He lifted her up into his arms, bending his head to kiss her slowly before walking down the steps and disappearing into the night.

Samuel turned to Madeline once they were out of sight. "When will they ever get enough of each other? It's…"

"Wonderful," Madeline interrupted, beaming. "I hope I meet someone just like Michael one day." She sighed deeply.

Taken off guard by her comment and the dreamy look in her eyes, Samuel could only stare at her. He pulled a cigar out of his pocket and lit it, never taking his eyes off her. "Michael, huh…I thought you preferred guys more like— like Jude, you know, kinda bookish," he said, as he clenched the cigar between his teeth.

"Whatever gave you that idea?" Madeline tossed her hair casually over her shoulder. "I love Jude, but he's not my type." She settled back into her seat and began slowly rocking.

Samuel narrowed his eyes, gazing at her through the smoke from his cigar as it circled his head before dissipating into the cool night air. Leaning against the post, he crossed his arms as he continued to observe her. The only sound he could hear was the slow and steady creak of the rocker. "So tell me, Miss Madeline…what *is* your type?"

Madeline rocked slowly as she seemed to weigh her words. "First of all, he's got to be a believer. Only God can give a man the strength he'll need to be *my* husband."

Samuel swallowed hard; very sure what had just crossed his mind was not what she'd meant at all. Clearing his head, he listened, trying hard to keep his imagination in check.

She continued, "I'm not going to be the easiest person to live with. I know I have…peculiar ways. Only a Godly man will be able to see past it and put up with me. And, he must love me and only me. I won't share my husband's affections or attention with other women. That's what I like about Michael. He's completely devoted to Telie…you can see it. A woman knows these things about a man. He's a one woman man."

Samuel cleared his throat before speaking. "Yeah, Michael's devoted. He was like that with his first wife, too. He never even looked at another girl, since grade school. And, I might add, he had *plenty* of opportunities. I've always admired that about him, even before I was a…" He let the sentence drop.

Madeline looked up. "You haven't always been a believer?"

"No."

As he turned his attention away, Madeline understood by his body language that the subject was closed, so she didn't pursue it any further. Changing the subject, she commented, "Nice night. These shortened days have me thinking it's later than it really is."

"I better head back inside...see if anyone needs anything." He silently walked past her and into the house.

Samuel looked like someone had let the air out of him. *What could be bothering him?*

Chapter 21

*L*ane Bennett stood in the dining room at Bell Bennier, gently swirling his glass with his eyes fixed on a portrait of a beautiful woman. "I can't believe I'm actually looking at a portrait by Jonathon White, unbelievable!"

Lane was Michael Christenberry's nephew and a close personal friend of Telie Christenberry. Lane and Telie had, in fact, dated for a short time before she became involved with Michael. Still, Telie and Lane remained close. She encouraged Lane's work as an artist and, much to Michael's annoyance, had many of his works scattered throughout their home and business. Although Lane was a well- known artist in his own right, his aspiration was to study under the man he most admired, and that man was none other than Jonathon White. The problem was, Jonathon White seemed to have dropped off the radar screen some twenty years earlier and hadn't been seen or heard from since.

Samuel stepped into the dining room. "She's beautiful isn't she?"

"Yes, very. Is that your mother?" Lane asked, pulling his attention away from the portrait to look at Samuel.

Samuel nodded. "Josslyn Camellia Warren and I adored her. She was the love of my father's life and the heart of this house. This room was her favorite; that's why we placed her portrait here."

Lane smiled as he ran his hand through his tousled blond hair. "I'm blown away…you actually have a portrait by Jonathon White. He's without a doubt the *greatest* American artist…in my opinion, of course."

"Well, you need to see all of his works, then; feel free to tour the house, they're everywhere. My mother shared your passion for the works of Jonathon White."

Lane looked as if he might pass-out from sheer astonishment. "You're serious? Your mother was an admirer of Jonathon White?"

Samuel laughed, patting him on the back. "As a matter of fact, my father once told me that Jonathon and my mother were very great friends and that's why the house is full of his works. They were gifts to my mother from Jonathon, even the portrait."

Speechless, Lane could only nod. "I'd be so honored. I can't thank you enough," Lane choked out.

The way Lane's face lit up reminded Samuel of a boy catching his first glimpse of a BB gun under the Christmas tree. He dismissed his words. "Don't thank me, just go and enjoy. Each room has at least one painting, sometimes more. All of the rooms are open tonight, wander around." He waved Lane away, noticing for the first time the young woman who stood silently on the other side of him. She looked familiar, but he was positive he'd never met her before; he would have remembered *her*.

Seeing the look on Samuel's face, Lane quickly apologized. "I'm sorry; I guess I was so taken by the portrait that I've forgotten my manners. Samuel, this is my girlfriend,

Elle Bragwell. Elle, this is our host, Samuel Warren. He and Michael are very close friends."

Elle extended her hand and Samuel clasped it. "I'm pleased to meet you, Samuel. Any friend of Michael's is a friend of mine."

Elle's voice was low and warm. Her clear blue eyes were penetrating and seemed to have the ability to look straight through you. Her light brown hair spilled down her back in soft, loose curls...she was a beauty. "It's always a pleasure to meet a beautiful woman. Let me know if either of you need anything." Samuel stepped out of the room, suddenly feeling a need to find Madeline.

After having searched the grounds and most of the house for Madeline, he'd almost given up; deciding she'd gone home, then he heard her laughter coming from the direction of the kitchen. As he stepped through the kitchen door, he froze. There, sitting at the bar across from each other, were Madeline and Josiah. And from the look on their faces, they were deep in conversation.

Josiah looked up, over the shoulder of Madeline and watched as Samuel entered the room. "Samuel, come join us." He pulled out a barstool. "I've got to tell you...I can't remember when I've enjoyed myself so much. Everything's been great. And, whoever made that brisket knows what they're doing. I think I've had three plates full already."

Madeline swiveled around on her bar stool. "I agree. You and Willa did a great job with the food. Everything is," she turned back to Josiah, "just wonderful."

Wonderful! Did she just say, wonderful? "I'm glad you two are having fun and enjoying the food." Trying hard to keep the annoyance out of his voice, he said, "I'll be glad to take you home now, Maddie. You've certainly been a trooper and stuck it out...longer than I expected, I might add."

"Josiah's taking me home in a minute; besides, Bree's looking for you. She came through here about an hour ago asking if we'd seen you. But, she went back outside."

"Bree? I thought she'd left hours ago. She said something about having a headache."

"I'll see Madeline safely home, Samuel." Josiah waited for his response. He could detect a note of protectiveness in Samuel's voice and he wanted to make sure he understood that his intentions were honorable.

"I know you will, Josiah." Samuel lifted his hand and nodded. "Well, goodnight you two, and thanks for coming."

"I had fun, Samuel. Thanks for forcing me against my will to come to your party," Madeline teased, looking back over her shoulder, but Samuel had already left the room.

Walking out onto the porch, anxious to get some night air, Samuel found Michael and Telie relaxing back in their chairs, talking in low tones. "Join us and relax; almost everyone has gone now. Bree left about an hour ago, right after Lane and Elle pulled up. She told us to let you know that something came up, but that she'd call you later." Michael hooked a chair with his foot and pulled it forward. "Sit."

Samuel dropped into the chair, suddenly feeling like he was made of lead. All was silent as he pulled out a cigar and lit it. Seeming to contemplate something, he stared up into the night sky as he said; "You know...its strange how you don't notice some things all that much...things you've been around all your life, until one day...boom, there it is and you suddenly feel like you can't live without them."

A moment later, Telie responded, "I know just what you mean. My first night in Moss Bay, I slept in the bunkroom at Christenberry's. I couldn't fall asleep. I suppose some of it was the new surroundings, but mostly, it was the sound of a train whistle I missed most. I used to lie in bed and listen to that whistle as it grew closer and closer, imagining the towns it rumbled through as it made its way to Cold Water. Funny how something can be so much a part of you when most of the time you never even notice it...until it's gone. I grew up with train whistles and rumblings, but I guess I never really thought about it much, until I didn't have it around anymore. Now, I miss that sound...it sounds and feels like home to me."

"That is *so* true," Samuel said, pensively. "Michael, you've got yourself one wise woman...you know that, don't you?" The orange-red glow from the tip of his cigar danced circles in the darkness as Samuel gestured pointedly with his hand.

"I definitely know that. I also know that I've got a pretty good friend in you. Thanks for all of this, Samuel. We've really had a good time...now let's help you clean up this mess." Michael stood up.

"Don't insult your host...just go on home so I can turn in. It's way past my bedtime. Oh wait, about my kiss." Samuel stood, placing his cigar on the rail of the porch. "I'm a man of my word, Michael, and I warned you that I was going to kiss the bride." Samuel's grin grew wickedly as he observed the crease deepening in Michael's forehead. Samuel lifted Telie out of her chair and very softly kissed her cheek. "You are a remarkable woman, Telie. My best friend is blessed to have you share his life."

"Thank you, Samuel. And I'd like you to know that there is someone very special out there for you, too. I have this notion about it." She turned and winked at Michael.

"Oh no...I knew you were sitting too close to that rosebush earlier!" Michael shook his head in disbelief.

"Did I miss something?" Samuel looked from Telie to Michael, then back again; not at all sure he wanted to know.

"Rosebushes...they have a habit of talking to my wife," Michael smirked.

Telie swatted at Michael's chest. "Go on and tease, but *we'll* see...you mark my word!"

As Samuel said goodnight to his friends, he quietly closed the door behind him. The grandfather clock in the upstairs hallway chimed out the midnight hour as he walked through the house, turning off lights.

Walking down the hall, Samuel caught a glimpse of a figure standing in the dining room. Peering in, he realized it was Greenberry, standing alone in the darkness and staring up at the portrait of his mother. The only light in the room was the faint glow from the picture light attached to the frame of the portrait.

"My mother reigned in this room. Some of my fondest memories are of her sitting there," Samuel motioned to the head of the table, "holding court like a queen. We were all so enthralled by her, especially my father. She held us spellbound with her stories and her laughter until no one ever wanted to leave the room." A half smile pulled at the corners of his mouth.

"I was in love with your mother," Greenberry blurted out, unexpectedly.

"Who wasn't?" Samuel said, dismissing the comment.

Greenberry pulled a chair against the wall opposite the portrait and dropped into it with a grunt, stretching out his legs in front of him. "She was mine before she was your father's."

Suddenly the room seemed brighter as pale moonlight spilled from the French doors, landing in irregular patterns across the glossy wood floor. Samuel's eyes fixed on Greenberry and he thought he saw a tear glistening on his rough and weathered cheek. Everything seemed smooth and still, like the deadly smoothness of quietly moving water on its way to the rapids. "You want to elaborate on that for me, Greenberry?"

"The biggest mistake of my life was leaving your mother behind to go chasing after my dream, my treasure. I moved to St. Simons Island, Georgia thinking that was where I needed to be. But, like a darn fool, I left the real treasure behind." There was a long pause before he continued. "We tried to carry on a long distance relationship for a while, but I soon got so preoccupied with my work and my...ambition that I let her slip away from me."

Samuel pulled out a dining room chair and eased into it, careful not to distract him so he would continue with his story.

"Your father was not as stupid. He met your mother in Charleston the first summer we were apart and never let her out of his sight. He pursued her with every ounce of moxie he possessed and waited...patiently until she'd finally given up on me."

Questions crowded in on Samuel's mind. He *had* to know some answers. "So...how did you end up here, at Bell Bennier? I mean...you and Dad weren't enemies?"

"Why heck no, I was the fool, not your father. You can't fault a man for picking up what I so casually tossed aside." Greenberry shook his head. "Jim came looking for me, right after your mother got sick. Seems when she was having a rough go of it she would call out for me in her sleep. Your dad…" Greenberry's voice cracked. Taking a deep breath he repeated, "Your dad found me on the island and asked me to come back with him and stay…until…" he let his voice trail off.

"Until she died?" Samuel finished, as his mind tried to understand the reasoning behind his dad's decision. *Is it possible to really love someone that much?*

Greenberry wiped his eyes with the back of his hand and cleared his throat. "He told me that Josslyn loved me…and it was killing him to see her in so much anguish." He stared up into Josslyn's face as if she held all the answers for him. "We all made our peace…and not that cold hard peace that comes from indifference, but a warm, accepting peace that comes only from love." He wiped his leathery hand down his face. "Aha, you got me bawling like a baby. But son, I want you to know that they just don't make men like your dad anymore. He was one of a kind. Don't get me wrong, your mother loved your father, in fact, she loved us all with all she had. That was your mother's way."

Samuel tried to absorb it all. Gathering bits and pieces from his collective memory, he finally gathered up enough nerve to ask. "So why did you decide to stay on after my mother passed away?"

Greenberry grunted. "Josslyn never did anything half-way. If she loved you, she loved you with everything in her, that's why…"

Samuel held up his hand. "Please don't tell me you're my real father. Is that where this is going?" Samuel was still shocked to learn of his friend Michael's discovery that Mr. Christenberry was in fact not his real father at all, but his adoptive father and that his real father had been a Mobile billionaire in the shipbuilding industry.

"Why heck no...you'd be a sight better lookin if I was your daddy, boy! But as I was sayin, your mother loved you boys more than anything in this world. She asked me to stay on and help Jim with you boys. Strange I know, but somehow it worked for us."

"Oddly, that makes perfect sense." Samuel stood, stepping near the open wall cabinets where his mother's silver was displayed, one side was filled to overflowing, the other side stood empty. He thought back to that night long ago, remembering.

During one of her fitful nights of sleep, Josslyn had jumped out of bed and rushed into the dining room and began removing her silver pieces from one side of the mahogany wall cabinet to the other. Hearing the commotion, Jim and Samuel rushed into the dining room. Seeing what she was doing, they questioned her softly, not sure what had caused her to act in such a way. She told them that the Lord showed her in a dream that one side of the cabinet would be filled with Samuel's wife's silver. She was so pleased and excited with the thought that Jim helped her remove the pieces out of the cabinet, grateful to see the light back in his wife's eyes. Jim later told his son that maybe that was his mother's way of sharing her life with them. It was like she knew that soon she would have no more years to share and she wanted to be a part of their lives somehow, like a connection across time. So, they left it that way, all through the years, just the way Josslyn wanted it.

Samuel smiled to himself. It was almost as if his mother was making her presence known through the shaft of moonlight illuminating the empty shelves. Although marriage was the last thing on Samuel's mind, the thought was touching.

Turning his attention back to Greenberry, he asked. "Did you ever regret staying, I mean, did you ever want to leave?"

"I almost did...once." He exhaled deeply before continuing. "I was going back home, to my work on St. Simon's Island. I went down to the dock the night before I was to leave, I'd left some equipment in my fishing boat or something, I can't remember exactly." He shook his head. "But, after what I saw, I knew I could never leave."

Samuel widened his eyes, gesturing with his hand. "Well, don't keep me hanging, what did you see?"

"I saw Madeline. She couldn't have been more than four or five, but there she was...all curled up in the bottom of my boat with her pillow and a blanket. I reached in and gently lifted her out. She opened her eyes and smiled at me," Greenberry shook his head. "You know...that smile still gets to me, and, well, that just did it. When I asked her why she was sleeping in my boat, you know what she said...she said, 'It rocks me.' If that don't put a lump in your throat, check your pulse."

An image of a younger Madeline flashed through his mind, then was quickly replaced by the current version. He prayed Josiah wasn't close enough to touch her, much less rock her. Trying to erase the thought, Samuel asked, "What about Willa?"

Greenberry smiled warmly. "That woman interests me. I was just talking to your mother about her."

Samuel thought for a moment. He'd always felt his mother's presence in the room; maybe Greenberry did, too. "I see...so what did she say?" he ventured.

A scowl formed on Greenberry's forehead. "Boy, I might talk to your mother, but I ain't crazy enough to think she'll ever talk back!" Changing the subject rather abruptly, Greenberry asked, "Did you know Willa's husband?"

"As a matter of fact, I did…we went to church together back in Charleston. He was a close friend of mine."

"What sort of a man was he?"

"The good sort…never heard him cuss, faithful at church, too." Samuel bit back a grin, knowing full well that Greenberry had trouble in those particular areas.

"That's kinda what I thought." Greenberry hung his head, slightly. "I wish God would hurry up and make a decent man outta me before it's too late and I lose Willa for good. A woman like that deserves a good church going man."

"Well, God's the only one that can do anything with any of us, Greenberry. You're on the right track." Samuel said, flashing a broad smile. Not willing to let the moment go, he had one more question to ask just in case Greenberry went into another decade of silence. "What about your business…whatever happened to it? Did you give it up for good to stay here with us?"

"Yeah, I gave it up…a long time ago." There was a pause. "I'm Jonathon Greenberry White and I was once an artist."

In the dead silence that followed, the elephant bell clanged to the floor and rolled, then came to a stop at the feet of Samuel.

Chapter 22

I don't want to join the ladies circle, Samuel," Madeline argued, as she slipped past him in the foyer. "All they do is talk in there. When the subject of God *does* come up, they just discuss Him...like He's an idea to be studied. No offense, but that's just not my way."

"None taken." Samuel wasn't about to come between Madeline and God. And for the life of him, he wondered if he might not be better off learning a few things from her.

Tucking her hair behind her ear, she explained, "I like to spend time with God, talking. That's what we do mostly, but...sometimes we never say a word, just enjoy being together. It's about a relationship, really."

Samuel had been surprised to see Madeline at church that morning, and even more surprised to see that she was sitting with Michael and Telie. Lane was also there, sitting next to her. His gaze swept over her, this time concentrating on the dress she wore. He hadn't seen that particular dress before, which was unusual. It was a simple pale yellow dress, but what it did to her skin, her eyes...she practically glowed. And her hair, all piled up on top of her head with soft strands falling loosely around her graceful neck was almost too much to take. And her lips, they shone with the barest hint of coral. He found he was having great difficulty pulling his attention away from them. A light fragrance of lilac floated like an aura around her, filling his senses.

He'd been anxious to corner her after service, so his mind raced, trying to find an excuse to talk with her and keep her around a little bit longer. That's when he suggested the women's circle. And, surprising him, she'd agreed and stepped into the room where the ladies held their meeting so she could get a closer look at what goes on in a women's circle.

"Bye, Samuel," Madeline finger waved, as she headed for the church doors.

He watched her walk away and felt a muscle twitch in his cheek as he spied a young man doing the same thing. He reigned in the thought of backhanding the boy across the bulletin table, before turning at the sound of his name.

Cricket Meadows, the mother of Trey and Bitsy, called for Samuel as she stood in the foyer of the church. He walked toward her, immediately regretting it as she took possession of his right arm and rattled on and on about one ridiculous thing after another.

A moment later, Madeline walked back inside the church, spying Samuel in the company of a woman. She noticed that Samuel made no move to pull away from the woman. Her back stiffened as a feeling of jealousy possessed her.

Samuel coughed uncomfortably and looked around for a way to escape. Oh, he had been propositioned before…but never at church! He was not that kind of a fool, and the very thought of it made his skin crawl. "Uh…Mrs. Meadows, I'm not the sort of man who…"

Just then, Madeline walked up boldly to them with a determination born out of sheer emotion, giving her the courage to interrupt. "Please excuse me for a moment, but I need to ask Samuel if I can have a ride home. My car won't start again."

Relief flooded Samuel's face. "Of course you can." He pulled away from Cricket's tight grasp, but was immediately seized again by her hand.

"The offer still stands, whenever, wherever," Cricket stated boldly, then released his arm with a seductive smile.

Samuel put as much distance as he could between them. But, before he could explain, Madeline said casually, "Sorry to interrupt, but I thought I'd better catch you before you drove off some place with that woman and I'd be stranded."

Her comment brought a stutter to his tongue. "Wh What! I'll have you know, I had no intention of driving off with her...or, or anybody else for that matter. What kinda guy do you think I am?"

"A weak one, where women are concerned anyway," she added, snidely. Risking a glance in his direction, she found him watching her with a confused look of amusement on his face.

"Your confidence in me is flattering. Your keys, please," he said gruffly, as he extended his hand remembering another time he'd asked for her keys. A vision of Madeline draped in a sheet briefly flashed through his mind.

Madeline dropped the keys into his hand.

Turning the key in the ignition, he stated, "It's your battery, again. This time it'll have to be replaced, right after lunch. Nothing opens until after lunch anyway."

"I can't. Josiah is coming over." Madeline brushed back a wispy piece of hair from her cheek.

Caught off guard for a brief moment, he recovered quickly, saying, "Well, you'd better call him. Here, use my phone. His number is in there."

Reluctantly, she called Josiah and explained the situation. Snapping the phone shut, she handed it back to Samuel. "Lead the way, Trail Boss," Madeline said, with a hint of sarcasm.

Time quietly passed as Samuel and Madeline sat outside on the patio of Pap's Cove. The weather was mild and breezy. With their meal finished, they relaxed in their chairs listening to the clamor of seagull's overhead, watching as boats bobbed in their slips, creaking and bumping against the dock as the sun warmed their faces.

"I can't enjoy my coffee with you glaring at me like that Maddie. Now come on, what's bothering you?"

"Nothing...I'm just sorry that I interrupted your plans; that's all. You should be having lunch with that woman right now instead of me."

"Cricket...you can't be serious." Samuel dismissed her comment.

Madeline chewed on her bottom lip, contemplating if she should continue. "*You* certainly looked serious before I interrupted. As a matter of fact...you seemed to be enjoying whatever it was she was saying to you."

"She's annoyingly talkative."

"What's wrong with being talkative?"

Samuel placed his coffee cup down on the table and leaned forward, dead-eying her. "It's not that she's talkative...she's just tediously pointless." Unable to resist any longer, he took a strand of Madeline's soft hair and gave it a gentle tug. "By the way…you look especially beautiful today. Yellow is your color."

Madeline raised an eyebrow. Her mood was lifting, rapidly. "Thank you. Sonny gave this dress to me."

He scraped back his chair, regarding her closely. "I made a promise to Jude to look after you. And, I'm a man of my word and I intend to keep it. But, if you keep dressing like that I'm afraid I may have to call in for back-up," he teased.

"Jude is gone, probably for good. So, you're released from your obligation to look after me for him." She swallowed hard as the words left her lips.

Compassion filled him as he observed the soft downward pull of her mouth. "It's my pleasure to look after you, Madeline," he commented softly. "I'll always be here for you, with or without Jude."

Madeline peered over Samuel's shoulder watching as Elle walked up to their table. "Hey you two, can I get you anything else before I leave?"

"No…everything was delicious." Samuel flashed one of his disarming smiles that could suck the air right out of you. His lop-sided grin was lethal and had the power to erase all reasoning ability. But Elle seemed immune to its effects.

Elle nodded, "Good, I'm glad you enjoyed it, now how about a boat ride to finish off the meal. Lane's on his way over. He would absolutely love for you to come along. We would ask Michael and Telie to join us, but it seems they like to spend their Sunday afternoons at home these days." Grinning, Elle knew they understood the meaning behind her words.

"Maddie?" Samuel lifted his brow as he waited for her reply. "You feel up for a little boat ride?"

"It's all right with me, just let me call and cancel my plans with Josiah...for now," she emphasized, cutting her eyes to Samuel.

Her plans with Josiah had more to do with helping him get back with the woman he loved than with her. Josiah reminded Madeline of Michael in the way he was so completely devoted to his former fiancée', even after their terrible break-up. She prayed Josiah had listened to her words of counsel and wouldn't give up trying to get his girlfriend back. It seemed like such a minor issue that separated them. She was hopeful for their reconciliation.

Pushing back from the table, Madeline dialed Josiah's number as she got up and walked toward the dock. After explaining to him, she was relieved to learn that he'd made plans with his former fiancée` to talk out their differences. Feeling excited and a little hopeful, she smiled as she closed the phone and stepped near Samuel, nodding. "Let's go sailing."

Samuel rubbed his hands together excitedly. "Good! It's been way too long since I've been out on a boat with all of that fresh sea air hitting my face."

They headed out across the open water just as the sun began to disappear behind the clouds. There was a slight chop rolling the water and a spraying mist on the breeze. Madeline held an expression Samuel had never seen on her face before, she looked mesmerized. The wind tossed and pulled at her honey amber hair, whipping it loose from the clasp that held it on top of her head, allowing it to blow freely in the wind.

The prow of the boat sliced through each wave. It swung high before dipping into the trough, plunging rather deeply. Samuel reached for Madeline with both hands to steady her in her seat. A muffled sound escaped her lips drawing his immediate attention. Samuel motioned to Lane and he brought the boat down low.

"Everything alright back here?" Lane questioned, as he made his way over to his guests.

Madeline surprised them all with her reply. "I've never felt more fully alive in all my life!"

Lane's face broke out into a full-blown grin. "You're a woman after my own heart; a true sea lover."

Samuel and Elle exchanged looks at the unspoken camaraderie that seemed to bond Lane and Madeline together in an instant.

"Well, this spot seems as good as any," Lane said. "Why don't we take a break and have some refreshments? On our evening cruises, we kinda use the boat like a floating bistro."

"Best table on the water," Samuel responded, eyeing Madeline. He could hardly believe the new creature before him. *Why am I surprised? Where else would a sea nymph come alive except the sea?"* All of a sudden he had a great interest in boats. "What's the length of this boat, Lane?"

"48 feet, six inches; dry weight, 32,000 pounds."

"What does it hold?"

"400 gallons...she's smooth isn't she?" Lane became animated, motioning for Samuel to follow.

Peering across the deck, Samuel stated, "I really like the open loft design. You can look down and see the galley and salon below. I've never seen anything like it." Samuel ran his hand down the smooth dark wood of the rail above the skylight.

Lane nodded, explaining, "I chose this boat for Elle. She's claustrophobic. Most boats have closed-in designs. When I saw this one, I jumped on it. I try and stay out of high following seas no matter what boat is under me, but this one...it's just too tempting not to take her out. She can handle anything that's tossed at her. I admire that in a boat."

"And in a woman," Samuel added, thinking of Madeline and how she endured times of adversity with such courage and strength of mind. Looking around at the white upholstery and dark stained wood with its clean sleek lines, he noted how the color only heightened the effect of spaciousness. "This is one sweet cruiser."

"Thanks, man. Want a beer? Oh, no wait...I'm sorry, old habits die-hard. I'm trying to back off so I don't stock them anymore. Elle and I decided to make a few lifestyle changes and drinking was one of them. How about coffee?" Lane offered, running a hand through his wind tossed hair.

"I'd love a cup."

They stepped down into the galley. Lane prepared the coffee, talking over his shoulder to Samuel. "My dad was green with envy when I told him I'd been at your house the other night."

"Oh, really...why's that?" Samuel leaned against the counter with his arms crossed in front of him.

"He has this fascination with all things French; especially anything having to do with France before the French Revolution. My art will never hang in the same room as his precious French works. I used to laugh at his obsession, now it just seems to annoy me."

Samuel narrowed his eyes as he studied Lane. "So, I take it he knows the history of Bell Bennier."

Lane threw his head back and laughed. "You could say that. Marcellus Bennier has long been a name thrown around our household. He was some kind of French Nobleman wasn't he? I should know this; I've heard the story enough in my life time to have it imprinted on my brain."

"He was," Samuel stated, confidently. He watched Lane with new interest.

Lane looked like he was made for the sea. Samuel glanced up the steps to where Madeline sat, thinking how similar she and Lane were. His eyes took in her tousled hair and tanned face. He wondered briefly if Lane and Madeline had met before, would they have connected. Pushing the thought from his mind, he took the coffee cup from Lane's hand, pausing briefly before taking a sip.

While the men were busy inspecting the vessel, Elle sat down next to Madeline. There was no sound, only the lapping of water against the hull. There was easiness about Elle that instantly made you comfortable around her.

"I'm sorry, Madeline. But I don't know much about you. Do you live nearby?" Elle inquired, in her honey smooth voice.

Madeline smiled as the wind whipped her hair. Tucking it behind her ears, she replied, "Uh huh. I live down by the sea on a stretch of land that was once part of Bell Bennier, on Bell Forest."

Elle smiled. "I love Bell Bennier. We were there for Michael and Telie's party you know. I saw you there."

The yellow dress Madeline wore billowed slightly around her knees. Smoothing it down, she said, "I remember seeing you, too. I love Michael and Telie and I'm so glad Samuel had a party for them. I enjoyed it." Madeline was more than a little surprised at her own admission. *Did I just say that I enjoyed a party?*

"That makes two of us. Telie is incredibly blessed to have Michael. He is one of the finest men I know."

"I couldn't agree more."

"So, are you a relative of Samuel's?" Elle asked, remembering that she'd seen a stunning blonde on his arm briefly the night of the party. It made sense that a relative would live on the same property. That was customary in the South. Most families kept the land and the wealth together.

"Oh no," she laughed. "Samuel and I have grown up together, but we're not related."

"Lucky for you, he's quite handsome. He seems so attentive to your every need. That's rare in a man."

Madeline raised her eyebrow. "Attentive to *my* needs? Oh, he's just bossy that way."

"You mean watchful and protective? I don't see "bossy". I see a lot of things most people miss. People have always fascinated me, I like to observe them." Elle lifted her hair off her shoulders, catching a stiff salty breeze. "Sometimes I wish I didn't have that particular gift, though. I'd be more content in life if I didn't see so much in the faces of others."

Madeline noticed sadness in Elle's clear blue eyes. "Why?" she asked, softly.

Elle's voice lowered. "Oh…it's just that Lane is so wonderful. I know I don't deserve him. We've grown to love each other, but I don't see it working out for us, in the long run. I wish so badly that it could. I feel so complete when he's near me. I spend my time thinking about him, waiting on the sight of his red jeep pulling up at my place. He's all I've ever wanted in a man...and, he makes me laugh."

Madeline straightened in her seat. "Why do you say that you don't see it working out, Elle? It's so obvious that he's crazy about you." Madeline looked perplexed. "What could possibly stand in your way?"

"Lane's father, Tommy Bennett." Her voice was barley over a whisper. "He despises me."

The dejected look on Elle's face caused defensiveness to surface inside of Madeline. "What are you saying? That the man doesn't have the good sense to approve of the match?"

"He thinks I'm trash and that Lane is too good for me." Elle paused. "And, he's right of course."

Livid, Madeline turned on her with a raised voice. "You're wrong! You're not trash! And, don't ever let anybody tell you that you are."

Elle shrugged. "You don't know my past."

"No...I don't, but whatever it is, it's in your past. If you've asked God to forgive you, then it's forgiven *and* forgotten! It's out there somewhere...on the ocean floor." Frustrated, Madeline stared at her. "Why did you move here? Where is your family?" She knew she was being forward, but she didn't care. She was mad.

Blinking back tears, Elle replied, "I was raised by a hateful woman whose only ambition in life was to impress those around her. I never measured up and she let me know it. About five years ago, right after I turned eighteen, I made a break for it. I haven't been back or regretted a single day since leaving." Elle's lips pulled down at the corners. "You see, that's why it'll never work between us. I've lived under that kind of hatred. I never want to feel that way again, and I feel that way around Lane's father."

"You've been taking care of yourself all this time?" Instinctively, Madeline reached over and smoothed a strand of light brown hair out of Elle's eyes.

The tender gesture was well received, causing Elle's throat to tighten and the tears to spill. Nodding, she explained, "Pap gave me a job and a place to live. I live in a small house on the property of Pap's Cove. It's really nothing more than a large room with a bed and bath and a kitchenette, but I've found peace there."

Madeline leaned over, wrapping her arms around Elle in a gentle embrace. She remembered how she felt, suffering at the hands of her grandmother and the malignant hatred that had long ago twisted the mind of Mrs. Linville. It was only the wish to be rid of Madeline for good that caused the old woman to hand over the deed to Bay Cottage. That, plus thinking Madeline had a desire to make Tarpon Springs her permanent home.

Relief flooded Madeline on that fateful day as she walked away from her grandmother's house with deed in hand. No more disparaging looks cast in her direction. She was free of the woman, forever.

Lane and Samuel walked up to the touching scene. "Looks like we've missed out on something, Lane," Samuel teased, smiling down at the two girls who looked up at them with tears in their eyes.

Lane shook his head. "Women...you give them everything in the world to make them happy and what do they do? They cry!"

Chapter 23

*L*ane angled the boat down the coastline, giving his guests a view of their homes from the water. Madeline stood transfixed, gazing at the colors of blue, green and white rushing under the bow. Lifting her eyes, she saw the coastal beaches, bleached white and running for miles in either direction. Beyond the shoreline stood lush forests stretching out into the distance until their colors faded into a misty blue. Bell Bennier sat perched on a slight rise like a shinning jewel in a setting of velvet green.

They rounded the point, passing St. Thomas Monastery. The structure looked medieval, rising up from among the ancient trees that surrounded her. Then, Michael and Telie's home, Bell Forest, came into view and Madeline smiled; thinking of her friends and how they enjoyed each other so.

"What do you say we all drop in on Michael and Telie...unannounced?" Lane joked, waiting for a reaction from the others.

"I can't speak for everyone...but I for one value my life. You forget I've known Michael all of my life; I've seen that temper. True, he's nothing like he used to be. But I know when to steer clear. Telie's got that man all wrapped up. I think it's wise to let them be." Samuel grinned.

After dropping Madeline off at Bay Cottage that evening, the battery for her car forgotten, Samuel pulled up in front of Bell Bennier.

So...my Maddie likes the sea, Samuel thought. He hopped out of the truck, realizing with a start that he'd just thought of Maddie as his, causing him to almost lose his footing. Quickly recovering from the almost fall, he mounted the steps and entered through the front door.

The house was still; only a faint ticking from the mantle clock could be heard. Reaching his study, Samuel made his way to his massive desk, pulling out a stack of papers from the top drawer before dropping into his chair. An hour or so later, he set the papers aside and opened the lid on his cigar box, took one out and rolled it between his fingers. He stood and stretched, then walked across the hall to the dining room and pulled open the French doors that led out onto the veranda. A soft wind out of the west set the chandelier tinkling. He thought again of his mother. A clang and a thump sounded as the elephant bell hit the floor once more, rolling near his foot. "All right mother," he mused, "you don't have to hit me with it."

Picking up the bell, he studied it, rolling it over in his hand. He caught a glimpse of a sparkle within the dark recesses. Flipping on a lamp, he searched the interior, finding nothing. He ran his finger inside, moving it around until his finger struck an object.

Joe Gregory dragged his feet, taking his own sweet time, moving like cold molasses toward the car his boss, Michael, had indicated. Under Michael's direction, he'd been instructed to help the lady by unloading items from her trunk, then he was to take them inside to Telie.

Rounding the corner of the car, he froze…dead in his tracts. His jaw fell open as if hung from its hinges.

Madeline looked up into Joe's gaping expression and smiled before reaching down to pick up another stack of soap. Once the soap had been carefully placed in a box on the ground, Madeline extended her hand. "Hi…I'm Madeline. And you are?"

Joe found his voice and took the hand she offered. "Joe," he stammered. His face turned three shades of red as he dropped his gaze to study his boots, fascinated all of a sudden by them.

Michael called from across the property. "Joe, admire your feet later, right now, help Madeline get her soap inside. Telie's waiting."

"I'm on it, Boss." Joe stepped cautiously near Madeline. *If she touches me*, Joe thought, *I'm liable to faint dead away.*

Madeline flashed a smile and Joe's knees grew weak. He swayed on his long and lanky legs, then braced himself on the side of her car to steady himself. Pulling off his camouflaged cap, he ran a hand through his poker straight brown hair then placed the cap back securely as if that small amount of adjustment was all that was needed to be presentable. He reached into the trunk and began lifting out soap, filling up the boxes near Madeline.

"Thanks for helping me out, Joe. When Telie called and said she needed this much soap, I panicked. I didn't know how I was going to haul this entire load inside. I need my little red wagon. She winked at Joe, trying her hand at flirting just as she'd seen Samuel do with the waitress in town. She was rewarded with an instant reaction. Joe got the lead out and began loading down the box with bar after bar of soap. He quickly ran off toward the back, then returned in a flash with a cart, filling it to overflowing.

Michael stepped away from the window in the front office and motioned for Telie. Clasping her elbow, he led her to the front window and pointed.

Telie took in a sharp breath. "I've never seen Joe move that fast. What has Madeline done to the poor boy...put a bee in his cap?" They stood watching the comical little scene play out before them. Telie turned her face into Michael's chest, laughing hard.

Michael said, "Oh no, here they come. They quickly turned away looking for a distraction as Madeline and Joe headed toward them.

Madeline pulled the door open as Joe forced the cart inside at the direction of Telie, steering it near the empty shelves along one entire wall. Madeline stepped inside and gazed at the empty rows of shelves lining the wall. They were painted an antique white and stood about shoulder high. The amount of space shocked Madeline. "Is all this space for my soap products?"

"I'm afraid so. You see...," Telie began to explain before being interrupted by Michael.

"You see...my wife has these weaknesses, two of which happen to be chocolate and bubble baths. I'm sure a chocolate shop is next on the agenda." Michael leaned down and kissed his wife briefly on the lips before stepping away. "You girls have fun and behave. Come on Joe. Let's leave the women with their soap; we've got work to do." Before Michael pushed open the door, he called back to Madeline. "What have you got Samuel doing today?"

Madeline turned, gently swiping the hair out of her eyes. "He's in Charleston on business, but he's due back later tonight."

"Oh," Michael nodded, and then seemed to consider something. "Well, make sure you have our number in your phone. If you need us, call and we'll be right over. We haven't seen anything suspicious lately, but we're keeping a close eye out. So are the monks at St. Thomas."

Madeline smiled. "Samuel made me promise to stay at Bell Bennier until he returns. Greenberry is staying there, too. He didn't want me and Willa there alone." Madeline blew out an exaggerated breath. "He treats me like a child...a simple minded child at that," she fussed. "I'm surprised he hasn't called. I haven't heard from him in the last five minutes. He's been blowing up my phone all day!"

Michael drew back, raising a startled eyebrow. "Huh...you won that bet, Telie," he grinned. "I'll gladly pay you later." Winking at his wife, he pushed the door open and left.

Madeline awakened later that night with a sense that Samuel was home. After tossing back the covers, she grabbed the robe from the foot of the bed before easing her feet to the cool floor. Making her way across the room, she went down the steps and out the front door to the veranda.

"I hope I'm not disturbing you," Madeline said to Samuel, as she hugged her arms in the cool night air.

Samuel sat peacefully rocking, staring out into the night. His voice, warm as embers carried the faint scent of vanilla from his pipe tobacco. It wrapped around her like a warm quilt. "Not at all, please, sit. I could use the company." Samuel's smile was hidden by the darkness as he took note of his blue bathrobe hanging well past her wrists. And then, in a move that surprised him, Madeline leaned over and took the pipe from his hand and puffed on it a few times before handing it back.

"I've always wanted to do that," she said, matter-of-factly.

Caught off guard by the action, he simply pulled his head back slightly and smiled.

Madeline sat down in the rocker next to him and asked, "What are you thinking about, business?"

Samuel drew in a deep breath. "No, actually I was thinking of my father."

"Oh...I think of him often, too; especially on nights like this." She smiled, as she always did when she thought of Mr. Jim.

After a long moment of silence, Samuel spoke again, only this time his voice was graveled with emotion. He rubbed his face, self-consciously. "I promised my father I wouldn't come home as long as he chose the bottle over his family. I even tried to take Jude from him...but Jude wouldn't leave. And...as you know, that's exactly what I did." A wave of guilt struck him as he realized how stubborn he had been. Running his hand wearily across the stubble of his beard, he let out a deep sigh.

A light wind blew through the branches of the mighty oak as if hushing his voice and caressing his face.

Madeline reached over and closed her hand over Samuel's. Her small hand was warm and reassuring. Without a word, she seemed to convey to him in a simple gesture all that needed to be said. He smiled at her, gently lifting her hand to press a soft kiss to it.

Only moments before, Samuel had felt like an orphan. Feeling the loss of his parents left him empty. He looked down at the young girl beside him offering him comfort and realized that what he missed, she'd never had, a parent's love and devotion.

"Did you enjoy your trip to the city?" Madeline asked, knowing that there was a good chance he'd seen Bree and the thought bothered her for some reason.

"Charleston? I number it among one of my favorite places. But, nothing compares to my home here at Bell Bennier. I guess my father was right; it's where I belong.

Samuel had been taught early the workings of the plantation and found that he enjoyed every aspect of farm life. He got pleasure from seeing the fruit of the ground, loving the everyday world of Bell Bennier. He'd inherited his father's determination and willful spirit. It was that same spirit that caused him to leave home in the first place and seek his own fortune.

"Did you happen to see, Bree?" Madeline turned her attention to her bathrobe, picking at it and brushing some imaginary piece of fluff away.

"Yes, I did."

"Oh…and how was she?"

"Just as beautiful as ever," Samuel teased, laughing as Madeline's head shot up to glare at him.

Taking on a serious note, he added, "We've set a trap. Bart and I got with a friend, a very influential friend, and he's going to play the part of someone interested in developing a resort on one of the islands off the Carolina coast. Hopefully the bait will be attractive enough to finally catch our man. Or woman," he clarified.

Chapter 24

A burst of splattered red broke over the darkened sky to the west. Samuel and Madeline noticed it at the same time, jumping up simultaneously, nearly colliding as their worst fears were realized. Bay Cottage was in flames.

Samuel jerked his phone out of his pocket and began dialing for help. After he finished with the 911 operator, he dialed Greenberry. Rushing into the house, he grabbed his boots, pulling them on as he shot out the door. Madeline ran up the stairs to quickly change, her heart pounding. With no time to think, she dressed and ran out of the room, passing Willa in the hallway.

"Madeline! What on earth?" Willa's confused expression begged for explanation.

"My house is on fire," she managed to say, before rushing down the steps and out into the night.

The house was fully engulfed as Madeline ran into the yard. Samuel and Greenberry worked to clear a path around the house to keep the fire isolated and contained so no further damage could be done.

The deep glow of embers illuminated the night sky as fickle sparks shot upward. Hissing flames greedily devoured Madeline's home. A stillness; like death seemed to permeate the air as the cottage moaned in sorrow with the last timber falling into the flames. With an aching in her chest, Madeline watched as her home melted from view. Her eyes shone, reflecting the fire light. Staring out at the destruction brought fresh waves of grief. Despair swept over her leaving her feeling weak and drained. It was all she could do to keep standing.

The fire trucks arrived, but too late to do anything more than extinguish the flames. Bay Cottage was gone.

Samuel and Greenberry relaxed their efforts, heaving air into their smoke filled lungs as they dropped their tools and stepped back from the site. Bracing his back on a nearby tree, Samuel wiped his brow with the back of his hand and scanned the area until he'd spotted Madeline. There she stood, looking helpless and lost. She'd been dealt yet another blow. Forgetting everything else, he pushed off the tree and made his way to her, thinking of her as a little girl in need of comfort. He wrapped his arms around her slight frame and held her tightly. She turned into his chest, giving voice to her loss with a low mournful cry.

Samuel held her tight, wishing he could absorb all the loss, all the pain. Caressing her hair, he felt helpless as he faced the destruction before him. *Was this an accident, perhaps started by one of Madeline's candles, or had this fire been intentionally set?* So many thoughts flashed through his mind, but none stronger than the thought that was sure to haunt him for the rest of his life, the thought that Madeline could have died in this fire.

As if adding insult to injury, the wind picked up, hampering the efforts of the firemen and scattering embers into the surrounding woods. Reluctantly, Samuel released Madeline, picked up his shovel and made his way to the brush. His attention was never very far from her. But, he was relieved when he saw Willa approach and wrap a blanket around Madeline's shoulders before leading her away.

Back at Bell Bennier, the night wore on as the wind tossed the trees cruelly in violent thrusts. Inside the house, the walls creaked and moaned under the vicious onslaught of the storm. Large raindrops pelted against the windows and trickled down the glass in wavy lines as the rain finally arrived. Relief was in sight for the men, and for that Madeline was grateful.

From her darkened room, she listened attentively to the sounds of the house. Earlier, she'd heard the voice of Telie, then muffled voices she couldn't make out. Willa had given her a dose of her "cure-all", Benadryl, and the drug was working its effects. Her eyes grew heavy and soon she'd succumbed to a tired and exhausted sleep.

Samuel and Michael walked up to the Fire Chief, extending their hands. "The back door to my house is open and the coffee is on. I'll make sure your guys have something to eat on the bar. There's a bathroom down the hall, help yourself. Looks like the rain has saved us a long night of fire fighting, we're heading back, but please make use of my house before you and your men start back to town. I appreciate everything y'all have done."

Samuel and Michael entered the kitchen in the early hours of the morning with daylight still hours away. Shaking out of their rain soaked jackets, they moved toward the smell of hot coffee. Samuel's eyes were red with strain, smoke and lack of sleep. The door blew open and Greenberry stepped inside, stomping his muddy boots on the doormat. Michael took a seat at the table with a cup of steaming coffee in each hand. He motioned for Greenberry to do likewise. Michael slid a cup in Greenberry's direction and watched as he drew a long sip, draining it in one long pull. "I'll pour your cup when you get back," Michael said to Samuel, as he peered at him over his coffee cup. He saw the look in Samuel's eyes and knew where his thoughts were. More than once he'd seen his friend glance up the back stairs.

After ridding himself of his charred and muddy boots, Samuel took the stairs, two at a time before stopping in front of Madeline's door. He listened. Hearing nothing, he eased the door open. Waiting for his eyes to adjust to the darkness, he quietly moved to the side of the bed and looked down on her sleeping form. Her body curled around a pillow and her hair fell across her cheek. Samuel fought the urge to brush it away from her face. But, seeing the peaceful way she slumbered, thought better of it. Watching the slow rise and fall of her breath, he was assured of her comfort. He stepped away, quietly closing the door behind him.

Michael hooked a chair with his foot and slid it back for Samuel as he entered the kitchen. Getting up, he poured his friend a cup of coffee, then settled back down at the table. "Greenberry went home," Michael stated. "He was worn out."

"Good, he needs sleep." Samuel held his cup with both hands, like a cowboy in front of a campfire. "You and Telie head on upstairs and get some rest. Willa will be clanging pots in this kitchen in a few hours. I'll wake you when breakfast is ready."

Michael stopped, not sure he'd heard him correctly. "Telie?" He'd thought Telie had gone home hours ago.

He motioned with his head toward the living room. "She's over on the couch asleep. I'd appreciate it if you'd stay the night. Madeline will need Telie in the morning. Take Mom's old room."

Michael nodded, then drained his coffee before heading toward his wife. He gently nudged her, waiting for her to stir, then slid his arm around her waist, helping her to her feet. Together they carefully mounted the staircase, leaning into each other. Once they were out of sight, Samuel placed his head in his hands and let out an exhausted breath, his thoughts were never very far from Madeline.

The sun-break beamed across the morning fog as cool vapors rose from the ground, swirling and dancing in the gray light. The stench of wet ash was heavy and pungent on the early morning air. A distance yelping of a dog drew Madeline's attention toward the fields. Resting her head on her drawn-up knees, she waited for his approach as she sat on the front steps of Bell Bennier.

The dog rushed up to her excitedly, jumping and plopping his two front paws across her lap. Wagging his tail with gusto, he panted as if thrilled to see her. "Where did you come from, boy? Are you lost?" The dog seemed to relax under the smooth strokes Madeline was giving to his fur. He settled on the ground at her feet, thoroughly enjoying the rubbing.

"McKeever!" Telie scolded, as she came up behind Madeline. "Where have you been? I'd given up on ever finding you again." Telie held her coffee cup tightly as she gingerly stepped down the steps to sit beside Madeline. "This is my dog, McKeever. He's been missing in action for the past few weeks. Michael thinks he probably has a girlfriend." McKeever raised his soulful eyes to Telie, but never moved a muscle. He seemed perfectly content to stay right where he was.

"Well, he's absolutely adorable. I'm sure he's quite the ladies man." Madeline reached behind his ear and scratched.

"Don't encourage him, he's rotten enough. All of our neighbor's have seen to that." Just then, McKeever's ears perked up and he raised his head, snarling as he looked down the drive. "Might have known, it's the mailman; for some reason McKeever can't stand him. Settle down, McKeever." Telie used hushed tones to quiet him. The mail carrier stopped in front of the mailbox at the end of the drive, then turned around and headed back out without completing the loop around to Bay Cottage.

News sure travels fast around here, Madeline thought, finding it almost funny that he would already know about the fire.

Telie cleared her throat. "While you were sleeping last night, Nathan and Sonny dropped by to check on you. Nathan went out to join the men, but Sonny stayed and visited awhile. You've met Nathan, right?"

Madeline nodded, remembering the day in Pastor Thad's office when she'd first met the former pastor.

"Sonny brought sacks of clothes and personal items. We sorted through all of it and found a few things we thought you could use. I slipped them into your room a minute ago."

Madeline turned her head to look at Telie who was sitting one step behind her. "Oh...my things are gone. I guess it all hasn't hit me yet."

"Yes, well that means you get new things. Now, I'm not one to shop, but I do love to order from catalogs and I just happen to have a few with me."

Madeline eyed her suspiciously, giving her a crooked little grin. "Just so happen?"

"I had Michael pick them up from the house before he left for work this morning," she confessed. "Anyway, I've been instructed to help you pick out several outfits including under garments and shoes. And I'm to make sure you have plenty of jeans, a pair of boots and something...yellow." Telie pursed her lips. "It seems the gentleman prefers the color yellow against your skin."

"Oh no," Madeline protested. "Samuel is not buying my clothes. And, just as soon as I decide where I'm going to live, I'm leaving here, too."

In the distance, wisps of smoke curled upward above the trees and Madeline's shoulders slumped in grief. The strain of the long night showed on her face. Her features were drawn and tight as she looked down, avoiding the sight of the last remembrances of her home.

Telie eyed her for a long moment. "You remind me of me," she said gently. "But, you'll have to get over your pride. We're doing nothing more than you'd do for us if the situation were reversed. Now, listen to me, you're going to sit right here and pick out clothes with me and you're going to do it without an argument. You and Samuel can fight about the other matter later."

With amused disbelief, Madeline turned her attention to the catalog in Telie's hand. She wasn't sure what to make of Telie's comments, but she decided not to argue about it and try to hang on to her remaining strength...she'd need it when she had to deal with Samuel later. Besides, any girl that could handle a machete the way Telie could deserves her full attention.

In a comforting and relaxed manner, Samuel sat next to Madeline at his desk in the study. Spreading out papers before them, he began the quiet discussion of seeing to her affairs. Once the financial matters were seen to, the conversation led into her plans to rebuild. Madeline was struck by the ease of their discussion. None of the usual fire and sparks she'd grown to expect when conversing with him entered into their talk. Just calm reason and soft inquiries. Although she enjoyed the pleasant way they interacted, something inside of her missed the fire and sparks that usually ignited every time they were together.

Samuel suppressed an overwhelming need within him to take charge of the situation and make decisions for her. But, as he had learned, Madeline needed to feel in control of something, especially when everything else in her young life seemed so out of control.

Truth was...Madeline had come to respect Samuel, not only as an overseer, but a leader as well. She looked to him whenever her doubts were too much for her. His presence gave her strength, reassurance and security, something no earthly man had ever done before. She now wondered if perhaps God had led Samuel to her, for such a time as this.

Madeline turned to find him watching her. She forced her attention back to the plans Samuel had spread out before them and calmly answered his soft inquiries. She knew she should have given more input, but her head ached from her near exhaustion and she struggled to pay attention.

"When I restore, I don't tamper with the character of the place. Character is what makes it unforgettable. I try and let the land and the environment dictate the style. How do you see it?" Samuel looked up from the plans, noticing the weariness in Madeline's eyes. "Are you not feeling well, Maddie? You look a little flushed." He placed a hand on her forehead.

Before she could answer, the pounding of footsteps on the wooden floor could be heard coming from the front of the house. "Madeline!" the voice of Jude echoed through the house. Madeline jumped to her feet and ran toward the voice, leaving Samuel staring after her. Rubbing his hand down his scruffy face, Samuel inhaled deeply before joining his brother.

"You look exhausted," Jude remarked, taking in the deep circles around Madeline's eyes.

She lowered her eyes from his searching gaze. "I'm fine, just a little tired."

"Look at me, Madeline," He placed both hands on her cheeks and searched her eyes. Turning toward Samuel, he gave him a questioning look. "How long has she been like this?"

Samuel didn't like the insinuation. He casually took a cigar from his pocket bit down hard, clenching his teeth as he commented dryly, "Since the moment you drove away, Jude, she's just been wasting away to nothing."

"Oh stop it you two, I'm fine. I just have a headache and I'm tired."

Samuel's brows grew together in concern as he noticed the weakness in her voice. "Upstairs, Maddie, I'll bring you some Advil. You need to rest."

Madeline was so tired and in pain with her throbbing head that she obeyed, walking toward the stairs. Samuel was surprised at her compliance and thought to himself, *I better enjoy it while it lasts because it isn't likely to ever happen again, but it sure makes an impression on Jude.* He noticed his brother's shocked expression which caused him to stand a little straighter.

Madeline turned back, walked over to Jude and lifted up on her tiptoes to kiss his forehead. "We'll talk later…when I get up."

Feeling like Madeline had just launched a stiff boot into his belly; Samuel crossed his arms over his stomach and waited for her to leave. Once she'd climbed the stairs and was out of sight, he turned to Jude. "Well little brother. I'm glad you're home…how about something to eat?" They crossed the foyer and went into the kitchen. Opening up a cabinet door, Samuel grabbed a bottle of Advil from the shelf, then reached inside a brown paper bag on the counter and pulled out a cellophane wrapped praline. "I ordered these from New Orleans," he explained, seeing the perplexed look on his brother's face. "They're Madeline's favorite."

"*I* know pralines are her favorite. What's been going on here since I've been away?" Jude asked accusingly, staring at his brother.

Samuel shrugged, enjoying the reversed roles they were playing. "Same as usual I guess. I mean other than the break-in at Madeline's home and oh, finding out that Beau Chambers tried to molest her when she was little…and her house burning down…other than that, nothing unusual."

Jude slid onto a barstool. "All right, start from the beginning."

Chapter 25

Samuel didn't know when it began to happen, but it was happening. Something had awakened inside of him. Something he'd never encountered. He could only grasp it in brief snatches, but it was there—a desire to leave all of his plans behind and follow his heart. He couldn't deny the relief he'd felt when Jude boarded the plane only hours before. It annoyed him greatly to see Madeline with Jude. Seeing the two of them together demanded every ounce of self control he could muster to keep from yanking them apart.

"Enjoying the view?" Samuel asked Madeline, as he came near. He'd found her sitting cross-legged on a patch of moss, overlooking the charred out remains of Bay Cottage.

"I wouldn't use those exact words," she replied, as a hint of a smile crossed her lips.

Inhaling deeply as his chest expanded, Samuel let out a breath. "Sea air and a wide horizon, what could be better?"

Madeline gave him an incredulous look as he dropped down beside her. She was grateful for Samuel's presence though, and felt better the instant she'd spotted him from a distance. Never had he looked more handsome as he walked toward her. The sun shone around his muscular frame. He looked solid and steady and she liked that about him. Her spirit was nurtured by the security he so easily brought to her. Whenever he was near, she dropped all guards.

Overwhelmed with loneliness over Jude's departure and her mother's absence, she'd sought comfort near her former home. Even though the memories she had of her mother were without much joy, what had only been presence was now only absence, and she missed her even more with the cottage gone.

The spot they shared under a copse of sheltering trees had been abandoned to thickets and undergrowth years ago. Perched on a small rise, the moss-covered knoll had a clear view of the sea beyond where they could observe the roaring and relentless pounding of the greedy surf. It rushed ashore, flattening dunes as it raked across the sand; it held the same steady beat, not concerned at all over the absence of what once had been her home.

A mourning dove landed in the grass not too far away, joining his mate and sounding the familiar, Oo-ah, coo, coo, coo.

"You know...I've always heard that doves mate for life," Samuel interjected. He eyed the bird skeptically. "But...I don't know about that one...he looks like a player."

With a burst of laughter, Madeline startled the birds into flight. "Well if anybody knows what a player looks like...it's you!"

Samuel studied the smooth curve of her neck as she tilted her head back. It was good to hear her laugh. He picked up a stone and rubbed it between his fingers. "You know, I'm really not the player you think I am...at least not anymore." Samuel drew back his arm and threw the stone into the ashes some distance away. "You might say that my life has been transformed…or reformed; whichever way you want to put it. The point is…I'm not the same as I used to be."

Madeline watched as a random breeze stirred his hair. She caught her breath as Samuel turned his steel gray eyes to her. There was something there she'd seen before—it was light. She didn't have to ask, she knew what had changed him. It was the very same light she'd seen in Mr. Jim's eyes all those years ago.

"God's way and not your own way anymore…that's it isn't it?" Madeline brushed back a wispy piece of her hair from her eyes.

"Yeah, pretty much. Can't say it's been easy," he gave a half-laugh. "But it's been an adventure. The best part is waking up to a new day knowing that no matter what life throws at you, you're never alone. Someone once said that God's middle name is surprise. I believe it. I always look for the surprise each day holds. Hang on to that hope."

Letting out a sigh, Madeline replied, "I don't want to end up like my mother." She let the desperation sound in her voice. "My mother closed her eyes to the world as if all the color had drained out of it. After she heard that my father had died, she died…on the inside. She was so overwhelmed by the loss that she refused to see anything else. I never want to feel that hopeless…ever." Madeline grew quiet, then choked out in confused anger. "But she had me, Samuel. She had me. Why wasn't I enough to make her want to live?" Madeline's throat tightened. Swallowing hard she raised her eyes to meet his.

Samuel's voice was low as he responded to her. "Come here." He reached over and lifted Madeline onto his lap, wrapping his arms around her. Leaning back against a tree, he whispered into her hair, "Everyone has their struggles in this life, Maddie. It's best never to forget that. But life is about the journey and where it leads us and how we grow along the way. Sometimes, though, change can cast a person in a place of paralyzing fear or a holding pattern. Either way, that person refuses to move forward. It boils down to a lack of trust in God, basically. But, He'll bring you through the trouble if you let him. Remember when he told us, 'In this world you will have trouble, but cheer up, I've overcome the world.' That's good to know when your house burns, or your parent dies or any other trouble that may hit us hard. This place is only temporary...we'll make it through, and with joy. Don't forget the joy. I for one, intend to experience my share of it. Somehow...when you experience deep sorrow, it makes joy that much sweeter."

Madeline folded her hands beneath her cheek and rested her head against his shoulder, staring out at the charred remains of her home. "Where would I be without God?" she whispered. A cry collected in her throat, but she swallowed it down. Too ashamed to admit she was weak and needed Samuel's strength and comfort if only for a moment. She'd never blubbered like that to anyone before, not even Jude. What possessed her to snivel about all of this now? "I'm sorry I lost it on you, Samuel. I guess I'm just tired and not feeling very well. My head still hurts."

He turned to her in a quick, almost startling manner. "Never apologize for sharing what's on your heart, Maddie. I'm just glad you shared your thoughts and fears with me."

Madeline cleared her throat. "So am I."

Floodwaters rushed out from the east fields, overflowing the banks of Bayou Bell. It hurried along, saturating the ground as it cut a path toward the sea.

Three days after the initial onslaught of rain, the sky began to lighten. Grabbing his jacket off a hook near the back door, Samuel stepped outside to walk the property and access the damage. His boots sunk into the soggy soil as he cut across the field in the direction of the monastery.

"Hello to the camp!" Samuel shouted across the grounds of St. Thomas monastery, as he spied Brother Andrew.

Brother Andrew turned quickly to the voice. Narrowing his eyes, he smiled as he recognized Samuel walking toward him. "For a moment there I thought you were your father," Brother Andrew said, as he reached out to clasp Samuel's firm hand. "That's how he always greeted me."

"If you hadn't beaten him so badly at chess all those years, you wouldn't have to worry about being haunted by him." Samuel grinned, noticing the sparkle in the old man's eyes.

"True, true...it's a weakness I suppose. I just loved playing chess with your father. You could almost see the wheels turning around in that head of his as he tried to out maneuver you."

Brother Andrew was a portly man with kind eyes and a ready smile. His white hair and reddened face made you think of Santa Claus, an impression that didn't trouble the old monk one bit, in fact, he liked the idea.

"Come inside my boy and visit. It's been much too long since I've seen you." Brother Andrew led the way down the stone walk and through the archways that outlined the perimeter of the courtyard. Opening the creaky wooden door, he motioned for Samuel to enter. Once inside the dimly lit room, the smell of old books, wood polish and extinguished candles hung faintly on the air as he looked around the study.

Very little had changed in the room since Samuel had last visited and it felt good, familiar and somehow comforting.

Samuel moved toward the leather wingback chairs that were positioned at an angle in front of a large stone fireplace. A fire burned low, spreading warmth throughout the room. Taking a seat, Samuel stretched out his legs in front of him, waiting for Brother Andrew to join him. "It feels good to be home, Brother Andrew. Even with all of this rain, I wouldn't want to be anywhere else."

Brother Andrew lowered his weight in the chair next to him with a grunt. "We've certainly stayed on our knees around here...first, with the passing of Della, then Jim, and all of the odd occurrences at Bay Cottage and now the fire... that poor, poor girl. What she must've suffered."

Samuel raised a questioning brow. "Madeline?"

"Madeline, yes, she has a very entrancing presence about her doesn't she?"

Samuel nodded, then half-laughed. "You could say that." At times he'd felt as if he needed to lash himself to the ship's mast so that he wouldn't respond to the alluring singing siren.

Brother Andrew smiled, "Our Brother Simeon, he's Irish you know," he said, as if that clarified everything he was about to say. "He has some notion that the girl is not of this world. We tease him about it. But, she never fails to command his almost hypnotized attention whenever she walks along the hillside. He even remarked once that her clothes were the same at each sighting, as if to give further proof to his theory."

Samuel shifted in his chair, covering his amusement with a cough to clear his throat. "Oh, she's real all right. I assure you."

"Oh, *I* know. She's a Bennier," Brother Andrew stated, proudly.

Samuel turned his attention around sharply. "What did you say about the Bennier's?"

"Madeline is a Bennier descended from Adella Bennier Linville." He took in a deep breath. "You see…I've always had this fascination with history…some even call me a historian. And, this place we call home is chock full of history. I know a great deal about it, including its legends and its people. Madeline is, as far as I can tell, the last Bennier." Brother Andrew smiled and nodded his white head, pleased with himself.

"Uh…do you mind throwing some light on the subject for me, Brother? I'm trying to follow you." Samuel leaned forward with his elbows on his knees, clasping his hands together. Brother Andrew now had his undivided attention.

"Of course, my boy, I have the documentation in this very room. It removes all doubt. Madeline is the sole remaining heir, unless of course her mother had other children that I'm not aware of." Brother Andrew got up and moved to the bookcase, pulling out several folders. "Come to the table and let's have a look."

Samuel joined Brother Andrew at the large French rectory table. Sliding out a chair, Samuel sat down, never taking his eyes off the papers.

"Although her title won't do her much good this day and age, it's still hers…about all that's left of the estate though, is the twelve acres she now owns. And for that, you can thank your benevolent ancestor." Brother Andrew tapped the papers on the table with his forefinger.

"*My* ancestor?" Samuel asked, waiting for clarification.

"Hold on…I'll have Brother Ignatius make us some coffee. Go settle in the chair again, this is quite an interesting story." Brother Andrew left the room, leaving Samuel alone with his thoughts. He returned shortly with coffee on a tray and two slices of pound cake.

Trying to contain his anxiousness, Samuel held tightly to his cup with both hands, his eyes fixed on Brother Andrew.

"Well, it all began with Marcellus Bennier," he said, reaching for his cup. "He built the raised Creole style home in 1830 for his wife, Eudora Leighton. Sitting juxtaposed between Mobile Bay and the Gulf of Mexico, the three thousand thirty three acre plantation seemed the ideal location for farming and rearing a family. Desperate to have children, Eudora prayed to have a son. That prayer was answered one February night when Eudora gave birth to Sergius. Sergius grew into a man of God, full of wisdom and compassion. But, those convictions soon found him in opposition with his father, especially over the issue of slavery.

Sergius married a gentle woman named Rebecca Pro-vines and they had two children, Alva and Adella. Their son, Alva had been sickly most of his life. But, his parents spared no expense when it came to their son. Years later, Alva died leaving the family without sufficient funds to keep Bell Bennier operating. They sold the home in 1877 to the Warren family along with most of their assets. This was the beginning of Warren ownership of Bell Bennier. Following me so far?" Brother Andrew took a long pull of his coffee. At Samuel's nod, he continued. "In the final sale of the property, Samuel G. Warren stipulated that thirty-three acres of bay front property be deeded over to Sergius Bennier, free and clear. When Sergius adamantly protested, it was said that Samuel Warren told him that it had been commanded him by the Lord. That ended all protests."

Samuel rubbed his chin with the back of his hand. "Wow...I never knew the history. So..."

"So Sergius, along with his wife and daughter moved to the property after building a modest house, Bay Cottage. In gratitude to the Lord for providing for them in their desperate need, Sergius bequeathed 18 acres along the bay to the Order of Saint Benedict, some of which was sold to the Christenberry's, having something to do with it being a former cemetery, I can't recall. But, most surprisingly, three acres were given to the family of the young slave girl that his father, Marcellus had put to death in the bayou. Our neighbor, Theda, who now lives on the property, is a distant relative of the young girl who drowned in the bayou that day. A former slave owning property was rare indeed and greatly frowned upon. But, Sergius was wise enough to keep the information between the two families until the course of time changed some thinking."

Samuel eased back in his chair. He propped his elbow on the armrest, contemplating what he'd heard.

Brother Andrew sat up in his chair, placing his coffee cup down on the small table beside his chair. "In France, Madeline's ancestor was the Noblesse de Cloche, meaning, Nobility of the Bell. Ironic isn't it?" He sat back, rubbing his fisted hand. "In this form of government, only the most prominent citizens rule. They were the elite aristocratic class, privileged by birth and wealth. Marcellus' father was a municipal leader in Toulouse, France, where Saint Thomas Aquinas is buried."

Samuel saw the old monk's eyes light up with the mention of Saint Thomas Aquinas. Clearly, the saint had an admirer in Brother Andrew. "Why did Marcellus move his family here? I mean, it sounds like the guy had it made in France."

"The French Revolution, my boy. That ended the reign of the French Nobles. As a matter of fact, there are only a few remaining families holding First Empire titles today. Madeline has a legitimate claim to a title. Oh, it wouldn't do her much good except on birth certificates and such, but still, it's hers. There are some who covet that sort of thing." A smile brightened the old monk's face. "I had this one gentleman spend an entire afternoon with me discussing the history of Bell Forest and Bell Bennier in particular. The man was obsessed with French Nobility and seemed almost driven to know more about Marcellus Bennier."

Samuel narrowed his eyes. "That man wouldn't happen to be Tommy Bennett would it?"

Brother Andrew looked surprised. "Yes, as a matter of fact it was."

"Did he ask about anything specific?" Samuel had an inkling something was about to be revealed.

"Oh…he seemed most interested in the signet ring worn by Marcellus. I told him all I knew about it." He pushed up from his chair. "I've got a picture of Marcellus wearing the ring." Rifling through the papers on the table, he said, "Ah ha, this is what I showed to Mr. Bennett."

Taking the picture from Brother Andrew, Samuel began to study it.

"In France, the signet ring bearing the coat of arms is traditionally worn by French Noblemen on their left hand. This picture was taken before he was married. If the wearer is married, the ring is worn in an inward position. But, as you see, the ring is quiet obviously displayed." Brother Andrew peered closer, then reached over and picked up his coffee cup, taking a sip.

"Not as obviously displayed as this." Samuel lifted his left hand and wiggled his finger. "I found it welded to the underside of an old elephant bell my family found in the attic."

Brother Andrew almost choked on his coffee. Clanging the cup down on the saucer, he reached for Samuel's hand. "In all my days," he declared. "I never thought I'd ever see anything so…magnificent. May I?" he asked, extending his palm.

"Of course." Samuel worked the ring loose and placed it in Brother Andrew's palm. He watched as the monk cradled it, turning it over gently, almost reverently.

"Now why would the ring be welded to the inside of a bell?" he asked himself, as he pondered the ring.

"Maybe they were hiding it from the Yankees." Samuel rubbed his jaw line. "No, that wouldn't make sense. They would have retrieved a treasure like this after the Yanks cleared out. You said my family bought the house in 1877. That's twelve years after the war."

Carefully handing the ring back to Samuel, Brother Andrew commented. "Well, my boy. You've certainly given me something to contemplate. I won't rest until I've come up with an answer. By the way, I wouldn't let it be known that you have such a treasure just yet. Something tells me it wouldn't be wise."

"Something told me the same thing."

Chapter 26

*T*elie was grateful the storm had run its course by morning. Bell Forest has taken on a wild dance in the storm, bending and swaying to the winds and rain that hammered her for three days. Finally subsiding, it left in its wake swollen streams and water paths that spilled into the bay from Bayou Bell. The water had rushed down the gentle slopes with a gradual downward inclination toward the bay, soaking the ground all along the way.

The erratic stop-and-start gusts of wind and rain all through the night caused Telie to snuggle closer to her husband, Michael. They'd talked deep into the night, listening to the tempest rage outside, but feeling warm and secure in each other's arms.

Early that next morning, Michael headed out to work, leaving Telie home to rest. She'd not felt well for the past few mornings, so Michael had insisted she stay home. Managing to hold down a few sips of ginger ale, she walked out onto the porch, looking over the property after the storm. From the porch, she marveled at the magnolia tree Michael had planted in her honor a little over a year ago. Planted along side Bayou Bell, it grew strong with sturdy branches shooting upward. Water droplets tapped a steady beat on the thick glossy leaves as a slight wind shook the branches.

Telie caught sight of a sharp corner, sticking out of the ground beneath the tree. She reached for her shovel that was propped next to the steps and made her way over to the tree. After a good soaking rain, it was common for an occasional silver fork or spoon to perk up out of the ground. Remnants of a bygone era where the owners of Bell Bennier had buried their valuables near the bayou to prevent the Yankees from getting their hands on them.

She tapped the object with her shovel, testing it before gently sinking the shovel into the muddy soil. Telie grew more and more determined to unearth the object pushed up from the ground by the roots of the magnolia. Ankle deep in mud now, she dropped to her knees and began scooping away the mud with her hands.

Just then, Michael pulled up. It was not the first time he'd caught his wife digging in the mud after a rain. In fact, it was a common occurrence. Slamming his truck door, he made his way over to his wife.

Telie looked up excitedly, calling to him. "Michael, there's something here; something this tree wants us to discover."

During the past year with Telie, Michael had learned that sometimes it was best not to argue with her and just let it be, especially when he could see the determination in her eyes and that certain set to her jaw. "Here, give me that shovel. You have no business out here in the mud feeling the way you do," he said, reprimanding her as he set to work.

As more of the object was revealed, Michael's heart sank as a thought struck him. "Uh...Telie," he swallowed hard. "You know this area was once a cemetery for slaves. We might actually be digging up a coffin here."

Telie stopped scooping and looked up at him. "It's not a coffin. I know it's not."

"And just how do you know that?" Michael stopped digging and leaned on his shovel, eyeing his hardheaded wife.

"Look." She wiped off the mud from a portion of the box. "Slaves didn't have ornately carved coffins. This box has fleur-de-lis images all along the side. A slave wouldn't have that on their casket. Keep digging."

Nearly an hour later, Michael lifted the case out of the hole. Visible now were the elegantly scrawled words across the top of the box, "Glory be to the Triune God."

Telie watched her husband with anticipation, waiting for him to pry open the lid. He took the shovel and pried the wood gently. After a few good pushes, the lid creaked open. Taking hold of the wooden lid, Michael pulled open the crate.

Telie gasped.

"I'd better call Samuel," Michael stated, as he stared wide-eyed into the crate. "He needs to know about this."

The room was dark and still, doused of light except for the flickering of the gas lanterns on the balcony that dimly lit the surroundings. The sheer fabric covering the French doors softened the lantern's glow, allowing the diffused light entrance into Madeline's room.

How long have I been asleep? Madeline groggily opened her eyes and peered around the darkened room. Throwing back the covers, she sat up, feeling light headed all of a sudden. After a moment her spinning head settled and she eased her legs over the side of the bed. Her legs trembled under her slight weight as she reached for the bedpost.

"Where do you think you're going? Get back in the bed." The voice was gravely and hoarse, but there was no mistaking it, it belonged to Samuel.

She peeked around the post of the Rice Bed, spotting the dark shape of Samuel sitting in a chair with his legs stretched out in front of him. His elbow was propped on the arm of the chair with his head resting against his fist. He never lifted his head as he watched her.

Feeling caught, she made an excuse. "Uh…I'm going to the bathroom."

The chair creaked under Samuel's weight. He crossed the room and slid his arm around her waist, leading her to the bathroom door. "Can you manage from here?" His rough voice held a note of concern.

"I've got it now, thank you." She entered the bathroom, leaving him to stare at the closed door.

"Don't lock the door."

Shuffling to the sink, she turned the water on, waiting for it to heat before washing her face.

"Are you all right in there?" Samuel called from the door.

"I'm fine." Her strength was too weak to hold a washcloth and fuss with Samuel at the same time, so she opted for the face wash. After that small task complete, she finished up in the bathroom and, feeling dizzy, called for Samuel.

She felt the strength of his arm around her and goose bumps covered her flesh. Not sure if her fever was climbing or if the chills were caused by his nearness. She leaned into him, allowing him to help her back into bed.

"What's the matter with me?" Madeline whispered through her parched throat.

Samuel scrubbed a hand across his bristly cheek. "Doc says you have a good case of the flu. Here, let's get you some water." Samuel lifted the glass from the nightstand and held it to her lips.

"Ah...thank you, I was thirsty," she said, adjusting her position on the bed. For the first time she noticed the nightgown she was wearing. It was soft and made of simple white cotton. It had a scooped neck and a small border of lace encircled the neckline. "What time is it?" she asked, smoothing down the fabric with her hand.

"Close to sunrise. Are you hungry?"

Shaking her head, she patted the bed, asking him to sit. "How long have I been sick?"

"Three days. Willa and Greenberry have been concerned about you. You had us all a little worried." Samuel propped his weight against the bed. "I think Greenberry even bargained a little with God. It wouldn't surprise me if we see him in church on Sunday." Samuel grinned, happy to see the smile across Madeline's face.

"Well, if *that* happens, I'll take all the credit," she teased; noticing for the first time his red rimmed eyes and lined face. "You look tired, Samuel. Go to bed. I'm fine now and I want to sleep. See," she held her hand to her forehead, "no fever."

He reached over and felt her head. "Thank God."

The days following Madeline's illness seemed to take flight. She was disappointed to learn that she'd slept through Thanksgiving, but relieved to know that they hadn't told Jude that she'd been sick. He was meeting Jenny's parents for the first time over the Thanksgiving holiday and she didn't want anything to spoil that. But, Madeline was more than determined to enjoy the Christmas season at Bell Bennier.

"What do you like best about Christmas, Samuel? What sticks out the most in your mind?" Madeline asked, as she and Willa sat at the kitchen table, peeling apples for a pie they were making.

Samuel shifted on the barstool. "Hmm, let me think about that for a minute. I think it would have to be the smell of Christmas. I miss that the most. My mother religiously adhered to the tradition of fresh evergreens around Bell Bennier at Christmastime. No artificial anything for her. She would go into the woods and gather evergreens of all kinds, magnolia leaves, cedar and pine. Sometimes she'd even take nandina sprigs, dried cattail or whatever else she'd find and spray them silver. Every mantle in this house had an arrangement on it," he chuckled. "The place smelled wonderful, like Christmas. Dad and Greenberry never had the knack for decorating. Do you remember some of those pitiful trees Greenberry would drag up?"

"Yeah, I remember. Jude called them his "Charlie Brown Specials,"" Madeline said, glancing back at Samuel. It warmed her heart to think that she shared a Christmas memory with him.

Willa laughed, "Would someone please tell me how a man that can paint the way Greenberry paints still can't seem to match his socks? You should see his cabin! Nothing in there even comes close to matching." Willa's face flushed brightly as she realized her mistake. She'd only visited

Greenberry's cabin once and that was to wait for him to change shoes. Still, the admission embarrassed her.

"He may be an artist, but he's a man first," Madeline said, in a tone that suggested she knew all about men.

"Let this rooster get out of the hen house before y'all start squawking," Samuel joked, snatching a piece of apple on his way out the door.

The first bite out of the north caused Madeline to brace herself against its chill. Zipping up her new Carhartt jacket, she crossed the open field, pulling a wagon by a long measure of rope tied to the handle. A half-smirk played on her lips as she thought about what Samuel had said to her earlier. She'd argued that she didn't need all of the clothes he had ordered for her, that a couple of outfits would've been plenty, to which he remarked, 'I'm just keeping it interesting, Maddie. Variety is the spice of life. It's all about the spice.'

Entering the woods she began gathering pine branches and pinecones, dried grasses and such when she spotted an old ancient looking twisted cedar tree up ahead. Yanking the wagon along over roots and fallen limbs, intent on her task, she reached the tree. Stretching up on tiptoes, she grabbed a low hanging branch. Pulling it down, she tucked it under her arm to secure it before she made the cut. Startled by a rabbit running across the path, she let go of the branch. That's when she noticed how very quiet everything was...how very still. Feeling strange, as if she were in someone's crosshairs, she shivered, then chided herself for her overactive imagination. "What's next...a harmonica?" she mumbled, under her breath.

Grasping another cedar branch, she snipped the limb and tossed it into the wagon. A twig snapped behind her. Madeline hesitated; listening so hard that all she could hear was the pounding of her own heartbeat in her ears. She reached down and lifted the rope on her wagon and began turning away, slowly.

Just then, a sinister voice called from the depths of the gray and eerie forest. "Get out!"

Wasting no time, Madeline let go of the handle of the wagon and fled down the path. As she neared the clearing, a man stepped out into the path a short distance in front of her. She halted, terrified as she contemplated her next move. A rush of adrenaline coursed through her veins as she looked on the figure. The man was tall and thin with a weather-beaten face half covered by the hood of his black jacket. Her mind raced as she tried to thwart the enemy's plan before he had time to make a move. Just then, she caught sight of Samuel, easing up behind the man. Holding his hand out, she understood the message he was conveying so she remained still. Everything inside of her wanted to run, but she held firm to the spot, trusting Samuel to protect her.

The hooded man approached her slowly, leering as if he expected her to flee and it seemed as if he wanted her to.

"How many more wolves are in Bell Forest?" Samuel asked calmly, his voice ringing out into the air.

Startled, the man jerked around to face Samuel.

"Are there any more of you circling out there among the trees?" Samuel always got calm in a crisis, and the calmer he was, the angrier he was. By the easy way he spoke, there was no doubt in Madeline's mind that he wanted to tear the man to pieces. A ticking on the left side of his jaw was all that was visible of the rage building within him.

The man let out a stream of curses, relating the possibilities of what might have occurred on the Warren family tree. He produced a deer knife from his pocket and waved it in the direction of Madeline. "Don't come any closer."

That was the final straw that flattened the camel. Samuel raised his rifle. His voice was clear and precise as his steel gray eyes looked down the barrel of the gun. "If you so much as twitch, you're a dead man."

The man didn't argue. Seeing the look in Samuel's eyes, he dropped the knife and held up his hands in surrender.

"Maddie...go untie the rope around the wagon handle and toss it to me." Samuel kept his finger on the trigger and his eyes fixed on the man. "It's back up the trail, a few yards behind you."

Madeline did as she was told and tossed the rope near Samuel's feet. He bent down and retrieved it, ordering the man to turn around and place his hands behind his back. Easing the rifle down beside him, he grabbed the man's hands and knotted the rope around his wrists tightly to prevent even the slightest movement; uncomfortably doubling up the binding to cause more pain. That gave Samuel a measure of satisfaction. He'd wanted to kill the man for threatening Madeline. "Now —get moving."

Back at Bell Bennier, Sheriff Kyle pulled up in front of the house some twenty minutes after he'd received the call. Slamming his car door, he strode over to where Samuel sat calmly rocking in a chair on the porch. His rifle aimed at the trespasser on the steps in front of him. The Sheriff halted his steps, recognizing the man in Samuel's custody. "Wayne Summers?" He looked to Samuel for an explanation.

"Yes, old Mr. Summers...our Mail carrier. He's been pretty chatty, too. Seems someone hired him to scare

Madeline off her property. I found these on him," he tossed a pack of cigarettes to Sheriff Kyle. "That's the same brand I found in Madeline's house and all around her property."

Sheriff Kyle shook his head in disbelief, running a hand through his hair.

"Right now you're looking at a possible charge of arson along with trespassing, brandishing a weapon with intent to do harm and possibly more," Samuel stated calmly.

Words spilled out of Wayne, "I was hired to run Madeline off her property, but I'm not the only one in on this. His so called girlfriend," he motioned with his head toward Samuel, "she's in on it, too."

"All right...so what's his name...who's the guy behind it all?" the sheriff asked.

"His name is...Breanna Behrends. She's Tommy Bennett's girlfriend and she's after Bell Bennier. She wants all the land along the coast to give to him, as a gift. She plans on torching the monastery next...but I told her I wouldn't set fire to nothing, especially a monastery. That's pure evil. Bree set fire to Madeline's house, I didn't. All I did was try and scare Madeline into leaving. I did kidnap that mutt of a dog that belongs to the Christenberry's. He kept coming after me. But, I let him go after the house burned."

"Go on and tell him the rest," Samuel urged. "It gets even more interesting."

"Bree took a liken to Samuel and wanted to prolong the little game for awhile. Kinda like what a cat does to a mouse...you know, toys with it before moving in for the kill. Well, she'd already figured out that the fire could be blamed on Madeline because of her love for candles. Samuel told her that she burned them constantly and how he was afraid she'd burn the place down one day if she weren't careful. That's when she got the idea to hire that cowboy. She had him follow them to Charleston and meet up with them on the road. His job was to take her out and get her drunk. So drunk that she'd pass out and supposedly set fire to the place. But," he shook his head in disgust, "I aint no killer. After I found out what she planned, I made sure the girl was away when Bree set the fire. Bree flew back from Charleston right after Samuel left from up there this last time. She thought she'd have a good alibi, since Samuel saw her in Charleston."

Samuel shuttered, thinking of how badly he'd been fooled and how it might have cost Madeline her life. "So…how does Tommy Bennett play into all of this?"

"He's not involved. Bree wanted it to be a surprise for him. Apparently he's some kinda fanatic about Marcellus Bennier and everything the man touched. The prize was Bell Bennier."

Chapter 27

I can't believe she would do such a thing?" Madeline wrung out her dishrag as if it were Bree's slender neck. "And all for what…just to impress her boyfriend!" She tossed the rag on the counter and reached for the broom. Staying busy always helped her work out the snarls in her mind. She swept the kitchen clean, then moved to the veranda, sweeping until she'd worked her way all around the house.

Madeline stepped down the back steps and headed for the servants' quarters. Noticing a large pile of evergreens stacked next to the cabin, she promptly sat down on the ground and began sorting through the pine and cedar. *Someone must've retrieved my wagon*, she thought, and began weaving the branches together. Somehow the working of her fingers soothed her mind. Getting up, she went into her shop and brought out all the necessary tools she'd need to make arrangements out of the evergreens. She twisted wire around magnolia leaves and nandina sprigs, pine and cedar, working until her fingers nearly bled, but it felt good.

She pulled the wagon around to the front of the house as the day melted into the soft evening hues of a winter sky. She felt a kind of exhausted relief as she mounted the step with her arms full of greenery. She quickly began hanging the fresh wreath on the massive front door, then moved inside to tackle the mantle.

Madeline smiled as Willa came into the room. "Everything is still a mess," Madeline apologized, "but I'm working on it."

"Oh, everything looks wonderful, Maddie. Samuel will be so pleased. It already smells like Christmas around here."

"When is he coming back? Did he tell you?"

"No, he just said he'd be back in a few days." Willa hesitated. "You know, Maddie. It's understandable if you're a little frightened, maybe even angry." Willa moved to the couch and sat down, patting the seat next to her. "Sit down, rest a minute."

Madeline crossed the room, pulling off her shoes as she curled up on the couch beside Willa. "I'm not afraid...just mad. Sometimes it's too much. I mean all of it, it's just too much. I've come to the conclusion that God must be punishing me for something."

Willa looked horrified. "Don't even think such a thing! God is not like that."

"Well, I don't understand. Some people never experience half the stuff I've had to deal with in a whole lifetime. I'm just twenty years old! Is this how my life is going to be, one tragic event after another?"

Willa clasped Madeline's hand, squeezing it reassuringly. "Sometimes being a Christian means being tossed on the Potter's wheel from time to time where you're pressed and pulled and shaped. But that process, as painful as it might be, is shaping you into something useful and beautiful." She patted Madeline's knee. "The clay of your heart is soft, Maddie. You'll be easy for the Master Potter to shape, if you don't allow yourself to become hard. Trust His hands. Those hands are both loving and skillful...very skillful in your case, my dear." Willa brushed a strand of hair case, my dear." Willa brushed a strand of hair off of Madeline's forehead. "Wait on the Lord and trust Him."

The night was clear and sharp, a winter's night where the moon illuminated everything, bathing it with silver. Lane Bennett sat in church listening to Elle practice singing with the choir. A hand landed on his shoulder and he turned around.

"Dad, what are you doing here? Is everything alright?" Lane asked, concerned. He'd never seen his father in a church except at funerals or weddings.

Motioning with his head, Tommy Bennett indicated the foyer.

Lane followed him out. "What's going on Dad?"

"I was told I would find you here. I came by to tell you that I'm going to be away for a few days, possibly over Christmas."

"Why? Are you in some kind of trouble?"

Tommy Bennett cleared his throat. "No, no. The woman I'm seeing is in a predicament."

Lane quirked his brow, "Oh, I see."

Tommy shook his head, giving a half-laugh, "Nothing like that I assure you. It's a legal matter. It's unlikely that it will get resolved before Christmas. I just wanted you to know where I'll be, in case you needed me."

Lane nodded. "I'm spending Christmas with Elle anyway. You see..."

Looking putout, Tommy interrupted, "Lane, why do you bother with that waterfront trash. You could have any woman you want...why her?"

Lane worked the muscle in his jaw, clenching his teeth. In a controlled voice he stated, "I'd appreciate it very much if you'd stop referring to my wife as waterfront trash."

"Your wife!" Tommy shouted, halting the sound of "Silent Night" drifting through the doors from the sanctuary.

"Yes, my wife. I didn't tell you because I know how you feel about Elle. But you're wrong about her, Dad, and I refuse to allow your arrogance to control my life. I hope you'll have a change of heart once you get to know her."

Tommy stared at his son in disbelief. Adjusting his coat up higher on his shoulders, he calmly stated, "You've made your decision and now, you'll live with the consequences." He turned away from Lane, hitting the bar of the church door as he made his exit.

From the choir loft, Elle grew concerned. She'd seen Tommy Bennett enter the church and watched as Lane followed him out. A short time later, Lane returned and took his seat again, only this time, he seemed distracted, troubled. Oh, he had smiled up at Elle, trying to reassure her, but she could tell something was wrong, very wrong. Anxious to get to her husband, she began rubbing her hands.

"Relax dear, we're almost finished," Mrs. Feldman whispered to Elle. "Your handsome husband will still be there when this is all over."

Elle turned to the woman and whispered back, "I'm sorry, I'm just a little nervous."

Mrs. Feldman patted her arm. "You're such a sweet one, Elle. You remind me so much of Madeline Linville, do you know her, dear?"

The meaning of Mrs. Feldman's words suddenly registered, hitting Elle with full force to the face as effectively as being doused by a bucket of ice cold water. "Linville?"

"Yes, Madeline Linville. She's the pretty little girl that comes to church with Samuel Warren. But, I have seen her come with Telie Christenberry, a time or two."

Elle's face went white.

"Are you all right dear?" Mrs. Feldman motioned for Lane.

Lane jumped to his feet and rushed toward Elle who was halfway down the steps by the time her reached her. "What's the matter, Elle? Are you ill?"

"I need to see Madeline, right now. I'll explain on the way."

Brother Andrew had eyes that seemed to look straight through to your soul. Sitting across from him, Samuel rested his chin on his fisted hands, taking in the council of the old monk.

"If we listen carefully to the promptings of our heart...to what's happening inside us, we should do our very best to follow those promptings." Brother Andrew widened his eyes. "Don't let failures and disappointments in your past keep you from experiencing what God has for you now, my boy."

Samuel crossed his arms. "So...you think that's what I'm doing?"

"I do."

"I've changed. I'm not the same anymore. I don't know how I ever did it, but with God's help, I did. I changed direction. This, this longing inside of me pushed me forward. I'm not perfect, not by a long shot, but I'm not just living for myself anymore. I'm trying to live His way, as well as I can."

Brother Andrew nodded, listening as Samuel talked in deep resonate tones. He noticed his eyes seemed to hold a strange resignation, as if he had come to a complete understanding of the importance of life God's way.

"You still resent your father," Brother Andrew blurted out, unashamedly.

Samuel pulled his head back sharply. The words of the monk were like a sledgehammer blasting a rock.

The monk continued. "Jim faced his demons squarely and decisively...he was not willing to put Jude and Madeline at risk once you were gone. He relied heavily on you while you were around...*too* heavily, I'm afraid. And, he knew he had failed you. He spoke to me about it often." Brother Andrew shifted in his chair. "Your father's weakness was not alcohol...but your mother. Your weakness is not women, but commitment. You're afraid of losing something valuable and being hurt...just like your father was hurt."

The chair creaked as Samuel leaned forward. His silence and thoughtful expression puzzled the monk. Then a vague impression began to register that perhaps this was the first time Samuel realized the resentment he'd held against his father and his fear of getting too close to women. In fact, it seemed he'd purposely picked women he knew he'd never get too emotionally involved with.

"I don't know if I'll ever be ready for marriage," Samuel stated, as if he were talking to himself.

"The challenges of marriage are preferable to a sexually tormented lifestyle, my boy. Celibacy is a simple life, but it's not for everyone. And if you find a woman whom you love, everything else will work out, if you let God define the life you have together."

Samuel looked up into the aged eyes of Brother Andrew. He was staring at him in a different way—a studied way.

"Ah...so I see you've found this *one* already." Smiling, the old monk tilted his head, tapping his fingertips together as he watched the stunned expression on Samuel's face.

Samuel hurried up the porch steps of Bell Bennier feeling more buoyant and alive than he'd ever remembered. Coming through the front door, he paused while holding the handle as he noticed the fresh evergreen wreath that adorned the massive door. Smiling, he stepped into the foyer, taking a deep breath. He turned his attention to the living room where lights twinkled from a large Christmas tree in the corner. It was then he noticed a gathering of people seated near the fireplace.

"Well...Merry Christmas!" Samuel called out, smiling. He crossed the room toward them.

Madeline looked up with surprise as Samuel crossed the room and extended his hand to Lane. "You're back!" she said, excitedly.

Samuel plopped down in his leather chair and extending his legs out in front of him. He felt himself grin, "Did you miss me?" Their eyes met and held until she blushed and looked away. It was then that he noticed her red-rimmed eyes and pinkish nose. He sat up quickly. "Oh, I'm sorry, I've interrupted." He made a motion to get up.

"No, no," Lane explained, waving his hand. "Sit down. The girls have just discovered they're sisters."

Samuel narrowed his eyes. "Sisters?" He looked at the girls sitting side-by-side on the couch, holding hands tightly as if clinging to each other made up for all the years of lost time. The resemblance was uncanny. Why had he never noticed before? Their eyes pooled with fresh tears, identical eyes except for the color; one set was sapphire blue, the other, light emerald green. "So…how did this discovery come about?"

Elle cleared her throat and spoke softly. "I moved here five years ago searching for my mother. I'd found some papers locked away in the attic of my grandmother's house that led me here. All I had to go on were a few pictures and, of course, her name, Della Linville. I changed my name to Bragwell after I ran away. I thought my grandmother might search for me. But, as far as I know, she never has." Elle hesitated, then squeezed Madeline's hand. "I didn't know about Madeline until tonight. At choir practice, Mrs. Feldman told me that I reminded her of Madeline Linville. That was the first time in five years that I've heard that name. I had to find out if there was a possible connection. And, now I know I have a sister."

"Did you know your father?" Samuel asked, leaning forward in his seat. He was more than a little interested in the recent development.

"No…I didn't. But, I did find some people in Tarpon Springs who knew him. His name is Alexander Gailen and he's Greek. His father and grandfather were sponge divers and both were killed at sea. Apparently, our father was told a string of lies and he left the area. One man told me he thought he joined the Merchant Marines. Knowing Grandmother, she would have done anything to keep her daughter away from a Greek sponge diver. He wouldn't have measured up."

"So...you're Elle Linville," Samuel stated.

"She's now Elle Bennett, my wife," Lane corrected, then gazed at his wife as if a halo encircled her head.

"Well...congratulations! This is definitely a night for surprises." At that moment, Greenberry and Willa walked in the room, carrying two trays; one with coffee, the other with an assortment of Christmas cookies and cake.

"We heard you come in," Greenberry spoke gruffly to Samuel. "Willa insisted I help." He dropped the cookie tray on the coffee table with a clang. "No smart alecky comments about it either."

"Did you make the cookies, Greenberry?" Samuel teased. He enjoyed seeing the rough man squirm, not quite sure what to do with his hands.

"I just watched." Annoyed, Greenberry stepped aside as Willa placed the coffee tray down on the table.

Willa turned around, slipping her arms around Greenberry's waist. "I couldn't have managed without him." Standing on tiptoes, she placed a light kiss on his lips. Greenberry seemed to recover quickly, giving Willa a sideways grin, forgetting all about his embarrassment.

Samuel turned to Lane. "I have a few surprises of my own. First, let me introduce you to my friend here." Samuel waved in the direction of Greenberry.

Lane smiled, "Oh...we've met; here as a matter of fact, at your party."

"Yes, but you didn't know who you were meeting. This...my friend," he gestured again toward Greenberry, "is Jonathon White. Jonathon Greenberry White, the artist."

Stunned, Lane couldn't find his voice. His mouth opened but no words came out as he struggled to comprehend what he'd just heard.

"And, Greenberry, this happens to be your greatest fan, Lane Bennett, another fine artist."

Greenberry reached over and tipped Lane's chin, effectively closing his mouth. "I've seen your work, boy, you're good. I've picked up my brushes again, so if you'd like to drop by sometime, it's alright by me. My cabin is around back." He motioned with his head.

Lane stammered, "I'd consider it an honor and a privilege."

"Good...well, if you'll excuse us, Willa and I have some decorating to do...at my place." He pulled Willa toward the door. She smiled back at them, giving them a simple wave.

Silence filled the space. Only the crackling of the fire could be heard as the warm glow permeated the room. So much had been discovered that night. So much had changed in a matter of a few short hours.

As if knowing instinctively what Madeline was thinking, Samuel said, "Now you're not alone in this world, Maddie. You have a sister."

"I'm still getting used to the idea." She smiled warmly at Samuel.

"I was waiting for the right time to tell you this, Maddie. I think this qualifies as the right time." Samuel cleared his throat.

Madeline watched his face, thinking, *what else could possibly be revealed on this magical night?* The soft white lights of the Christmas tree twinkled behind him.

His next words were spoken almost reverently, as if not wanting to break the spell they were under. "You and Elle are direct descendants of the original owner of Bell Bennier, Marcellus Bennier. Brother Andrew informed me and he has all of the documentation to prove it, which makes you both of noble decent. You're bluebloods from French aristocracy."

Shocked, Lane's eyes widened. "I can't believe this! I just can't believe it! Do you realize what this means?" Lane laughed out, as he pushed up from his chair. "My father will have a coronary when he finds out. Just think...my little wife is a direct descendant of the infamous Marcellus Bennier. This is rich." Lane pulled his wife up, hugging her.

Elle pulled back slightly, and whispered, "It's not the blood that runs through us that's important, Lane, it's the blood that runs over us. That's what Telie said, remember?"

In that moment, Madeline met Samuel's eyes. "Telie's right. The blood of Christ...it covers us, giving us life... like—water on a sea star."

Caught off guard by her comment, Samuel titled his head. "Well spoken, Maddie."

Samuel's admiring gaze captured her attention. Only a second passed before he smiled a lazy smile. The dark stubble on his face made his teeth gleam brighter than usual. His face astonished her; he was so ruggedly handsome he seemed to always take her breath.

"Well...this calls for a toast." Samuel lifted his coffee cup. "To the grace of God who allowed these two lost sisters to find one another."

Madeline interrupted the toast. "Of course, Elle, you and Lane will now own six acres of Bell Forest coastline. That's your inheritance."

Chapter 28

Christmas morning arrived enshrouded in fog. The cool misty air drifted in through the open bedroom window, stirring the curtains and waking Madeline from a sound sleep. She shivered in spite of the down coverlet that cocooned her in warmth. Sliding her feet down the vintage sheets, she pulled the covers close and rolled over on her side. Pressing her cheek into the cool softness of her pillow, she thought, *Christmas Day*. She'd never felt such excitement on Christmas before. Hurriedly, she threw the covers back and eased her feet to the floor. After a quick shower, she slipped on a simple dress then ran a brush through her hair until it fell smoothly down her back. Lifting a small package from her nightstand, she left the room, making her way down the stairs.

Madeline was instantly aware of a difference in the atmosphere. The smell of Christmas was everywhere. She stepped into the living room, watching as Samuel stoked the fire. "Merry Christmas," she said, in a faint whisper.

Turning his head suddenly, Samuel smiled, "Merry Christmas."

She eased over to the Christmas tree and placed her package neatly under the branches.

"How about some coffee, Willa made a fresh pot before she left."

"Willa's not here?"

Samuel shook his head. "No, it's just the two of us. She's with Greenberry. They're sharing Christmas at his place this morning, then driving over to Mobile where her daughters will be staying. They're flying in later this morning. I think they're anxious to meet Greenberry."

"How's Greenberry handling it? Is he nervous about meeting Willa's girls?"

Samuel stood and stretched. "I think as long as Willa's by his side, he can handle anything."

"I suppose you're right."

Samuel lifted a small present from the mantle. "This is for you."

Taking the gift, Madeline looked up and smiled. "For me?"

"Go ahead…open it."

She ran her finger under the folds, loosening the paper as she freed the small box. Opening the lid, she gasped. Displayed on a sheet of velvet was a fine chocolate-brown leather cord knotted with lustrous pearls. It gave the appearance of seaweed gathered from the depths of the ocean with tiny latching pearls encircling the strand.

"I saw this piece and thought of you. It looked like jewelry made for a sea nymph or a mermaid. I had to get it for you."

"Oh…it's beautiful," she breathed, never taking her eyes off the necklace. "I've never seen anything like it." She fingered the small pearls, then quickly fastened it around her neck. "I love it, Samuel. Thank you." A giggle bubbled up to the surface, surprising them both. She felt almost giddy.

Samuel laughed. He loved the way her eyes danced. He'd never seen that side of her before and it secretly thrilled him.

"Here," she said, reaching under the tree to retrieve his present. She smiled with genuine pleasure as she handed him the box.

Samuel eyed her suspiciously. "What could this be? A plane ticket back to Charleston?" he teased.

"Open it," she said, impatiently.

Tearing open the wrapping paper, he removed a shaving mug with three bars of freshly scented soap. "Whoa…did you make this soap for me?"

She shook her head. "It's a three inch soap puck so it fits inside the shaving mug. It's my special blend for you, West Indies spice with a hint of sandalwood. I put eucalyptus and tea tree oil in there so the cleansers won't strip the natural oils from your skin. It will feel good and smooth and also condition your face."

"What about the fragrance?"

"It's a sensual blend," she stated, then immediately regretted her comment as the words spilled out of her mouth. The slow smile that crept across his face didn't help matters.

"So…this is *my* blend…the soap you made especially for *me*? This…*sensual* fragrance reminds you of *me*?"

Crossing the space between them, he tipped her chin up a notch. "Thank you." He kissed her softly on the lips.

"You're welcome." She kissed him back, just as softly.

"Don't mention it." He returned the kiss, more thoroughly this time.

Caught up in the moment, enjoying the little tit-for-tat game they were playing, she lifted up on tiptoes, "It was my pleasure."

Before she could kiss him back, a knock sounded on the front door. Madeline walked over to the window and peered out. "It's Mary Grace." She moved across the room toward the stairs. "I'll leave you two alone. It looks like she has another cobbler."

Before he could respond, she was up the stairs. He stared after her retreating form until she was down the hall and out of sight. He lifted his hand in a gesture of futility. *So much for Christmas joy,* he thought, as the door to her bedroom shut. He stepped to the front door, forcing a smile as he welcomed Mary Grace.

The glory of the early morning demanded to be noticed as streaks of pink and orange colored the sky. Samuel was an early riser, yet he almost always found Madeline up and steadily working with her soaps in the little cabin behind the house. It was fast becoming a routine for him to have his coffee there before heading out to work. Taking a seat at the large wooden block table in the center of the room, he casually sipped his brew. An easy familiarity began to develop between them. This unspoken bond seemed to be getting stronger as they talked each morning over coffee. He'd come to respect her, seeing her less as a girl and more as a woman, a very intriguing woman.

"I'll be moving to town soon," Madeline spoke over her shoulder. "You've been very kind to allow me to stay here this long. But, I need to go before I wear-out my welcome." She smiled back at him. "I've found this little shop in Moss Bay with an apartment above it. It's perfect for what I need. And, hopefully, I'll be able to sell more soap in town."

Samuel swallowed down the tightness in his throat. "So, when do you plan to move?" he asked, forcing his voice to remain calm and steady. He felt his lips quiver under the strain.

"Uh…tomorrow, actually," she said, smoothing her hair as she pushed it away from her face. She sat down across from him.

A strange ache came to life within Samuel. "If you need help moving…"

Madeline shook her head, "No, I've got it covered. That's one advantage of not having anything." She smiled over her coffee cup. "Greenberry and Willa are helping me move my shop later today."

Misunderstanding the sadness in his eyes, she asked, "So, how is your business going? I've noticed you've been coming in late these days. Is Bart still in town?" She looked deeply into his face.

She would notice, he thought, then smiled. "Oh, we're about to recover from the damage. It's been demanding…but it could have been worse."

"Jude says that you're at your best when facing a crisis," a smirk played on her lips. "I talked to him this morning. He told me to tell you that if you need him to help you out, he could take a semester off." She peered over her cup at him.

Samuel laughed. "Yeah well, that's not going to happen. But I appreciate the offer." Shifting in his chair, he added, "I figure another two months and we'll be on our feet again."

He looked at her, taking in her sparkling green eyes and the attentive way she watched him. "Did I tell you that Bart got back with his wife?" He felt light and weightless in her presence and wished, now more than ever, that he could stay and talk.

"What? That's wonderful!"

"Yeah, he's a different person. A better person...I guess it's true, she really is his better half."

"Do you enjoy your job, Samuel?" Madeline watched his face intently as she sipped her coffee.

The question caught him off guard. No one had ever asked that question of him. "It has its benefits, but I wouldn't use those exact words."

Smoothing her hair back with her hand, she asked, "So what *do* you enjoy doing?"

"Farming," he answered without hesitation. "I have this desire to live on my own good earth, to raise my family there and be a part of the land."

"Well, you just so happen to own a very nice farm with lots of land."

"Yeah," he half laughed. "But, it's not very profitable."

"Profits aren't everything you know."

He studied her a long moment. "Let's go for walk, down the beach." He pulled her to her feet. "This may be the last time we get to do this for awhile."

A fine shell sand mix crushed beneath their feet as they approached the beach. Samuel looked longingly at Madeline as she walked a step ahead of him, noticing the subtle effects of a sea breeze as it lifted her hair, the scent of lilac following close behind her.

The morning cry of seabirds called out as they walked along in silence. Listening to the rhythmic sound of the surf, they fell into an easy step as they walked along, just out of reach of the waves.

"Are you nervous about the move into town?" Samuel asked, as he picked up a shell and threw it into the water.

"You might say that." She brushed back her windblown hair from her eyes. "Life with my mother instilled a caution in me. I don't like change and I don't like to feel closed in, especially at night. I like to be able to see the stars. But, I need this change...for my own good. I've never been away from..." she made a wide sweeping motion with her hand, "this, for any length of time. Too much of my life has been cheaply spent living in fear and worrying about things I can't control."

Samuel looked over at the bare hayfield, soon to be plowed, and said, "Sometimes fear and isolation can form a hard crust over the top soil of our hearts. And, like that field over there, it's necessary to plow it up in order to get ready to receive a harvest. Without the pain of the plow, Maddie, there will be no harvest."

Madeline listened intently to Samuel's words, seeming to contemplate them. Oh, he was accustomed to people paying attention to him; it wasn't that, he'd just never had such rapt attention focused on his every word. She'd obviously gotten over her aversion of looking him in the eye. It now seemed hard for her to pull her attention away.

She halted abruptly, biting her lip as his brow raised questioningly. "So...what you're saying is, 'get ready to get plowed.'"

"Yeah, that's exactly what I'm saying."

"How did you get to be so wise?" Madeline remarked, as she glanced over at the sand dune that concealed her little sanctuary in the sand.

Samuel straightened slightly under her praise. "God alone gives insight, Maddie. As much as I'd like to take the credit for it," he said winking, then flashing a bright grin.

The plantation seemed lonely. Life moved on as usual and was busier now that spring had arrived, but at night the house seemed to be sighing as if in mourning. Samuel tried to keep busy, working late into the night, getting the farm ready for planting. The long days wore on, without much relief. It seemed as if the doldrums had set in and nothing stirred. Madeline's absence had all the feeling of a lull before a storm, making it hard for him to find ease for his mind.

Lighting a cigar, he opened the French door in the dining room and stood, staring out into the night. A piece of his mother's silver clanged to the floor causing Samuel to turn around. He reached down and picked up the tray, studying it thoughtfully before placing it back on the shelf gently. It was then he noticed the empty shelves beside his mother's silver laden ones, and paused. Twisting the signet ring on his finger absentmindedly, he suddenly remembered how he'd planned to give the ring to Madeline. It was one of the few family heirlooms she had. The thought of seeing her again cheered him. He closed the door on the sound of crickets softly chirping and headed upstairs to face another lonely night.

In spite of his exhaustion, Samuel couldn't sleep. The warm night air drifted in from the bedroom door, stirring the sheet that draped across his leg. With his hands behind his head, he lay staring at the ceiling. The absence of Madeline weighed heavily on him. He'd grown accustomed to her light movements in the next room. The sound of her bath being drawn and the splashing sound of water, the smell of lilac seeping through the door; even the creak of her bed as she crawled into it at night, he missed it all. *I'm acting like some kind of lovesick fool.*

He thought of Michael and of how much his friend would enjoy his predicament. *I'm looking you up tomorrow, my friend.*

A bird sang a shrill little tune from the railing of the balcony as Samuel folded his pillow over his ears. After a night of unrest, he dragged himself from bed, showered, dressed and tugged on his boots before buttoning his shirt and rolling up his sleeves. Sliding his loose change, keys and pocketknife off the dresser, he filled the pocket of his worn-out jeans and eased down the hall. He hesitated momentarily at Madeline's door before heading downstairs and out the door toward his truck.

Pulling up at Christenberry's Landscaping Company, Samuel stepped out of the truck, spying Michael near the tractor shed. He dangled the keys in his hand as he approach his friend, dreading what he was about to admit to his friend.

Michael turned to Samuel with a shake of his head. "That boy's as lazy as a bloodhound." He took off his sunglasses and motioned with his eyes toward the back of the shed. There, on a pile of wood chips was Joe, all sprawled out like a turtle sunning on a warm rock.

Samuel grinned. "Come on, let's go rattle his cage."

They approached the boy quietly, staring down at his peaceful form. Samuel spied a partially filled bucket of water near a wagon. He motioned for Michael to pick it up, then said, "You know, Michael, it's said that Alexander the Great would walk around, observing his men on occasion and if he ever found one asleep on the job, he would douse him with kerosene and set him on fire. I've always admired his style." Michael tossed the water on the boy, then Samuel struck a match.

Joe scrambled to his feet, tripping over his feet as he bolted away. After reaching a safe distance, he looked back at them and yelled, "Y'all are crazy!"

Michael threw his head back and laughed. "I see we haven't lost our touch."

"Speaking of touch...where's that beautiful wife of yours?" Samuel teased, then came the grin, wider than before.

"Far away from you." Michael faced Samuel, firmly taking hold of both of Samuel's shoulders. "I want you to be the first to know. We're expecting a baby!"

Samuel's eyes widened. "What! Oh, man that's great. When did you find out?"

"Yesterday," Michael said, unable to contain his joy. "Telie had been feeling tired and a little dizzy lately. I thought she just needed to rest. The girl never slows down, but..." He let out an exaggerated breath, "I was wrong. We're having a baby."

"This calls for a celebration. I've been looking for an excuse to fire up the grill." Samuel clasped Michael's hand, squeezing it firmly.

"Definitely...so how are you doing, Samuel?" His eyes took in Samuel's two-day growth of beard and lined face. "You look awful."

Samuel dead eyed his friend. "Yeah...well, I'm afraid you've lived to see the day. I've fallen...and pretty hard, too."

"I thought I recognized that look on your face. Is it Madeline?"

"Yeah, it's Maddie," he nodded.

Michael leaned back on a post, crossing his arms. "You gonna tell her?"

"You think I should?"

Michael nodded. "Yeah...and the sooner the better, for your sake, trust me on this. I've been there."

Chapter 29

Samuel and his men kept a steady pace as they worked the fields, moving with the sun. Wiping his brow with the back of his gloved hand, Samuel hopped from the tractor; the sun was just touching the treetops when his cell phone rang. "Samuel Warren," he said, as he tugged off a work glove to wipe the sweat from his eyes.

"Samuel, this is Nathan. I'm here at Pap's Cove and it looks to me like there might be trouble. Madeline is here and she's getting a lot of attention from some guys I'm not familiar with. I sure could use some back…Samuel, Samuel?" the phone went silent.

Moments later, Samuel stepped into the bar. After a brief glance around, he spotted Nathan staring at a man on one side of Madeline. Nathan glared in a way that didn't fit with his Godly reputation. With his arms crossed, he stared the man down until the guy finally pushed back from the bar and slipped out the side door, leaving only one man closing in on Madeline. The man was leisurely mouthing a cud of tobacco, deliberately taking his own sweet time as he chewed. His massive jaws worked the tobacco as a thin line of juice trickled from the side of his mouth. "Well now," he drawled. "What have we here?" He twisted on the bar stool so he could get a better look at Madeline. "How about a drink beautiful, then we can take a nice boat ride…enjoy a sunset together…sound good?"

"What he's trying to say, Maddie, is that he wants you in a boat, out to sea with him, drunk and easy. Is the picture clear in your mind yet, or do I need to keep painting?" Samuel's voice was steady and smooth, but resonated clearly from across the room.

Madeline turned to find Samuel leaning heavily against the doorframe. His clothes were dirty, as was his face, but his devilish smile caused her to shiver with fear.

"You stay out of this," the stranger threatened, as he spied Samuel near the door. "She's coming with me." He stood and leaned over her, leering as he pinned Madeline to the bar. His well-muscled arms blocked her way of escape.

Madeline reached back and picked up a half-empty glass and whistled it by the man, dousing him with water and ice. It sailed off into the dining room, bouncing on the floor.

Samuel reached the man in two strides and swung his fist with a vengeance. He caught his jaw, sending him flying across the bar, rattling bottles with the sheer force of the blow. Samuel drew back; ready to slam him again but Nathan caught his fist from behind.

"Hold-up, Samuel. You'll kill him…and he's not worth killin."

Samuel eyed the stranger, watching him shift his jaw with his hand, working it as if to see if it had been broken. He pointed his finger in the man's face and spoke in clear measured words, "If you ever come near her again, you'll never come out of the bayou. Do I make myself clear?"

The stranger nodded slightly, then scrambled to his feet to put distance between them. As he fled, Samuel stared at the empty doorway for a moment, waiting to see if the man returned with a weapon. When he was sure he had gone for good, he gathered his composure before turning his attention to Madeline. "Are you okay? Did he hurt you?" he questioned, as his eyes moved over her.

"No," she replied, in a weak voice. "They just scared me a little. I was all by myself until Nathan showed up. I thought Elle was working. I just dropped by to see her, but they told me she doesn't work here anymore." Madeline suppressed a shiver as she thought of the all too familiar hungry look in the eyes of those men.

Samuel looked at her for a long time. "Well, thanks to Nathan here, no harm has been done. Next time, don't come out this way without an escort. This time of day, you get all kinda men coming in off the water. These guys weren't from around here."

Nathan reached for Samuel's hand, grasping it in a tight grip. "See you Sunday," he said, and smirked. "Madeline, take care, and listen to Samuel."

Samuel placed his hand in the small of Madeline's back and led her to the door. "Come on, I'll take you home."

Madeline lifted her chin and forced herself to stare right into those steel gray eyes of his. "I can take care of myself now, Samuel. You can go on home. I'll be fine."

Samuel squared off in front of her as solid as an oak beam. "If you insist I'll follow behind you, but I will see that you get home safely. Now, quit arguing and get in your car."

She wanted to run away and bawl like a little spanked baby at the sharpness of his tone, but she stood her ground. There was no way she was ever going to let him think she had been scared. "Have it your way, but I need to stop by the store before I go home. You'll have to wait on me if you insist on following me home."

"I'll wait.

The bell hanging over the door jingled as Samuel entered the quaint little shop on Main Street, it had been weeks since the incident at Pap's Cove and he hadn't seen Madeline since. Looking around the shop, he noticed glass jars with colorful soaps and lotions. Decanters filled with lavender and other dried herbs lining the shelves. The smell was intoxicating, as was the atmosphere. Just then, Madeline stepped around the corner with an elderly woman close on her heels. She froze at the sight of him.

Madeline was breathtaking, even lovelier than he remembered. Her honey amber hair was twisted into a French braid with loose strands falling around her face, accenting her golden green eyes. Her lips parted slightly in surprise.

"Samuel," she breathed out his name in a whisper.

Moving near her, he said, "I like it. All of it." His eyes never left her face.

"Thank you. There's still so much to do, but I'm getting there." Forgetting her customer for a moment, she stared back at Samuel, taking in his striking appearance.

"I'd say you've arrived."

Madeline jumped slightly, remembering her customer. "Oh...please," she extended her hand. "I'll take those for you." Stepping behind the counter, she rang up the sale.

After the customer left the store, Madeline turned to Samuel. "So," she let out a breath, "what brings you by?"

Lifting his hands, he explained. "I was driving down the street, minding my own business, sliding some Texas Blues into the CD player when all of a sudden my truck practically steered itself into this place."

"Uh huh…can't control your truck anymore than your horse, I see."

"Guess not." A slow smile spread across his face, reaching his eyes. "I like what you've done to the place." He looked around noticing the color scheme for the first time. Everything, including Madeline, seemed to match.

Reading his thoughts, she spoke up, "This pale shade of blue-gray has sort of taken over my life. I've been obsessed with this color. I've made soap this color; painted the walls this color and I even bought this dress the same color." She smoothed the front of the little sundress. "I think it's the calming effect it has on my mind that makes me love it. It's my drug, I guess." As he turned to face her, staring at her, that instant she realized his eyes were the very same shade of blue-gray, matching everything around them.

"I'm feeling the effects myself," he said, taking in her pretty form and smiling his wicked smile. Then, turning serious he asked, "Do you miss home, Maddie?"

"I miss the sound of rain on my tin roof. I miss the stars, the ocean, but besides that, I guess I'm managing."

Samuel made a mental note to add "metal roof" to his list of additions to be made at Bell Bennier.

"Greenberry and Willa drop in from time to time. It looks like they're getting along well these days. I wouldn't be a bit surprised to hear of a wedding sometime soon."

Samuel nodded, changing the subject. "Do you live upstairs?" He pointed to the ceiling.

"I do. It's small, but comfortable. Would you like to see?"

"I'd love a tour."

"Okay, just let me turn this 'be back in a minute' sign around and we'll go up."

She locked the front door and led him up the back stairs. Stepping into the compact kitchen, he noticed two coffee cups and two small plates at the table.

"There's just one bedroom," she said, turning to open the bedroom door.

As he entered the tiny room, he saw a bed in the corner with a small table next to it. A lamp with a short stack of books covered the nightstand. At the foot of the bed was a pink and green quilt, neatly folded. He tried to shake an unwanted image that formed in his head, an image of Madeline with someone else. Turning away, he glanced out the door, looking for a distraction. "It's quiet up here. You wouldn't think it would be so noiseless like this in town."

"It does get quiet *and* lonesome up here at night. I miss hearing the sea. It becomes so much a part of you that you never really miss it until it's gone."

He quirked his brow and said, "You shouldn't be too lonesome. It looks like you've had company." He indicated the two coffee cups. The stubborn tilt to her chin silenced his next comment.

"Josiah stops in to check on me once in a while. This morning, he brought breakfast."

Something seized him in the pit of his stomach. "That was nice of him," he responded, trying his best to maintain control of his raging emotions.

The accusation in his tone infuriated Madeline. Her foot began to tap out a warning. "I think so. Anyway…why did you stop by? Could you not find anyone at Bell Bennier to argue with you?" She threw him a scathing look.

All too aware of the recent stirrings inside himself, sadness replaced the anger, squelching it. At the moment, nothing else mattered, nothing except seeing Madeline. "No, I didn't come here to fight. I just missed you."

The sad and dejected way he looked and sounded sucked the very air from her body. "Oh…"

"I better get going." He turned, walking slowly back down the creaking stairs. "Thanks for the tour, Maddie," he called over his shoulder as he reached the door. The door opened, then softly closed as the bells rang, sounding hollow in the room.

Days after Samuel's visit, his face still burned in Madeline's mind; robbing her of peace. "Why does that man affect me so?" she said out loud, as she filled a jar with lavender scented soap. She was tormented by thoughts of him. She needed to talk, but to who? Who would understand what was going on in her mind? *Telie,* she thought.

That evening, fog drifted eerily silent as it twined through the marshland and across the lands of Bell Forest. As Madeline shut the door of her car near the charred remains of Bay Cottage, a distant reverb of a ship's horn hung on the air like the low notes of an old pipe organ. Madeline shivered. Stepping over a fallen log, she seemed to drift in a sea of fog as she made her way across the field toward Telie's home. Passing the monastery, with vapors swirling around her, she stepped into a low spot where the mists had gathered. There were no stirrings in or about the monastery, only stillness. And, to all appearances, it seemed forsaken, all enshrouded in fog until a movement from within the dwelling caught her attention.

Madeline stopped. Her long honey colored hair fell in wild disarray about her shoulders. The gray dress she wore made her seem to disappear in the thick fog. Peering closely at the darkened glass, she noticed a rather old looking monk, standing at the window. His white hair stood out from his weathered face like fluff. Wide eyed, he gave the impression he was startled. Madeline smiled and gave the old monk a tiny wave.

Seemingly astonished, the old monk fell back into his chair as if he'd seen a ghost. Twisting her lips to keep from smiling, Madeline waited to see if the monk would recover. Just then, the old monk wiggled his bony fingers in a tiny wave, with a somewhat bewildered look on his face.

Madeline smiled and was more than a little relieved as she continued across the lawn toward Telie's house.

McKeever bounded out of the fog, running up to her as if expecting her, his tail wagging his whole body. "Hey boy, are you the welcoming committee around here?" Madeline reached down and patted McKeever on the head. "Lead the way, my friend."

Telie opened the back kitchen door and stood waiting as McKeever and Madeline approached. "Get in here, girl. This is not a night to be roaming all over the countryside. You'll scare us all to death!"

Madeline laughed, "Yeah, I think that's just what I did to one of the monks over at the monastery."

"That you did. Brother Raphael called to tell me you were on the way. Seems Brother Simeon is convinced you're some lost soul in need of guidance to find your way to the other side. He's in the chapel now praying for you."

"That's comforting. Don't stop him; I need all the prayers I can get." Madeline climbed the few steps to the back porch. "I hope I'm not interrupting anything."

Telie's smile was warm. "Not at all, Michael is still at work and I'm baking cookies. I hope you like chocolate chip."

"My favorite."

"Good, have a seat, I've just made a fresh pot of coffee." Telie opened the cabinet door and pulled out two cups.

"Sounds good." Madeline looked all around the small cottage. It was cozy and warm and consisted of only three rooms and a bath. The kitchen was white and cheery with blue and green glass pieces scattered all around. From her chair at the kitchen table she could see the living room with a huge stone fireplace taking up much of one wall and above the fireplace hung a beautiful painting of an oak tree. The furnishings looked overstuffed and comfortable. Overall, the cottage was charming.

"I know what you're thinking. You're thinking where in this world are you going to put a baby?" Telie's voice held laughter and you were drawn to it like lips to sweet butter on bread. "We have the house in town, but this place suits me. I'm a much simpler person here. That's why we're going to add on another bedroom for the baby." Telie smirked, as she poured their coffee and placed a plate of cookies on the table. "I won that argument." She winked.

Warm heat rising from the cup caressed Madeline's cheek as she sipped her coffee. "I'm here for a little advice," she said, as she placed her cup down in the saucer.

"Okay, shoot."

Madeline inhaled deeply before explaining. "You know what kinda life I've led, don't you?"

"For the most part," Telie answered. She'd learned long ago to listen well and talk little.

"Fear has played a major role in my life and I've missed out on a lot because of it. Love is one of those things I've missed out on, and now I don't know what to do about it. I've been so busy trying to safeguard my heart from pain that I've missed out on life and love and all that's important. How do I start? How do I let someone know that I love them...where do I get that kind of courage?"

Telie cleared her throat. "Being the border-line control freak that I am, I need to be reminded from time to time that God is in control. So, turn it over and let Him do the directing."

"I've done that, I'm just not sure where He's directing. Something inside me wants to confront Samuel with my feelings, but how do I know that's God directing me?"

"Talk to Samuel straight out. Being straightforward and honest is usually the right way, then, be prepared for whatever happens. That takes courage, but you must be willing to take a chance on love. What happens if you don't ever take a chance...nothing?"

"Nobody has ever gotten to me the way that man has. When I'm around him...well, he's just so infuriatingly wonderful. It's worth a chance."

Chapter 30

Dogwood blossoms warmed by the sun made the air smell of spring. Madeline watched as bees buzzed in random patterns around the new clover of Bell Bennier. Rain would soon fall, but not before dark. Right now, she was going to find Samuel and tell him how she felt about him.

The weeks that followed his last visit were miserable. She found she'd lost her appetite along with the ability to sleep a full eight hours. All she could think of was Samuel. Well, she was going to put a stop to all this foolishness and talk it out with him, today. Her very life depended on it.

Greenberry caught sight of her in the field and made his way to her. In the distance, the sun began sinking behind the treetops as it lowered in the sky, bathing everything in golden light.

Greenberry knocked the dust off his hat as he slapped it against the side of his leg. "You lookin for Samuel?" he asked, squinting in the dim light.

"I am," she said with determination.

"He's out there." He waved in the direction of the woods. "Chopping more wood that we don't need." Greenberry tugged his hat down over his eyes and mumbled under his breath.

"Thanks." Madeline continued on, heading for the trees in the distance and following the sound of Samuel's axe.

"Samuel!" Madeline called out.

Samuel halted the axe in mid-air, slowly lowering it as he spotted Madeline making her way toward him. Her tone remained friendly, but her demeanor stiffened ever so slightly. "We need to talk."

"Yes...we do." He dropped the axe, reaching her in three quick strides.

Madeline spoke plainly—something not all that common in the women he'd been acquainted with. She could hold her own and didn't wallow in self-pity. Two traits he greatly admired...in a man. But here they were in this woman...and not just any woman, but the most appealing creature he'd ever known. He reached for her hand and brought it to his lips, placing a gentle kiss to the top of her soft hand.

Madeline caught her breath. Surprised by the gesture, she'd forgotten everything she'd planned to say to him. The rush of emotions that filled her felt warm, like brandy coursing through her veins.

The faraway drone of a passing plane filled the uneasy silence between them. Samuel's gray eyes deepened with intensity. He watched her mouth tremble slightly at the corners. In a deep, low voice Samuel said, "I want to take you home with me and call you my own." He paused a moment, then continued. "What I'm saying, Madeline is that I love you and I want you for my wife."

Breath she didn't even realize she was holding escaped her lips. She stared up at him, speechless.

"Uh, Madeline, you're killin me here."

Snapping out of the trance, she blinked once then asked, "You want to marry *me*?"

"I do." He fixed his eyes on her trembling lips, noticing how they began to pull down at the corners as if by an invisible string. Her green eyes sparkled with tears. He waited.

Drawing in a jagged breath, she released the word, "Samuel."

"Is that a 'yes, Samuel,' or a 'no, Samuel.'"

After a long tormented second, she said, "That's a yes, Samuel."

Grabbing her firmly, he kissed her long and hard. Pulling away, he said, "I didn't mean to propose to you this way...I had it all planned out. There's my mother's ring I want to give you." He shook his head. "I guess I just got ahead of myself. But, you've made me the happiest man alive. Come on...let's go get your ring. I want it on your finger this minute."

Confused, Madeline felt herself being pulled along behind Samuel. Impatient with her slow steps, he turned and scooped her up into his arms and carried her the rest of the way.

Madeline seemed to burst into bloom like a crocus in the thawed spring earth. She shifted her hand, watching as the Old European cut diamond sparkled on her finger. Crafted in platinum, the brilliant diamond was surrounded by six round diamonds, three on each side, bead set along the shoulders of the ring. The sparkling white diamonds against the coolness of the platinum stole her breath.

Madeline snuggled closer to Samuel on the couch in the living room. "This is the only ring I'll ever wear on my fingers."

"Is that a proclamation?"

"That's a declaration. I'm declaring my love for you and only you for the rest of my life."

"How did Jude take the news?" Samuel asked, pulling back to look at her expression. "Am I going to have to fight my own brother for your hand?"

Madeline shook her head. "No...he seemed a little shocked at first, but by the end of our conversation he was calling me his sister-in-law and laughing about it."

Samuel pulled Madeline into his lap and was about to kiss her when Willa stepped into the room. "How about some nice hot coffee and some chocolate cake... fresh from the oven?"

Madeline smiled, all too aware of Samuel's intense gaze on her. "Thanks, Willa. I love your chocolate cake."

"Well, I thought I'd make your favorite in honor of your engagement. Now...Greenberry and I are going into town, so," she paused, not quite sure how to proceed, "the house is all yours."

Samuel took a sip of coffee and nodded appreciatively. "That's good, Willa. Just the way I like it."

Willa left the room, smiling, not sure if he was talking about the coffee or being left alone with Madeline.

Madeline turned her attention back to Samuel. "Now, where were we?"

"Oh, I think we were just about to…" He dipped his head and found her lips, kissing her thoroughly. Pulling away, her half-mast eyes spoke volumes as he reluctantly lifted her off his lap. "There's something else I want to give you."

"Oh?" Madeline's deep blush caused a light laugh from Samuel.

"You're safe…for now," he said, grinning. "But, we do need to hurry up with this wedding," he added, cocking his eye at her. "I'm no saint, you know."

Taking her hand, he led her into the dining room and flipped the light. There, on the mahogany dining room table, gleaming under the light of the crystal chandelier was piece after piece of the most beautiful silver Madeline had ever seen. Silver serving trays and water pitchers, candle sticks and tea urns, bowls and glass and silver cruet sets all glowing and brilliant under the chandelier.

"I've never seen anything so magnificent. Is this your mother's silver?" She turned, finding the shelves still full of Josslyn's silver. With a confused look, she turned to Samuel for an explanation.

"This is *your* silver, Madeline. Telie found it under a magnolia tree in her yard. After all that heavy rain, it just perked up out of the ground."

"My silver…I don't have any silver?" Her arched brows drew together in sudden doubt.

"Oh yes you do. This is Bennier silver, see?" He pointed to the tea urn. "This is the original Bennier crest. Michael called when they discovered it and helped me load it up. I took it to a friend of mine in Charleston; he's a silver restoration specialist. I trusted him to remove the corrosion without weakening the silver. Most of the pieces were just tarnished, and that never actually hurts silver, but I wanted to make sure it was done right. And, as you can see, he did an excellent job with your silver...oh, and one more thing." He twisted the signet ring off his finger and held it out to her. "This also belongs to you."

Madeline stared down at the ring in Samuel's hand as her mind tried to take it all in. "I don't understand."

"This ring belonged to Marcellus Bennier. It's yours now."

"No." She closed her fingers over Samuel's hand. "It's yours now and will one day belong to our son."

At her words, Samuel smiled, placing the ring back on his finger. "I'll keep it for him."

"So...all this is mine?" She swept her hand across the table."

"All of it." Samuel watched her, enjoying the play of emotions across her face. "And, I've got the perfect place for it, too." He nodded toward the empty shelves that stood next to where his mother's silver was displayed. "That's where your mother-in-law said you're to place your silver."

Madeline's lifted her brow. "Well, I'm certainly not one to argue with my mother-in-law. It will go exactly where she wants it." She reached behind Samuel's head and pulled him toward her. A sudden clang sounded behind them, pulling them apart as the elephant bell rolled to their feet.

"Mother always did like to make a show of things." Samuel drew Madeline into his arms once more. "Now, let's talk some more about that son you promised me."

By the time summer arrived at Bell Bennier, the place was a frenzy of activity. The sound of boots hitting the back porch caught Madeline's attention. She looked up from her papers, scattered all about the kitchen table, waiting for Samuel to enter.

"How's the wedding planning going? You workin on grandmother Linville's invitation?" He grinned at her as he roughly wiped his hands on a kitchen towel, tossing it into the sink. His teeth gleamed white against his dirty face. Recklessly, he grabbed Madeline up from her chair and looked down at her in that ageless way a man looks at a woman.

Madeline's mouth softened into a lazy smile. She reached around his head and pulled his face toward her lips.

"Whoa...I'm filthy. Let me go clean up before I get you dirty."

"I've always found dirt appealing on a man. Its evidence he's been working," she teased. Grabbing a fist full of his hair, she forced his lips to meet hers as she kissed him more intently than she meant to.

"You keep kissing me like that and I'll be forced to roll around in the dirt first thing every morning."

Madeline smirked. "That will suit me just fine."

"Now, back to grandmother Linville," Samuel said, as he dropped down into his seat. He leaned forward with his elbows on the table. "What are you going to do about her?"

Madeline gave him an incredulous look. "Nothing...oh, she'd be thrilled to learn that I landed a man with a name and a little wealth to bring her recognition." As painful as the thought, she knew her words were true.

"You keep forgetting, Maddie, that between the two of us, I'm the one who will be marrying "Up". I'm the common blood—you're the one with the lineage no one would dare question."

Madeline tucked her hair behind her ear. "As if all of that matters; after all, we all go back to Noah." She looked up at him through a veil of darkly fringed lashes. "I know that eventually I'll have to deal with my grandmother, but not on my wedding day."

"Well, it's your wedding and whatever makes you happy makes me happy."

"I want a small affair, just our family and a few close friends. But, I guess if I had all of my wedding dreams come true, I'd have my own father walk me down the aisle, to give me away." She shrugged. "Oh well, you can't give away something you've never had. It's odd...but I've always felt him," she patted her chest, "in here."

Samuel moved to gently cover her hand with his and said in a husky voice, "He'll have to move over. That spot belongs to me now."

Samuel glanced again at the man seated next to him as his truck bumped its way down the dirt road. It still surprised him that, with Lane's help, they'd been able to locate the seaman without difficulty. From the look on the man's face he guessed that he might not be accustomed to narrow and restrictive places such as the cab of a truck. His broad shoulders seemed to fill every square inch of the space. A ship could be seen in the bay as they made their way toward Bell Bennier. Samuel noticed the glint in the man's eyes as he watched the ship with keen interest.

"Is that a sense of adventure I detect in those eyes of yours, Alexander?" Samuel asked, as he pulled down the visor, allowing a package of cigars to fall into his hand.

"Care for one?" he asked, before his thoughts turned toward the remarkable resemblance the man bore to Maddie. To have sired such an interesting person as Madeline, he knew the man seated next to him was well worth knowing.

Alexander waved his hand, declining off the offer. "Yeah well, I guess it's all I've ever really known...the sea and ships. But, I'd be lying if I said I wasn't excited *and* nervous to see my very own children." He shook his head as if to clear it. "It's still hard for me to believe. Who would've thought that my Della and me would've set to seed two fine girls?" He grew quiet and stared through the truck window. "If I'd only known; all this time and all those lies kept me away from my Della." He turned and looked pointedly at Samuel. "She tried to tell me...Della...she tried her best to tell me but I wouldn't listen. I thought that if I just went out to sea I could make enough money to please her mother and she'd change her mind about me." His voice was choked and broken. "I was a fool to ever think that money could ever make a difference to that woman. When I returned, she told me that Della had run away after putting our child up for adoption. I didn't know that she was expecting our second child. I have no one to blame but myself for ever believing that hateful woman."

"All of that is behind you now, Alexander. New days are ahead and you've got a future with us if you want one. And, I might add, you won't even have to give up your sea legs. Your son-in-law, Lane, has a job waiting for you at his family's shipbuilding business. I'm sure a seafaring man such as you has heard of the Bennett Shipbuilding Company. Of course, if you'd like to stay closer to home, I could use an extra pair of hands around the farm. That daughter of yours is going to require one of my eyes on her nearly every waking minute."

Moments later, with a squeak of brakes Samuel's truck rolled to a stop in front of Bell Bennier.

"Alexander twisted his rough and calloused hands. "I've never been this nervous in all my life." He swallowed hard. "I hope they won't hate me."

Samuel patted the man's leg. "You'll do fine, I promise you. They're more nervous about this than you are. I just told them that I was bringing home a guest and to be waiting. That's them, waiting on the veranda."

The moment Samuel and Alexander stepped out of the truck, Madeline rose to her feet. Elle crossed the porch and clasped her sister's hand tightly. No one needed to make introductions; they knew instinctively that the man standing in front of them was their father.

Alexander's long, muscular frame was superbly proportioned. His bronze-hued skin showed dark against his white collared shirt as his deep brown eyes held an emotion neither girl was prepared for. Seeing the rugged man before them choked with tears caught the girls off guard as compassion mixed with relief filled them.

"Is that any way to treat your daddy girls?" Lane said from the doorway. "You could at least invite the man inside."

At Lane's words, both girls flew down the front steps and into their father's arms. Samuel stepped past them, watching the exchange of hugs and kisses as they enveloped each other in their arms. As Samuel passed Lane, he casually remarked, "I never get tired of tossing out sea stars, Lane. No...I never get tired of it."

"Huh? I don't understand?"

Samuel pulled out a long cigar from his pocket, bit off the tip of it and spit it over the porch rail. "I'll have to tell you that story sometime," he said, putting his arm around Lane's shoulder and squeezing it as they made their way into the house.

There, in the circle of the driveway, near the old box-woods stood Madeline, Elle and their father, Alexander. Bell Bennier stood silently, witnessing the exchange. Change was coming once again, just as quickly as the encroaching season of summer. But, of all the changes sure to come none will be more welcomed than the sound of children's laughter and secrets being whispered through the trees and along the sacred grounds of Bell Forest, once again.